D0438322

THE
VIRGINITY
of FAMOUS
MEN

Paris, He Said: A Novel
Little Known Facts: A Novel
Portraits of a Few of the People I've Made Cry: Stories

THE VIRGINITY *of* FAMOUS MEN

STORIES

CHRISTINE SNEED

BLOOMSBURY

NEW YORK · LONDON · OXFORD · NEW DELHI · SYDNEY

Bloomsbury USA
An imprint of Bloomsbury Publishing Plc

1385 Broadway   50 Bedford Square
New York   London
NY 10018   WC1B 3DP
USA   UK

www.bloomsbury.com

BLOOMSBURY and the Diana logo are trademarks of Bloomsbury Publishing Plc

First published 2016

ISBN: HB: 978-1-62040-695-3
             ePub: 978-1-62040-697-7

LIBRARY OF CONGRESS CATALOGING-IN-PUBLICATION DATA IS AVAILABLE.

2   4   6   8   10   9   7   5   3   1

Typeset by RefineCatch Limited, Bungay, Suffolk
Printed and bound in the U.S.A. by Berryville Graphics, Berryville, Virginia

To find out more about our authors and books visit www.bloomsbury.com. Here you
will find extracts, author interviews, details of forthcoming events and the option to
sign up for our newsletters.

Bloomsbury books may be purchased for business or promotional use. For
information on bulk purchases please contact Macmillan Corporate and Premium
Sales Department at specialmarkets@macmillan.com.

For Melanie Brown
and for Adam Tinkham

CONTENTS

BEACH VACATION

THE TRIP WAS HER SON'S reward for earning As in all of his classes the preceding year, and she and his father had told him that he could choose anywhere in the country. To their surprise, he did not pick Los Angeles or New York, Aspen or Maui. He wanted to go to Captiva, a tiny island off the Gulf coast of Florida that was nearly split in half during a hurricane a few years earlier. The island was the sort of place that families went to vacation with other families. She did not realize until a few hours after they arrived that he had chosen the island because a girl he liked planned to be there with her parents at the same time.

But there were other problems, worse ones, that she would have to face, the first being her husband's absence. At the last minute, he was informed by his boss that he could not go to Florida, despite having already been granted the week off. The day before they planned to leave, he was ordered to fly from their home in Chicago to Shreveport, Louisiana. A warehouse had burned down, one where his linens-manufacturer employer stored cotton for its looms. The fire had taken two adjacent warehouses with it, neither of which

1

the manufacturer owned. Steven was apologetic and worried and told her and Tristan that he would try to join them after a couple of days. He hoped that it wouldn't be as bad as it sounded in Louisiana and that they might let him go after the insurance adjusters visited the site and the police and firefighters were done poking around.

They had not taken a vacation together as a family in two years, aside from a few tense weekends at a lake cottage in central Wisconsin, where Tristan had pouted over not being home with his friends and his computer. She was alternately enraged and morose that Steven would not be going, and she would have canceled the trip if he and Tristan had not argued so convincingly that they go ahead as planned. Why Tristan still wanted to go when it was only the two of them had perplexed her, but at the time she had been flattered: they did so little together outside of the house because he had turned seventeen in February and could rarely be bothered to have dinner out with her and his father, let alone travel with her to a beach resort more than a thousand miles away for one entire week.

It was mid-March and crowded and seventy-eight degrees when they arrived at the resort, where they had booked two rooms with a view of the Gulf. She had held on to the second room because she hoped her husband would join them but didn't really believe he would. She also knew that her son was too close to adulthood for them to share a room, his body more manly than boyish now, with whiskers and wiry leg and armpit hair that she tried not to see but it was aggressively there, as were his dirty clothes that smelled like his father's after an hour of yard work or a visit to the gym. The previous fall, she'd made Steven talk to him about condoms and pretty, vulnerable girls, which they had already talked about when Tristan was twelve, but it seemed necessary to her that they have this talk a second time. He'd gotten his driver's license the preceding spring and for a while was taking out the same girl, who then suddenly he wasn't taking out anymore and Jan didn't know what had happened because he would tell her and Steven only that it hadn't worked out and what was the big deal?

The resort had been badly damaged by the hurricane and many of the little villas and apartment buildings were still being repaired or completely rebuilt, though the hibiscus and oleander bushes had survived or else had been replanted and had grown again to a floral effusiveness that reminded her of bridesmaid dresses and frilly tuxedo shirts, but beautiful ones that people wouldn't have cringed over.

"This place is a dump," Tristan announced as they drove from the front office to the square yellow building that housed their rooms.

"I don't think so," she said.

"When was that storm? Four years ago?"

"Two and a half."

"What's taking them so long to fix things?"

"Everything on the island probably needed to be repaired. There are only so many people nearby who can do this kind of work."

"This place charges enough that you'd think they'd be able to afford more construction guys."

"It probably doesn't work that way."

"Well, it should," he said dismissively.

Before and during the plane ride from O'Hare to Fort Myers, they'd argued over his shoes and neither of them had recovered yet. Despite the freezing weather in Chicago, he'd insisted on wearing his Tevas without socks, and Jan hadn't been able to deter him. Steven had already left for Shreveport and couldn't gently bully Tristan into backing down. More than once during the three-hour flight, she had looked at his feet and sighed, and he had scowled back at her and barked, "What, Mom?" loud enough for the people in the row ahead to hear. Two of them had corkscrewed their necks to stare back at her and Tristan with a gleeful frown.

Their rooms were connected by an interior door that locked on both sides. Jan had misgivings when she saw this, even though she had keys for the hallway doors of both rooms. Despite his gruff dismissal of the resort's grounds, Tristan seemed to like his room, which was light-filled, smelled of lilacs and had two queen-size beds, along with pastel paintings of regional seashells. There were several large, fluffy taupe towels in the bathroom, seashell-shaped soaps, shampoo, a shower cap, a thick terry cloth robe. The minibar was locked and, she hoped, unbreachable. She had called from Chicago to request that the code be removed from the room before check-in. It appeared that it had been—no instructions sat on top of it or were taped to the minibar's door.

It had been a mistake to come. She could not ignore this fact anymore, but she said nothing to Tristan, who had flopped down on one of the beds and was now giving her a calculating look. "Don't you want to get your stuff unpacked? Or are you going to hang out here and stare at me all day?"

A fact she had been trying to ignore for the past year: she and Steven had witlessly, indulgently, allowed their son to cultivate the least appealing characteristics of a privileged teenage boy. At home it was easier to ignore his occasional snits, his snide comments and self-absorption. Hormones, Steven would sometimes say, shrugging off most of her complaints about their son's irritable moods. He wasn't getting arrested, was he? Driving drunk or crashing the car or doing drugs, was he? He wasn't stealing or not coming home when he said he would. Most boys his age didn't seem to be much different from him, she could admit, and she had tried to believe that this was only a temporary, unpleasant phase of their development—many of his friends were distant or smug too, prone to giving her benignly vacant smiles, then snickering as soon as she left the room at a remark one of them had made under his breath. Tristan's good grades, his sudden striking looks and popularity with girls and other boys made his egotism understandable, if not forgivable, but she had hoped that once he learned to see these gifts as conferred by the illogic of biological heritage and blind good luck, he would become more generous. There were also others with even more to offer than he had, which surely he would understand at some point?

At present, this did not seem so likely. Her only child could just as easily, perhaps more easily, grow up to be selfish for as long as he would live, unless she and Steven drastically changed the way they responded to him. This week alone together, however, did not seem the ideal time for her to start behaving differently to his provocations. But if not now, when? she wondered wearily, her stomach tense with worry and self-contempt.

"If you can't speak to me politely, don't say anything at all," she said.

"Fine," he said. "No problem." He closed his eyes and kept them closed until she left, unlocking the shared door on her way into her room, one that was the mirror image of his. She threw herself down onto one of her own beds and stared blankly at the glass doors that opened to a balcony over-looking the Gulf. It was a gorgeous view, on a gorgeous, beleaguered little island where only a day earlier she had imagined Tristan and herself being happy together.

The sun was on its downward trajectory but still bright. The alarm clock by the bed read three thirty; she did not want to stay in her room for the rest of the afternoon but was reluctant to go to the pool or the beach if Tristan stayed behind. After a few minutes, she got up when she heard him stirring next door and put on her swimsuit, a modest one-piece, despite her trim figure, one she had kept by exercising and eating light, which, because of her sweet tooth, was hard to do. She knew she wasn't old yet either, only forty-two, and despite how tired she sometimes felt when faced with the pretty young girls and boys who often draped themselves across her and Steven's furniture, she believed that she was still attractive. Whether her son or her husband thought so too, she wasn't sure. Steven was a nice man, even-tempered and sincere, but often preoccupied by the stressful responsibilities of his job. He had recently been promoted to vice president of sales and marketing and was rarely at ease anymore. He needed this vacation much more than she did, and then, hatefully, it was taken from him at the last minute.

She got up and knocked on the connecting door. "Do you want to go down to the pool?"

When there was no reply, she knocked again. "Tristan?"

"I guess," he finally said, his lack of enthusiasm obvious despite his muffled voice. "What the hell."

She turned the knob, realizing too late that he might not be dressed, but he was still lying on the bed in his clothes from the plane. He gave her an angry look. "I didn't say you could come in."

"I'm sorry about your sandals," she said.

He blinked. "What?"

"I'm sorry that we argued about your Tevas earlier."

He propped himself up on his elbows. "I'm used to it. Not a big deal."

"I was just worried that you'd catch a cold."

"I feel fine. We're in the tropics."

"But Chicago isn't the tropics."

"Let me get my suit on. Can you go back to your room?"

She could feel her face reddening, her temper close to a rare flare-up. "I'll see you down by the pool." She went over to the glass doors. "That one right there," she said, pointing to a kidney bean of turquoise water, white chairs arranged around its perimeter. Some of the chairs were empty, but most had people or bright towels covering them. There were three pools at the resort; the kidney-shaped one was only twenty yards from their building.

"I might want to go to the beach."

"Okay, but if you do, please stop by the pool and let me know."

He was silent.

"Did you hear me?"

"Yes, I heard you," he said, irritated.

"Let's try to have fun, okay?"

"Uh huh," he said. His green eyes were on her pale feet, her hot pink toenails garish in the natural light. His light brown hair was fetchingly disheveled, his face shadowed by a dark smear of whiskers along his jaw and upper lip. He had so many of the best advantages— a different bold girl calling almost every day, the car Steven and she let him use gone from the driveway until eight or nine o'clock most weeknights, midnight on weekends, but his grades held up. He was a fast study, naturally smart, and took this fact for granted. He wanted to go to Yale or Princeton or Stanford. She hadn't told Steven, but she almost hoped that he wouldn't get in to any of them. He could go to the University of Illinois or Michigan State and in time be just as happy there. It seemed possible that she had turned into a terrible mother.

At the pool, she chose two chairs that faced the afternoon sun, hoping but not really believing that Tristan would join her. In her beach bag, she had a book and two magazines and a large bottle of water they had bought at the Publix before the causeway to the island. She rubbed sunscreen into her white arms and legs and adjusted her straw hat to keep the rays from her face. She glanced at the other people—a few silent couples, several shrieking children, two or three single women in bikinis. She had never cheated on Steven and did not think that he had ever cheated on her. Her impression had long been that it did not occur to him to cheat. At the few parties they went to each year, he rarely seemed to understand when a woman was flirting with him. She had often wondered if this obtuseness was an affectation, but whatever its source, it had held. Some of their friends, inevitably, had had affairs. Over the years, some had divorced, but she and Steven remained a fixture. *The perfect family*, she had once overheard someone say mockingly at a neighbor's Fourth of July cookout. *I wonder what it's like to go through life without ever being miserable?*

Tristan came down after she had drained half of her water bottle and read one chapter. A girl was with him, a long-legged, curly-haired blonde in a red string bikini. Others turned to stare at them. Jan knew instantly that the girl was from home, that this had been Tristan's plan all along. "Mom, this is Patty," he announced.

The girl smiled and offered a thin, suntanned hand. She wore a braided silver ring on each index finger.

"Hi, Patty," said Jan, trying to smile.

"She's here with her parents this week too," said Tristan. "Can I have dinner with them tonight?"

"Tonight?" she repeated.

"Yeah."

The girl couldn't look at her. Jan knew that she understood something complicated was happening. She kept her eyes firmly on her toes. Patty's toenails had pink polish on them too but it was paler than Jan's.

"I thought it'd be nice if you and I had dinner since it's our first night here," Jan said quietly. "Why don't you have dinner with your friend and her parents tomorrow?"

Tristan gave her a stony look. "Because they invited me for tonight."

She thought that she might shout at him or cry. Steven would never understand how fraught things had become between her and their son, and she didn't know if she would be able to forgive Steven for this. She looked up at the girl. They were both hiding behind sunglasses. Patty's face looked almost iconic in her dark glasses. She most likely had many boys after her, something Tristan must have been aware of. "Do you think your parents would mind if he joined you tomorrow night instead?"

The girl looked at Tristan. It was clear that she didn't want to wait. "No, they probably wouldn't," she said reluctantly.

"Mom," said Tristan. "They asked me to go tonight. It's rude to make them change their plans."

She hesitated, wondering for a second if the girl would come to her rescue and tell Tristan that he should stay and have dinner with his mother. It was only fair, she could almost hear the girl saying. But neither of them said a word.

"Fine," said Jan, resigned. "Go ahead."

Patty smiled nervously. Tristan said nothing. He stared down at her for several seconds and then mumbled that he was going to the beach. The girl said good-bye and followed him. She was so thin and tall, only a couple of inches shorter than his long-limbed six feet. Jan watched them leave, their hands not yet touching, and thought unhappily of the room he had to himself. They might be going there now and if he got her pregnant and had to marry her and keep the child . . . No, no, she had to stop thinking like that. She was not the only woman in the world with a teenage son. Millions of other women had survived the same affliction. Just barely, she thought bitterly. She forced herself to sit by the pool for another hour, reading and rereading the same two pages in her library book, her mind a bubbling morass.

When Steven called a little before six, after she had returned to her room and made sure Tristan wasn't in his with the girl, she had trouble keeping her voice down. "You have to come. Tomorrow, at the latest. I mean it. Tristan is driving me crazy."

He didn't speak for a long time. Finally, he said, "I can't, Janet."

"Why not?"

"Because a little boy was playing in one of the other buildings that burned down. They found his remains this morning."

She felt panic flood her chest and then she was shivering. A little boy's remains. There were few words on earth more terrifying.

"I don't think I'll be able to leave for at least another three or four days," he said when she didn't reply. "At the earliest."

She still couldn't speak.

"Janet?"

"What do they want you to do?" she asked.

"I'm not sure, but Rick needs me to stay here for the time being."

"I don't understand him. The day before you were supposed to leave for vacation and then guess what, you can't go."

"You know this is serious," he said. "More serious than we ever thought it would be."

"But why do they need you to stay? Is everyone else in sales and marketing down there? Unless you or someone you know started the fire, I don't see—" She recognized that she was being selfish but could not stop herself. She wanted her husband in Florida with her and their son. He presumably wanted to be with them too.

"The boy's mother's going to sue us, I'm sure."

"I suppose she will."

He sighed. "I'm sorry that you and Tristan aren't getting along. Maybe you should cut the week short and go home on Tuesday or Wednesday if things don't get better."

"I don't know. We'll see." She told him about the girl, the dinner invitation, the argument over the sandals. Steven murmured that he was sorry, that he wished he could be there to help. Before they hung up, she said, "I don't know how to talk to him anymore. He's so rude to me all the time."

"I really think that'll pass, sweetheart."

"I'm not so sure."

"I think it will."

"He's not a good person, Steven. He just isn't. I feel sick to my stomach saying it, but it's true."

He exhaled heavily. "He's not that bad, Jan. Come on. I'm not in the best frame of mind to talk about this right now."

"No, I guess not."

"I'm sorry, but everything's such a mess here and I can barely put a coherent thought together about anything, especially you and Tristan."

"All right," she said. "I'll let you go. You're tired and I'm bothering you. We'll talk tomorrow then, okay?" She said good-bye and hung up, cutting off his own good-bye, not giving him a chance to say he loved her.

She gazed listlessly at the TV, listening for Tristan's return. He came in from the beach a half an hour later, took a fast shower, and before he went out again, opened the adjoining door and said good-bye. He was wearing khaki shorts, his irritating Tevas, a navy blue linen shirt. His face and arms were already turning brown. "Please be back by ten," she said.

He patted his pockets, found what he wanted and stopped. "Yeah, okay."

"Three hours should be enough, don't you think?"

"I'll have to see," he said. "I can't rush them back here if they want to hang out for a while."

"I'd like you to tell them that your curfew is ten o'clock. Please do that, Tristan."

He was silent.

"Please."

He nodded, not meeting her eyes, and shut the door.

She knew that it would have been stupid to insist that he stay and have dinner with her. It would have been an ugly, public joke: him glowering at her all night and refusing to talk, their waiter and the other diners noticing. They might have pitied her, guessed that it wasn't her fault, but no one had any reason to pity her. She had a home, a husband, a healthy son who hadn't been killed prematurely by cancer or a drunk driver or a warehouse fire. She had two college degrees, neither of which she used anymore because she no longer worked at St. Luke's, the hospital where she had been a nutritionist for eleven years. Now she worked part-time at the library and helped a caterer friend with her biggest parties; Steven earned most of the money. The nutritionist's job had absorbed too much of her time and energy, as was the case now with Steven and his job. She had missed most of Tristan's childhood, and it seemed to her a malicious irony that her current freedom was more of a burden to her son than a boon.

She ate dinner in a seafood restaurant outside the gates of the resort and watched young parents chastise their tired, impatient children when they overturned a water glass or got up and ran around the table for no reason other than unruly excitement. Some of the other vacationers had red faces with a sunglass shape of ghostly skin around their eyes. No one seemed to notice her, but she didn't mind very much. She brooded over Steven and how impatient she had been with him on the phone. It was difficult sometimes to picture them together for the rest of their lives, but she did not know where she would be if not with him. The prospect of losing him to another woman filled her with a dull horror. She knew that it could happen, that it would happen if she did not learn how to be happier. Still, it was easier for him—he had a sense of purpose, despite his job's current unpleasant demands, and Tristan at least respected him. It was she who bore the brunt of their son's bad moods. Steven saw this sometimes and responded with a rebuke, but he continued to believe that their son would grow up to be a charming, charismatic man.

After dinner she took a walk on the beach, the sun already having dropped below the horizon. Several couples and a few families still ambled along the beach, some greeting or smiling at her. No one else looked remotely miserable. She wished that she could enjoy herself. If she didn't feel better in the morning, she might change their tickets and leave early, as Steven had suggested, but if Tristan threatened to stay behind, she could imagine a screaming match. It was absurd that she could feel so bad in such a beautiful place. She could not imagine ever wanting to return.

By ten, her son had not yet come back from dinner. At ten thirty, she called his cell phone, but he didn't answer. At ten fifty, she called again, so furious that her voice shook as she left a second message.

He finally called her at eleven twenty, from a hospital in Fort Myers. The girl was not well. She'd had a reaction to something at dinner—the oysters or the shrimp, they suspected, though no one else was sick. She wouldn't stop throwing up and they had to put her on an IV. The doctor wanted her to spend the night in the hospital and her parents would probably take her back to Chicago early if she were well enough to travel. When Jan arrived at the emergency room entrance to take Tristan back to the island, he was very surly, refusing to meet her eyes when she opened the car door and said hello. The girl's parents were staying overnight with her and did not come outside with Tristan to say good-bye.

"This place sucks," he said as he got into the car. "Why did we come here?"

She looked at him, smelling on his breath what she thought might be alcohol but was too tired and demoralized to ask him if it was. "Is Patty going to be all right?"

"She'll be fine."

"Are you sure?"

His hands gripped his knees. He still wouldn't look at her. "I said she would, didn't I?"

"I know you're upset, but treating me rudely isn't going to help things."

"I'm really fucking tired, Mom. I've been sitting—"

"Don't swear at me, Tristan."

"I've been sitting in the hospital for three hours. I can't be the perfect son all the time."

"No, but some of the time would be nice."

She could feel his furious eyes on her as they drove away from the hospital with its boxy windows and sick girlfriends and foiled teenage hopes. "What's that supposed to mean?" he said.

"I wish you would have called when you got to the hospital so that I didn't have to spend an hour and a half worrying about why you weren't back yet."

"I forgot," he said flatly. "With everything that was going on, I forgot that I was supposed to be home by ten."

"I called you twice and you didn't pick up."

"I didn't have a strong signal in the hospital. It kept fading in and out."

He would have an excuse for everything. He would lie and never admit that he had done something wrong. She could not bear the thought of it and started to cry. She stared at the road and let her eyes turn blurry and blinked back as many of the tears as she could but soon her cheeks were wet and neither of them said a word. They drove the whole way back to the resort without speaking, Tristan sulking and playing with the radio, trying to find a station that he liked for more than one song. She could have yelled at him but was too tired, too disappointed, and still not sure whether she should change their tickets and insist that they leave early, which now Tristan would probably have welcomed. For this reason alone she thought they should stay but knew the impulse to be a juvenile one, and with neither of them happy and Steven off in Louisiana dealing with a dead child and the loss of millions of dollars in goods and property, the vacation was an unequivocal disaster.

When they got back to the resort, Tristan mumbled "Goodnight," and disappeared into his room, and within a few seconds, she heard his television droning. It was now after one A.M., and they'd left Chicago only eighteen hours earlier, but she felt as if she'd been shoved into someone else's life, her own passable life in Illinois now unreachable, as if a malevolent trickster had spirited her away from it with the promise of sunshine and renewed youth.

She fell asleep in her clothes and dreamt of a forest fire, awakening just before seven with a start, her face hot, as if she had stood too close to the dream fire. Her head felt hollow and achy. She made herself stay in bed until eight, knowing that Tristan wasn't likely to be up until ten or eleven. After pulling on her swimsuit, she went down to the beach to try to walk off her headache and search for a few shells worth keeping. The morning air was cool and the sky clear; on the sand she saw that some people had already staked out their places for the day. Beach chairs and towels were arranged in neat rows but almost no one reclined on them yet.

Despite the ordeal of the previous night, she realized that she did not want to leave the island yet. It seemed best to stay, to refuse failure. With the girl sick, Jan hoped that she and Tristan might now be able to spend some time together, that they might have a conversation that didn't devolve into a hostile argument. She walked a mile down the beach, toward Sanibel and the mainland, before turning back, feeling more hopeful as she watched the sandpipers on their twig legs scurry against the tide and the pelicans hover just above the water, scouting for whitefish. She did not slow down until she'd returned to their rooms and knocked on Tristan's door, asking if he wanted to go out for breakfast. He didn't respond, and when she entered his room through the adjoining door, he wasn't there. The bed was unmade and his clothes from the night before were in a heap next to the dresser, a pair of blue underwear in a wad on top.

The keys to the rental car were still in her dresser drawer, as was her purse, all her money and traveler's checks inside of it. She went out to the balcony and looked down at the pool. Her son was there, sprawled across a chaise longue, a suntanned woman in a yellow bikini sitting in the chair next to him, her head close to his, her slender back to the balcony where Jan stood. This bikini-clad woman wasn't Patty. She seemed older, though Jan couldn't tell for sure. She hurriedly checked her hair in the mirror, put on some lipstick, and went down to the pool.

Up close, the woman in the yellow bikini didn't look much younger than Jan was. Too old to be talking so conspiratorially to a boy who couldn't have been mistaken for someone much older than eighteen, despite his broad shoulders and the hair that had started to grow on his chest. As Jan approached, Tristan leaned closer to the stranger and said something that Jan couldn't hear. The woman looked up and smiled at her as if to say they were all friends, everything was fine, and wouldn't she like to join them?

"I'm Liz," said the woman, offering her hand.

Jan hesitated, long enough to make it clear that she wasn't pleased. "Jan Wright," she said.

Tristan's face was unreadable. "Liz is down here because she just got divorced."

The woman shook her head and laughed. "No, no. I just filed for divorce. It hasn't come through yet."

"But you're still down here celebrating," he said.

She laughed again. "That's exactly right."

Both the woman and Tristan looked up at her, expectant. She had to keep herself from blurting, "Why do you think you can say things like that to my son? Don't you realize he's still in high school?" Or, "Will this be your first divorce?"

But all she said was "Oh."

The woman shaded her eyes and squinted up at Jan. "I know how that must sound, but my husband isn't a good person. I never should have married him."

Jan nodded. She did not want to act the killjoy her son expected her to be. She was close enough to smell the coconut lotion the woman had applied to her slender body, her beauty undoubtedly having been noticed by Tristan too. When had it happened? she wondered. When had he become a boy who felt that his mother did nothing but limit him, that she lived only to hold him back, to keep him from experiencing the things adults claimed as their inalienable right? He wanted sex, possibly love, and he was determined to have them, whether she wanted him to or not.

"If you don't mind," Jan murmured, "I'd like to take my son to breakfast."

"I already ate," he said.

"But I haven't, and I'd like you to go with me. I'm sure you can still find room for juice or a piece of toast."

"You should go with your mom," said the woman.

He didn't move.

"Tristan," said Jan. "I'd like to go now. I'm hungry."

He stood up, yanking his towel from the chair. "I'll see you later," he said, glancing at the woman.

She smiled. "It was very nice to meet you and your mother, Tristan. I hope to see you both later."

"I don't know if it's appropriate for you to talk to someone like her," Jan said as they walked toward the restaurant near the resort's entrance.

Tristan rolled his eyes. "Someone like her? What's that supposed to mean?"

"She must be at least twenty years older than you."

"She's thirty-one."

"You're seventeen."

"It's not like we were fucking by the side of the pool. We were just talking."

Jan stopped, her breath coming in a single panting gasp. "You are never to talk to me like that again. Do you understand? I should slap your face right now."

He made a harsh, ugly sound. "Why don't you? What's stopping you?"

They stood glaring at each other under the morning sun, beside the brilliant oleander bushes where bees drifted from blossom to blossom, she standing on the balls of her feet, looking up at him, one hand in a fist at her side, and in the next second she was opening it and raising it to his face. Her palm met his stubbled cheek hard and then it was over and he didn't jump back or touch his face in injured surprise. He only stared at her while she panted and dropped her eyes, her body trembling with fury and shame. A few people were close enough to see what she had done, their conversations temporarily stalled before they resumed with a note of false brightness. Soon she and Tristan were moving again, as if nothing had happened, but she knew that something irrevocable had. They would not be able to forget it. She had hit him, for the first time in his life, and she was certain he had no doubt now that some part of her hated him too.

THE FIRST WIFE

I.

THE FAMOUS DO RESEMBLE the unfamous, but they are not the same species, not quite. The famous have mutated, amassed characteristics—refinements or corporeal variations— that allow their projected images, if not their bodies themselves, to dominate the rest of us.

If you are married to a man whom thousands, possibly millions, of women believe themselves to be in love with, some of them, inevitably, more beautiful and charming than you are, it is not a question of if but of when. When will he be unfaithful, if he hasn't been already? It isn't easy, nor is it as romantic as the magazine photographers make it look, to be the wife of a very famous, memorably handsome man. There are very few nights, even when you are together, when you don't wonder what secrets he is keeping from you, or how long he will be at home before he leaves for another shoot or another meeting in a glamorous city across one ocean or the other with some director or producer who rarely remembers your name. Marriage is a liability in the movie business, despite the public's stubborn, contradictory desire to believe that this particular marriage is different, in that it will endure, even prosper, with children and house-beautiful photo essays in *Vogue*.

There were always so many others lurking about, hoping to take my place, if only for a few days or hours. It was like being married to the president of an enormous country where nearly everyone was offering him sexual favors, ones he really wasn't scorned by anyone but me for accepting.

2.

He married me in part because I wasn't famous, not as famous as he was, in any case. He was the beauty in our household, and I was not the beast but the brains. I wasn't ugly or plain, and I remain neither ugly nor plain, but in college, when for a while I fantasized strenuously about becoming an actress, it soon became clear to me that I liked making up the characters more than playing them. I also realized early on that men age much better in Hollywood than women do. My husband will never be old in the same way that I will be. Even if my fame were as great as his, I would be called an old woman much sooner than he an old man. But I will never be as famous as he is, and although he can be blamed for many things, this isn't one of them.

How did it end? Before I say what it was like to be courted by him, to fall in love, however briefly or genuinely, I prefer to talk about the end because it is rarely ever given its due. It is the filmmaker's and the writer's most reliable trick to seduce us with the details of a marvelous and improbable coupling while hinting darkly that things did not end well, that some tragedy or tragic character flaw in one or both of the principals brought on a heartbreaking collapse. And when the collapse comes, it is seldom given more than a few pages, a few sodden minutes at the end of the film.

My husband was Antony Grégoire; this is the name he was born with, not a stage name chosen for him by an agent. It is regal-sounding, I suppose, a name that demands our attention or at least a moment's pause. His father was French, his mother Swedish, he their only son, the one masculine bloom raised in a garden of sisters. He and his sisters got along well enough most of the time, but he was the favorite—a fact their parents did little to disguise, despite the three daughters' spectacular scholastic and athletic achievements. Antony was bookish, quiet, and sheltered during early adolescence, but then he became handsome and, eventually, the best-looking man in the room. He attracted the heated attention of his sisters' friends, and in time, one of their fathers who was a film producer.

"If I'd met Anna's father even a couple of years earlier than I did, I bet I wouldn't have become an actor," Antony told me not long after we met. "If I'd been seventeen instead of nineteen, I probably would have rolled my eyes and been a sarcastic jerk to him. I was the kind of dork who smoked alone in his room with his Doors albums and Kerouac novels. I used to spend a lot of time wondering if Jim Morrison and I would have been friends."

I laughed. "You did not."

"Of course I did. Every punk I knew was like that where I grew up."

"You would have found your way to L.A. eventually. Especially since you were only an hour and a half away."

He shook his head. "No, I'm telling you, it wouldn't have happened. Bakersfield is like another planet. It was luck, nothing else."

His rise was fast and without real difficulty, a fact he admits to most people because he thinks it adds to his appeal. There is no odor of desperation about him, no stories of violent hand-wringing or sobbing before the security gate of some powerful director or casting agent's Bel-Air mansion. He embodies the most glittering American dream—the version that dictates success is one's birthright and should come easily. Americans romanticize struggle and hard work but do not, in fact, like to work hard.

It was January when our marriage split open, traditionally the coldest month of the year in North America, but in L.A., we hardly noticed, and it hadn't taken me long to prefer winters in Southern California to those in my snow-choked hometown of Minneapolis. "You probably knew this was coming," said Antony. He wasn't lying next to me or sitting across from me at the dinner table, avoiding my gaze. He didn't have to look at me at all because he said these words over the phone. I hadn't seen him in three weeks. He was in Canada filming a movie about caribou hunters, and I'd heard that he was with another woman. She wasn't in the movie and she despised cold weather, but I knew she was up there with him. We had friends in common, this woman and I. The film industry really is a small world, its tributaries and rivers and landmasses having all been mapped out by our mentors, our adversaries, our lovers past and future.

"I didn't think this would happen so soon," I said.

He hesitated. "You don't sound upset."

"I am upset."

"You don't sound like it."

"I'm not going to yell at you, not over the phone. I want you to come home and talk to me about this in person. Ask Jeff for a couple of days off. Tell him I'm sick, that I'm in the hospital. Tell him to shoot some of the scenes you're not in."

"I'm not going to lie. He could easily check."

"Then tell him that your wife of five and a half years has asked that you come back and talk to her before you try to divorce her."

There was a tense pause. "Try to divorce you? What do you mean by *try*?"

I hung up on him. When he called back, I didn't answer. He called me fifteen more times that night, maybe even twenty-five—I can't remember the precise number, but I didn't answer any of those calls, each new sequence of rings sounding more and more desperate and enraged. I didn't turn off the phone because it felt better to hear his distress than to sit in stunned silence. There was no prenuptial agreement; we had talked about it, but the idea had deeply embarrassed both of us. He had ignored the advice of his friends and his agent before our wedding because, again, he believed in success, not failure. He also thought that as a writer of character-driven screenplays, of political and romantic satires, I was not as interested in money as other people were. He was right, maybe, but I was interested in revenge.

I wanted him to come home and tell me to my face that he was leaving me for another woman. As you can see, I wanted to make it difficult for him.

3.

When you are thirteen, a recent initiate into the tragicomedy of adolescence, you imagine yourself marrying the boys whose dazed or beaming faces greet you from the dog-eared pages of teen magazines. You imagine yourself marrying your girlfriends' older brothers, those with driver's licenses and beginners' mustaches and possibly an alarming tattoo or two they have tried to hide from their parents. You imagine yourself, after the prom or on the night they propose, being deflowered by these boys, both the famous and the unfamous ones. You peer at your face in the mirror for hours after school and worry about your nose and cheekbones and slightly crooked teeth. You know yourself to be pretty enough, but probably not beautiful. Your legs are bony, or else they are too fat—you unwillingly, helplessly, wear the evidence of a loving mother's after-school cupcakes and cookies, her pancake breakfasts and Friday-night deep-dish pizzas.

Antony Grégoire is only three and a half years older than I am. He was a senior in high school when I was a freshman, and from a young age, he did not carry with him the sense that he would be famous, as many other stars apparently do. The same night that he had talked about serendipity, he'd told me that he'd planned to become a structural engineer and design vast, intricate bridges; he had always liked science and math. He was not a spendthrift, not in the hysterical fashion that many famous people are. There was never any fear of bankruptcy, because he did not insist on having seventeen vintage Rolls-Royces in storage or a large staff of servants who all lived in his palatial home. We had a cook and a housekeeper who each worked four days a week. Someone came to do our landscaping; someone else came to take care of the pool. This is, of course, the manner in which many people live in the wealthier towns and cities of the world. I loved Antony and did not want to lose him. I thought that I might be able to forgive him if he appeared at the foot of our bed the morning after his call from Alberta and proclaimed that he had spoken too soon, that he had made a mistake.

4.

I know that contradictory examples do exist. Paul Newman and Joanne Woodward's long marriage almost defies belief, but people forget that he left his first wife to marry her. If Joanne had been his first, I'm not sure it would have lasted.

I wonder about Elizabeth Taylor, hardly an example of spousal fidelity, but nonetheless—would she have stopped at three if her beloved third husband, Michael Todd, hadn't died in a plane crash a year after their marriage, in a plane he had named *Lucky Liz*? Or would Richard Burton's appearance have been inevitable, their own two marriages and divorces, and the 69-carat diamond he bought for her at Cartier, also inevitable?

5.

Other men I have had relationships with have not been as famous as Antony, but hardly anyone on earth is. He is in an exclusive club, the .01 percent of the world's population with instantly recognizable faces. The members are musicians, miscreants, politicians, movie stars: Mick Jagger, Cher, Che Guevara, Hillary Clinton, Bozo the Clown.

I was seeing someone else when I met Antony, one of my former graduate-school classmates who was trying to earn a living as an actor. His name was James, as in Jesse, he liked to say, not Henry, which confused most people who heard this because James was his first name, not his last. By the time we started dating, he had been hired to act in a few commercials and had also had nonrecurring parts on four or five TV shows. He was funny and a little strange and often unpredictable in that he might tell me to meet him for dinner at a nice restaurant where he would show up wearing a police uniform and handcuff me to him. We would walk into the restaurant and he would tell people that it was all right, I wasn't dangerous, no cause for alarm. He loved attention, and not surprisingly, I did too. I liked him quite a lot, though I couldn't imagine that we had a real future. He was probably depressive and sometimes would descend into days-long funks when he didn't get a callback, but most of the time he was sexy, spontaneous, enthusiastic. As far as I was concerned, we were having fun. We made each other feel less lonely, and in a big city, especially one like Los Angeles, this isn't so easy to do. Ordinary people feel lonely in a way that the famous do not, and despite how it might seem to those who do not live in Southern California, there are so many more ordinary people than movie stars sitting in traffic jams or buying their coffee beans and wheat bread at Vons.

6.

What happened is nothing new or surprising: Antony left me for a popular actress, one he'd met a year earlier on the set of his fourteenth feature film. The film flopped, which pleased me. Before marrying him, other people's failures had rarely made me happy, but when I began to sense that his interest in me was fading, I turned petty, often mean. The actress was his lover in the flop, and I'd known as soon as he told me that she had been cast to play the female lead that things I could not hope to control were going to happen. She was impossible to dismiss. It wasn't only her beauty and fame, both greater than mine, or her age, which was less than mine. She is the type of person who cares about causes. She cares about them publicly but genuinely, I will admit. She has raised and donated sizable sums of money for the construction of schools and hospitals and women's shelters in countries I had never previously considered visiting, let alone donating any portion of my earnings to. Hers, somehow, is a voice that people in power, here and abroad, listen to. More than any other reason, I dislike her because she reminds me that I am not good and kind enough, that my causes are laughable because few extend beyond my front door. I am aware that most people live their lives the same way that I do—no one is more important to us than ourselves. It is simply the nature of our species, of any species, I suppose, but this thought is not a comfort.

We had one phone conversation, accidentally, while Antony and I were in the process of divorcing. She picked up his cell phone one morning, probably forgetting to look at the display to see who was calling. But I also wonder if she saw my name in the liquid crystal, and for a wild, breathless second, she needed to know the words that I'd been saving up to say to her.

We both froze when we heard each other's voices. I finally mumbled, "I guess Antony isn't free?" I couldn't even pretend that I didn't recognize her voice.

"He's not here." There was something in her tone I couldn't pin down—shame? Or only wariness?

"When will he be back?"

"I'm not sure. A few hours, maybe?"

If I'd been capable of organizing a coherent thought, I would probably have said something unforgivable to her then, something she would remember and worry over, possibly for the rest of her life. Something that she would think was true, even if it wasn't—that she had no talent; that he would cheat on her too if he hadn't already; that he was cheating on her now with me.

I only asked her to tell him to call me back, my heart beating so hard I was sure that it would have burst from my chest if my breastbone hadn't been there to hold it down.

The caribou movie was his sixteenth feature film. It ended up doing very well, its box office receipts respectable, the director and one of the costars winning prestigious awards. I didn't go to see it. Antony did not appear at the foot of our bed the morning after his breakup phone call. He did not appear in person at our home until two and a half weeks later, during a scheduled hiatus in the film's production. Instead, he sent emissaries, three of his closest friends, one at a time, to tell me how embarrassed and regretful he was, how he hoped we could both be reasonable, how he hoped I'd eventually understand and forgive him. Coward, I said. Stupid fucking cowardly bastard. I wanted him to fall through the Canadian ice. I wanted him to get frostbite. I hoped that certain crucial body parts would fall off. I said these childish things to anyone who would listen, and at first there were many people who did.

Then, within four days, the news of our collapse began to appear in the papers, a big headline in a few of the sleazier ones, along with the most unflattering pictures of me that they could find, ones where my eyes were half-closed or I appeared to be snarling, ones where I looked drunk but wasn't at all, each printed with falsehood-riddled articles. Antony looked angelic, innocent, desirable—the onus, somehow, on me, as if I had driven him into the arms of a more beautiful and worthy woman. In some photos, her head was superimposed onto pictures where my head had actually been: Antony with his arm around my waist, whispering in my ear, kissing my cheek, looking the adoring husband; his hand at the small of my back, his body leaning protectively toward mine. These were old pictures, ones from our courtship and first year of marriage. I wanted to sue these sleaze rags but knew that it would be wasted time and money. The pictures and the stories were already out there. Nothing could be done to take them back.

7.

"No." When I thought about it, I realized this was a word we said to each other often.

We didn't have any children. Nor did we adopt. We thought that we would do one or the other, possibly both, but after two years, then three more, it hadn't happened. There was always a bigger, more important movie to make, more time to be spent apart, another topic that I hoped to research, another screenplay to adapt or write. I had known after year four that it wouldn't happen. I had stopped wanting a baby as much as I did at the beginning, and he had stopped talking about becoming a father. There was, at least, no vicious custody battle to add to the war over our finances.

"You didn't earn any of this money that you're trying to take from me," he said not long before the divorce was set in motion, angry that I wasn't going to settle for four million in cash and the house in Laurel Canyon, leaving him the New York co-op and the Miami villa and over sixty-seven million in stocks and other, more liquid assets. "You have your own fucking money, Emma."

"I know that," I said, "but I'm not the one leaving you for someone else."

He exhaled loudly. "You know that I'm really sorry this has happened."

"That's hard for me to believe."

"You don't have to believe me, but it's still true. I don't want us to be enemies. Maybe we could eventually be friends."

I snorted. "Sophie would love that."

"She'd understand."

"I really doubt that, Antony. Not everyone wants the same things you want."

When the outrage and jealousy dissipated, there was only abjectness. I knew in those moments that I would have taken him back. I knew that I would never be as close to another man like him. Whether or not I wanted to admit it, he was extraordinary, and being with him had made me feel as if ordinary concerns, ordinary disappointments and sorrows, had less to do with me than they did with other people. This is what celebrity signifies more than anything else—it is the strict refutation of the banal.

"How can you still care about him?" asked one friend, a divorced woman herself. "After all of the things he's done to humiliate you? You have more self-respect than that, don't you?"

"I don't know," I said, because maybe I didn't. I had the idea, obscenely childish and predictable but one that could have been a very potent kind of revenge, of writing a book about our marriage. In a self-righteous fever, I wrote ninety pages before I knew that I didn't have the will to finish it. By this point in our separation, Antony doubtless considered me a hardened opportunist, but I was not completely unhinged. In spite of my lingering bitter feelings of betrayal, I knew that it would be better for me to retain my self-respect and the notions of decency that had been ingrained in me by my Midwestern upbringing: you do not let people know what you're thinking, especially if your thoughts are uncharitable; you do not profit (emotionally or financially) at other people's expense; you do not intentionally hurt the people you care for or once cared for very much.

I missed him fiercely at times and awoke in the middle of the night, my face damp with tears, wondering if I could win him back. The clock on the bureau ticked ceaselessly, its answers all in riddles. After several consecutive nights of this, I couldn't bear the sound of its ticking and threw it away.

Friends, my parents, my one sibling (an older brother who liked Antony quite a bit) thought that if nothing else, I should have been relieved that the pain and anxiety and implacable jealousy were ending: the innumerable days during our marriage when I had been at home, trying to work, picturing him having a very good time with the other cast members in a film that was shooting in Moscow or Key West or Nairobi or Paris or Kuala Lumpur, picturing all of the fans who hoped to get close to him, to smile at him and be smiled upon in return, the fans who wanted to touch him, hold his hand, look him directly in the eyes and then go home to remember this one-minute interlude for the rest of their lives.

As I saw it, he was always off somewhere, living the best days of his life. If I went with him on a shoot, I wasn't precisely welcomed, by him or by anyone else working on the film. I was a potential fuck-it-upper, though some people were kind and decorously curious about my current writing projects. Antony needed to concentrate, memorize his lines, rehearse, get into character, which I understood but resented. I wanted love, physical proof that he needed only me—an outrageous and absurd desire.

N.B.: No one who marries someone famous knows precisely what will happen to their self-esteem. You might search fan sites, as fruitless and stupid as this would be, to determine who your far-flung enemies are, who has proclaimed the most ardent love for your husband, who plans to act on it as soon as possible. Despite how pitiful these sites and their custodians are, you feel corrosive jealousy. You want to go through the fan mail that arrives at the studio before your husband sees any part of it, throw most of the letters away, threaten with bloody bodily harm those who have sent lewd photos, written bad erotic poetry: "I Want to Suck Your Dick for Sex Days Straight, Mr. Grégoire."

If they all weren't so stupidly earnest, it might have been funnier.

8.

After seven months of bickering, I got much more than four million in cash and the Laurel Canyon house. As soon as we both signed the papers, we didn't speak again for two and a half years, not until our paths overlapped at a fundraiser for an AIDS research foundation that his second wife had insisted he attend with her. He married her a year after leaving me, and this time he insisted on a prenuptial agreement. Five months later, they were parents.

I'm not sure why I did it, but I started seeing a married man. He had been a friend for a number of years, one I was always mildly attracted to but didn't do anything to encourage. His name was Otik, a Czech man who directed commercials and music videos. Barring the gambling addiction, he wanted to be Dostoyevsky. I had read some of the novel he was writing before I became his lover and it impressed me, though it wasn't likely to be published—there was nothing American about it, no irony or levity in its pages, false or otherwise. I did not see how it could possibly sell. I didn't tell him this and I turned out to be wrong. When his book, *The Monk's Arsenal*, sold, he sent me three dozen roses—red, yellow, and pink. I tore off the tissue paper and felt the heated rush of tears because this was something Antony had done during our first two or three years together. Enormous bouquets with quotes from Keats or Shakespeare scribbled onto the cards would arrive for no reason. I liked to imagine the people in the flower shop, the young girls who took the order from Antony's assistant, knowing that this Antony was *the* Antony and wondering if they would ever be loved by a famous man who supposedly could give them everything they desired.

I met him when I was in graduate school at UCLA, where I spent four fevered months in my second year writing a screenplay for him. In a moment of bravado, I sent it to his agent. And then, as if it were an elaborate waking dream, Antony called a dozen weeks later and said that he loved it, he wanted to meet me, he was so flattered and impressed. I was twenty-seven, prematurely cynical about love, but then suddenly, every woman I knew hated me.

We met for lunch on Olvera Street, Antony's bodyguard, who was also his driver, waiting outside on a chair the restaurant owner smilingly set by the entrance for him. I couldn't speak for the first several minutes without laughing nervously. My face was flushed, my legs unreliable, my palms so sweaty my napkin became damp. I was terribly lonely and had feebly hoped for someone like him for a long time. It was why I had moved from Minneapolis to California. I had the same dream as millions of other hopeless people: to be discovered and declared worthy by someone far above me in stature.

He was tall, taller than I was by several inches, and smelled like he had just stepped from his bath. His hair was longer than when I had last seen it—in a film that had been released a couple of months earlier, one in which he had appeared naked and raving over a brother's death—and he touched my arm several times as he told me that he already had a director and a couple of producers interested and they were probably going to film my screenplay if I would allow them to. They would buy it from me, of course, for a fair price. I shook my head, incredulous. "It's a gift," I said. "I couldn't possibly make you pay for it."

He laughed. "If someone offers you money for your work, you take it. Rule number one. Maybe the only rule in L.A. Do you act too?"

I was smiling so hard that my face hurt. "I wouldn't dream of it," I said.

He touched my arm again. People in the restaurant were leering at us. I could feel them trying to decide what was going on, who I was. How in the world had I arrived at this table? Why not them? "Really?" he said. "I thought everyone did."

I couldn't tell if he was being facetious, but I didn't think so. "I'd rather direct," I said, hoping he'd laugh. More than feeling his hands on me, I wanted to make him laugh. Other women, prettier ones, probably couldn't do that, not often.

Instead, he winked. "It's always one or the other. Often both."

They paid forty-two thousand for my screenplay, more money than I had earned in a year, two years, probably, at that time in my life. The film, *Two Things You Should Know*, was a success. Later I learned that I could have gotten a lot more if I had tried to sell it through an agent. The film made money, sold overseas to European and Asian distributors, won a few big awards in the United States. Suddenly, I had become someone kind of important. A year or so later I wrote a sequel, *Two More Things You Should Know*; it wasn't bad, but it wasn't ever produced. By then, Antony was being sought out by the Italian American directors he had always fantasized about working with.

For a while, we were friends, nothing more, and met from time to time for lunch or dinner; we talked on the phone and went to parties where we knew we would see each other. I was in love with him from the beginning, more or less, but didn't admit it to myself. I felt an immense, heart-heavy gratitude toward him; he was, it seemed, responsible for my life becoming what I had long hoped it would. He appeared to care about me too, and not just because the film I had written for him was the first one where most of the better-known critics took him seriously.

I told myself that I didn't want to get involved with him. I could see that he had every woman's ardent attention wherever he appeared. From what I knew of him, he did not date any one woman for more than a few months. He was as restless as many famous men are believed to be—there are so many options, so many willing participants. If you don't feel the pressure to make one momentous choice, you don't; it is easier to make a number of small choices, to keep making them.

But I loved that he liked me, that he kept track of me, sent me gifts, called occasionally. I knew that it was better to be his friend than his short-lived lover. But after *Two Things* debuted, a year after he finished filming it, he bought me an expensive German car because the film was such a remarkable success.

After Antony delivered the car, he started to court me. I didn't know it was a courtship, but to most others, especially to James, my depressive boyfriend, it was obvious. "You're being obtuse," he said. "Or else you're just lying. I can't believe you can't see what he's up to."

"He has so much money that I'm sure it's not a big deal to buy me a car."

"No, probably not, but the gesture is the big deal. You don't buy a car for someone you don't expect something from in return. How often does he call you now?"

I looked at him, feeling his unease, his desire to give up on me, but he didn't want to, and I didn't want him to either, not yet. His lips were very red right then, as if he'd been pressing them together hard. He was an attractive guy, a tall, sturdy man who had played high school basketball well, something he was still proud of. I liked his long limbs and solid frame, his tangled dark hair. I liked, too, that other women noticed him.

"Not that often," I said, which was a lie. Antony was calling me every few days. Sometimes he wanted me to read a script, which I always did, scorning most of them. But mostly he wanted to talk and flirt. He told me he didn't know anyone else like me, and of course this was the best compliment I could imagine, aside from "I can't live without you."

"He's just thanking me again for the screenplay," I said.

"He paid you for it."

"He's still just my friend." I had never told James that I'd written the screenplay specifically for Antony. It would have been a stupid, possibly cruel thing to do.

James rolled his eyes. "If that's what you want to call it."

9.

He asked me to marry him when he was sitting next to Tom Petty on the *Tonight Show* sofa. Petty had just played two songs and talked to Jay for a few minutes, and then Antony came out wearing a beautiful shirt, one made of indigo linen, which I had bought for him during a trip to Chicago a few months earlier. They chatted for several minutes before Jay, with his friendly, squinting smile, asked him about his love life. Antony smiled back and said, "Everything's going well. But it'll be even better if Emma, my girlfriend, says yes to my marriage proposal."

Jay looked at Antony, blinking several times, and said, "Have you asked her? Are you telling me that you asked her and she said she wasn't sure?"

Antony shook his head. "Actually, I'm asking her now. I hope she's watching."

The audience started shrieking and hooting and kept it up until the producers broke for a commercial. I was with my friend Jeanie, another transplant from the Minneapolis area, and hadn't been watching as attentively as I usually did when Antony appeared on TV (it was later, after I saw the show again, that I memorized every detail of Jay and Antony's exchange), but when I heard my name and realized what was going on, I started shaking so hard that Jeanie had to hold both of my hands for several minutes before getting up to pour us both a large glass of wine and then another. The show had been taped only a few hours before it aired, much less lead time than usual, and no one had leaked Antony's proposal before then, at least not to me. Very soon my cell phone began to ring without stopping for most of the night. Friends from home, my parents and other relatives, were calling to congratulate me, to weep and exclaim with me. I could not believe that he wanted to marry me, and I suppose I should have paid attention to this disbelief, but who says no when someone you love, famous or not, asks you to marry him?

Soon after his proposal, a few of my friends started to show their jealousy and doubt but tried to pass it off as bracing observation, meant only to make me think.

One friend from home said, You'll always have money now. What's the point of you working anymore? Why don't you go with him when he's shooting his movies and try to have fun?

A second friend said, What about all his gorgeous ex-girlfriends? Is it really over with all of them? How would you even know for sure?

A third friend said, Is he actually going to go home with you for Christmas and family reunions?

Someone else, my brother's girlfriend, asked, Will it be an open marriage?

10.

Antony's favorite joke:

What did the bra say to the hat?
You go on a head, I'll give these two a lift.

For a while I thought that he didn't take himself too seriously. After all, he could easily have ignored the script I'd sent to him, never bothered to meet me in person to tell me that he liked it and wanted to buy it. He could have had his agent contact me instead. He could have gotten swept up in the cult of his own fame and completely left everyday life behind.

I suppose it was inevitable that he would meet another woman who interested him more than I did, one who did the same work he did, who understood all of the lurid fan mail and far-away meetings and the sheer exhaustion he felt on some days simply being who he was.

II.

James did not say that he hated me when I admitted to my feelings for Antony. For one, he was a little in awe of him. He might even have hoped that somehow he would benefit from my new fantasy relationship, that I would feel guilty and ask Antony to go out of his way to introduce James to directors or casting agents. He was probably even more talented than Antony was, and for a while, I thought that he would succeed—it might have been on television rather than in film, but his eventual success did not seem at all far-fetched. His depression, his self-sabotaging tendencies, his impatience and manic intensity, however, conspired to keep him from the breakthrough he hoped for.

This is something few people talk about in Hollywood, or anywhere else, despite how obvious it is: most people don't succeed as actors simply because they can't handle the near-constant rejection that confronts most beginners. Rejection is the relentless, powerful hazing that disables ninety-seven out of a hundred talented people. No one tells you that for your first two hundred auditions, you would be lucky to land one or two parts, minor ones at that. No one says this because it is stories like Antony's that have convinced most of us that it should be easy, and if it isn't, if you're not immediately chosen and declared the next Harrison Ford or Robert De Niro or Meryl Streep, then you're just not good enough.

12.

Otik, the married man I started seeing after my divorce, never asked what it was like for me to be with Antony, whether I expected to be as happy again, or as miserable. He did not care to know, nor did he seem concerned that his life was not as glamorous as Antony's, at least not in the same highly visible way. He was a dozen years older than I, and due in part to the close relatives and friends he had lost to various wars and self-destructive habits, he was unimpressed by the things that impress most of us.

He said a few things at the beginning of our affair that I thought did have to do with Antony, though he was never named.

"Certain events that happen to us," he said, "we spend a lot of time trying to forget, or else we try to live as if they are about to happen again, even when we know they won't."

Immediately I felt defensive. "I don't live in the past," I said.

"That's not what I'm saying, Emma. I don't mean you in particular. It's something I've been thinking about a lot lately. My wife is dependent on me for things she believes I provide for her but I don't. Half of what we see isn't really there."

I didn't believe she was as needy or as deluded as he made her sound. She ran a Montessori school and was raising two children on her own before meeting Otik. She intimidated me with her direct gaze, her air of always knowing the answer before anyone else. "She seems very grounded to me," I said.

He shook his head. "She doesn't have a lot of confidence in herself. She thinks that I keep her life from falling apart."

Along with Dostoyevsky, he idolized Milan Kundera. I think this was part of the problem. Not that I didn't like Kundera too, but in addition to their celebratory sexiness, his books had a surreal fatalism to them, as did Otik himself, and sometimes when we were together, it seemed as if I were facing a grinning cement wall.

"I don't feel like that," I said. "I know what you do and don't provide for me."

"I'm not worried about you. Your weaknesses are well policed."

I stiffened. "Thanks."

He laughed. "That's a compliment. Most people can't wait for the chance to tell you what's wrong with them."

13.

As a lover, what was Antony like? Was I too nervous to enjoy it the first time? Or was it so extraordinary to be alone with him, naked in his embrace, that it was the best time of my life?

These are a few of the questions my less discreet friends have asked.

Whether or not they realize it, these are also the questions everyone who reads celebrity magazines asks themselves about the featured couples as they turn the pages. *What could it possibly be like for them? Is each time always the best time?*

I have heard that a man in New York, a clever guy with social influence and connections, holds parties meant to seem like old-fashioned salons where he and his friends discuss questions such as Do people who can afford it deserve to have more than one or two kids?

Is sushi a big con?

Is sex overrated?

My answer to that last question is a qualified no. The actual physical rewards of sex, because they are so often inconsistent, probably are overrated, but its emotional heft, its implicit statement that another person desires you, possibly more than anyone else, if only in that moment, is, in a way, unrivaled. I loved sleeping with Antony because in those moments, no one else was as close to him as I was.

The first time was at my home, not his, and I wasn't ready for it, not amply perfumed or dressed in something ridiculous and remarkable. He came over unannounced, and it was raining and February and the previous day had been Valentine's Day. He'd sent me a card, and flowers, and four pounds of Swiss chocolate. He was in New York that day, doing publicity for his latest project, apparently dateless. When he appeared at my front door, his hair was damp, his face tired but smiling; he asked if he could come in, if he could stay for a while, possibly for good?

This isn't real, I kept thinking all that night and the next morning. This is a joke, isn't it?

THE PRETTIEST GIRLS

WHEN I MET HER, I had the kind of job people always think they want until they try it for a few weeks. I was working for a studio in Hollywood that made a lot of profitable, mediocre movies, and one of my primary responsibilities was to find locations where other movie people would eventually show up with millions of dollars' worth of equipment, a couple of irritating stars, and an overworked crew to shoot a feature-length film. It was a job where you had to trust quite a few strangers, where dead ends were time-consuming and predictably infuriating. We were in Mexico, in this dusty little satellite of Guadalajara called Tonalá, where, within an hour after my arrival, I saw a guy in a red vest and black cowboy hat, probably a laborer from a nearby farm, riding on horseback through the streets at rush hour. He sat high on a chestnut horse, clopping through the honking streams of bus and taxi traffic as if he did it every day, which it more or less looked like he did.

The girl was in the marketplace, selling ceramics with her great-aunt, a very wrinkled, fiercely smiling woman. The girl spoke good English and told me that her name was Elsa

Margarita, offering me her small, cool hand. I've seen a lot of beautiful women, many of them famous, but I couldn't stop staring at this girl. She reminded me of Sophia Loren in *Houseboat*, a movie she made with Cary Grant, one where he fell in love with her both on and off camera. His interest was not returned, which left him and many of the film's fans heartbroken. They wanted life to mirror the movies as badly as they wanted anything. I told Elsa that I was visiting from Hollywood, scouting locations for a film. This line worked nine times out of ten because girls her age always wanted to be famous. She said that she would help me find the church the director needed for a wedding scene near the end of the film, one that was supposed to take place in a dream sequence. He needed a bone-white chapel with a stark steeple and a glaring blue sky behind it and one arching doorway wide enough for a woman with a baby in each arm to walk through. I asked this girl what she wanted in return and she looked at me for a long time before saying, "I want to be in your movie. An extra? Is that what you call it?"

"Yes, that's the right word, but I'll have to see," I said.

I could have told her yes and meant it, but she might have had eight friends who also wanted to be extras, and if I wanted my church, they would have to be hired too. Something along those crooked lines had happened before. Beautiful girls had raked their stiletto fingernails across my back and balls and my blind, dumbly thumping heart a few more times than I wanted to think about. I was forty-seven with two divorces and two kids in East Coast colleges and I knew that women like this ambitious girl could be as cruel and status-hungry as any multimillionaire studio head with his one P.M. foot massage, two P.M. blowjob, and sixty-thousand-dollar dinner parties.

If I had said yes, she'd have known she had me, and likely as not, I'd keep saying yes. But then she gave me a look of such abject disappointment that after a few seconds of feeling my stomach twist into a tangle of knots, I said, Okay, fine. A second or two later I realized that she probably considered herself an actress and had been practicing certain looks for years in front of the mirror and her mother and siblings and the neighborhood gossips who stood around in her family's crowded kitchen, chests out, feet splayed, eating sweets and drinking all the coffee. She had it down, but despite recognizing this, I didn't want to let her out of my sight. It was painful to look at her too closely, everything about her so perfectly ordered, so soft and gleaming and implausible that she didn't seem real.

Strange as it might sound, I had the sudden disturbing feeling that things would soon start to go wrong for her, if they hadn't already. I could see her marrying some brute who would beat her when drunk and impregnate her every year until she was round and mute as an eight ball, or she would end up crossing the border illegally and get picked up by another kind of brute who would rape her and leave her for dead somewhere along the parched, murderous road. I realized that I was prone to melodrama, but this was a pitfall of the trade that had paid my bills for almost twenty years.

I got my church later that afternoon, and that night, after a new pair of sandals and a leather knapsack for Elsa, several drinks and a plate of *chilaquiles y frijoles*, I also got her into bed. I wasn't sure how old she was but she looked at least twenty. She told me she was twenty-three. Twenty in Mexico wasn't quite the same thing as twenty in America. If a girl was over twenty, came from a family with no money, and hadn't yet been handed over to a passable husband, she might never find one she could stand to look at in the morning. The girls roaming the streets in most Mexican cities, the ones hoping for lonely, horny men with cash, were anywhere from eight to sixty-eight, but I didn't usually look at them. It wasn't that some of them weren't worth looking at, but you didn't know what would happen to you. Some had pimps who would take your watch, wallet, and shoes, then laugh and tell you to go to the police. There were far worse things too, obviously. And some of these girls worked in places partitioned like an emergency room, with only a piece of cloth to separate one groaning john from the next.

Elsa wasn't a prostitute but she wasn't a virgin either. She didn't even pretend to be. I did not want to be her first anyway. It was always better with a woman who knew what to expect when she was with a naked man.

I took her back to my hotel a few more times over the next couple of days, and I remember her going into the bathroom at one point and rummaging through the things in my kit bag. My shaving brush was of great interest to her. She came out holding it and asked what I did with it. I pretended to smear some cream on her chin, the bristles tickling her. "American men are so funny," she said. "Why don't you use your hands to put it on?"

"Because we're a complicated breed."

"Breed? What is that?"

"The kind of animal you are."

She gave me a funny look. "You're not an animal." She was wearing one of my white T-shirts and had her hair pulled back with a red headband. No one I'd touched had ever looked more beautiful than she did in that moment, and I felt this crazed unease, like I couldn't let her out of my sight because the minute I did, someone would harm her.

But I had to leave the next day, and when I did, she cried and told me that I'd been kinder to her than any other man she knew. I didn't believe her, but her tears affected me. She gave me her number and asked me to call her from California.

I said I would but didn't end up keeping my promise. I had no idea what I'd have said to her over the phone: *I miss you are you okay what's new do you miss me?* She was so young, probably no older than my twenty-one-year-old daughter, Lily. It would have been a pathetic joke. But I did miss her, thought of her a stupidly huge fraction of the time, and had sex with my girlfriend, Lisette, because I couldn't have it with Elsa. I almost called her twice, but I'd look at her number on the hotel stationery and feel like a fool, my vanity overwhelming— who knew how many boyfriends she had, how many guys my age or younger she was playing around with. Someone as beautiful as she was had to have admirers, maybe some with more to offer than I did.

Several weeks later, however, I saw her again. When I came back with the crew to shoot the church scene and a few others, I called her and kept my promise that she would be one of the hundreds of extras in *The Color of Exile*, a film that eventually ended up on some of the worst-films-of-the-year lists. No surprise, but I wasn't paid to tell the director he would blow it.

"I was waiting for you," she said as soon as she heard my voice. "I knew you would call me. Come and get me right now. I want to stay with you tonight."

I didn't ask what her mother thought. Her dad was long gone, off with another woman in another city. I didn't want to get wrapped up in her family's unhappiness anyway.

She was wearing a pale pink dress when I picked her up, her beauty a blow to the knees. Her mother, a plump woman with her graying hair in a bun and a face as friendly as a slammed door, stayed inside their tiny beige house, which was on one of Tonalá's narrow, steep streets. Elsa answered the door by herself, leaping at me and kissing me noisily on the lips. I wondered if anyone in the neighboring houses was watching us, people who might have been used to Elsa carrying on with strangers. "Should I come in and say hello to your mother?" I asked.

"Okay. *Venga*." She pulled me into the house, her smile so large it had to be sincere. In the little hallway that led in from the street, family pictures had been taped to the walls. Several pairs of worn-out flip-flops had been lined up beneath the photo gallery in a neat row. The house was dim and stuffy, and within seconds Elsa's mother appeared before us, surprising me with her blue jeans and man's black T-shirt, no apron or floral housedress. Elsa looked nothing like her. She shook my hand and said, *"Mucho gusto, señor. Gracias."*

I returned the greeting, not knowing what she was thanking me for. We nodded at each other but said nothing more.

"It's okay," said Elsa. "She's cooking. We can leave."

I could smell frying beef, chilies drifting with it. I was relieved that her mother didn't invite me to stay for dinner, even if the food would have been good. We would have had nothing to say to each other. I didn't know what my intentions with her daughter were, and she understood this, I'm certain, even better than I did.

But it didn't end after the two days she spent with me. I lived those two days in a state of hypersensitivity—everything brighter, louder, heavier, but also softer. There was Elsa in the center, all else background, a high-speed blur. I allowed myself to do something few sane people would have congratulated me for: I brought her with me to Pasadena, where I was living at the time. If I hadn't, I wouldn't have been able to stop thinking about her, missing her, worrying that she was letting herself be hurt by some violent idiot. When she said, *"Tráigamelo.* I want to go wherever you go," I turned to her, my eyes stinging.

We were lying on the bed, housekeeping banging on the doors down the hall, the carpet soggy from years of humidity and dirty feet, Elsa already dressed for the day in a yellow blouse and short blue skirt, her toes brown and tiny against my hairy leg. I looked at her hard and saw how unmarked by time and disappointment she was, how unaware that the best possibilities of her life would probably become missed or failed chances. She was pre-reality in a sense, pre- most of the experiences that lead so many people to their final resting place of bitterness, cynicism, regret. Looking at her, I felt the staggering threat of my doubts and loneliness and lust. I didn't know if I would get this close again to another girl like her. "All right," I said. "You can come."

"But you have to do what I tell you," I said. "When I tell you. No fucking around, because you could be sent back here so fast you'd get dizzy."

She cried out, loud enough for the maids down the hall to hear. "I've been waiting so long to leave here," she said. "I will be good. *Te lo juro*, Jim."

I had money, enough for most of the things I wanted, and could take her across. A couple of the border guards knew me, and in those days, their price wasn't very high, but I worried that they'd want her for themselves, that they'd despise and harass me for taking her out. Neither of them made any trouble though, let alone a hostile remark; they took my money and waved us through. Seconds after we crossed the border, she told me that she loved me. She turned to me with her starving eyes and soft mouth and flushed cheeks and whispered, *Te quiero.*

I looked at her. "*Te quiero* too." I don't think it was a lie.

Something else: it shouldn't have, considering how many immigrants were dying every week trying to get across in the worst conditions conceivable, but it still astonished me that without taking much time to reflect on the implications, she was willing to pack a bag, say good-bye to her family and friends and everything that was familiar, everything that was safe, and go with me, a stranger whose past was unknown to her, to a future she could not have imagined, not with any authority, but she did. She did it without sentimentality too, as far as I could tell.

We drove up from Guadalajara, a very long drive, desperation its chief geographical feature much of the way— ramshackle houses, fruit peddlers' morose little stands, gas stations, and desiccated land. We didn't fly because I didn't know any of the immigration people at the airport on either end. We crossed near Tijuana and then drove up to San Diego, where we spent our first night together in America and I don't think Elsa slept for one second. She had to touch everything and smell it too—not just the soap and lotion and shampoo in the bathroom, but the bed linens, the curtains, the paint on the walls, the armchair next to the TV, even the telephone. "It all smells so clean," she said blissfully. *"Me encantan los Estados Unidos."*

"In English," I said.

"Sí, Mr. California," she said, flashing me a gorgeous, maniacal smile.

"You've really never been here before?"

She shook her head. *"Jamás."*

"English, Elsa."

"If you marry me, I won't have to worry about getting deported."

I didn't say anything, only forced my mouth into a noncommittal smile. It wasn't going to happen, but I didn't tell her this. Two marriages were enough. I didn't have any doubts that I'd be able to screw up a third one too, especially to someone who could easily have been mistaken for a friend of Lily's or my son, Patrick's, who was only a year and a half younger than his sister. My kids and I weren't enemies, but over the past few years, it had started to bother me that we didn't know one another very well, something that was mostly my fault. We hadn't lived in the same house in almost twelve years; when they were still children, they visited me during summer vacations and one weekend a month, when I went to see them, or else flew them out to L.A., after I'd moved from Chicago, where they and their mother had remained. One of my first thoughts after I brought Elsa to California was that Patrick would be attracted to her too—any straight guy would have been. I could imagine us competing for her, the end result being that my son would win, but I didn't see myself introducing them, at least not anytime soon. This should have been warning enough that bringing her north was a reckless, lunatic idea.

At the time, however, I wasn't interested in thinking about how or when it would end. You don't buy a car that you've coveted for years and imagine yourself crashing it into a wall a few weeks later. I didn't like endings, having lived through a number of bad ones already. Lisette was enough for me to worry about. I didn't know what she would do when she found out that not only was I breaking things off, I had already found her replacement.

"You're a coward" was the first thing she said. "A stupid, selfish coward who's so afraid of dying he has to fuck the life out of every girl he sees."

"That's not true," I said lamely.

"I think it is," she said. "Because you're a liar too."

I didn't let myself snatch at the bait. After two divorces, one of them acrimonious and prolonged, I knew it helped nothing to start accusing her of neglect or selfishness. She was still young, only thirty-four, a very pretty real estate agent with a well-trained singing voice she had given up trying to sell to record companies at twenty-five. "I thought we were going to make it," she said angrily. "I really thought some-thing was finally going to work out."

She said a few things more, forced me to take back the jade bracelet I'd given her a few weeks earlier, and told me to leave. I left her in Silver Lake and drove home, worrying the whole time that I'd made a mistake. Lisette was reliable, mature, an American citizen, a known quantity, as much as any woman could have been.

Elsa was very jealous that I even had to see Lisette—couldn't I have broken up with her over the phone?

No, I couldn't have. Lisette deserved better treatment, even if I wasn't capable of offering it with any consistency.

"How many other girls are you with?" Elsa asked. "I'm not the only one, no?"

"You are the only one," I said. "Now that I've talked to Lisette."

"Swear it," she said in a high, urgent voice. We were in the downstairs hallway, posters from a few of the better movies I'd worked on lining the walls. Her hair was damp; she'd just gotten out of the pool. I tried to touch her, but she backed away. "Cut your finger and swear on the blood," she said.

I stared at her. "I'm not going to cut myself, Elsa. You're going to have to take my word for it. For everything, not just Lisette."

"I don't believe you. *No soy la única.*"

"You are the only one. I'm not lying to you."

She retreated to the kitchen and I went upstairs to lie down, my head throbbing, but a minute or two later she appeared in the bedroom. She had a steak knife in her fist, the blade pointing at the ceiling, the exact opposite of how my ex-wife and I had taught our children to carry scissors and knives. "Cut," she ordered, thrusting the knife toward me.

I got up and grabbed the knife from her, sweating now. "I'm not going to cut myself," I said. "You're the only person I'm with. You have to trust me. I don't want anyone else."

We stared at each other, her delicate face rigid with anxiety. Mine couldn't have been much better. The knife made it clear that she could do whatever she wanted to me when I wasn't looking, a fact that somehow hadn't occurred to me until then. She might actually have been crazy. She had only been with me in Pasadena for four days by that time, not long enough for me to know, not by any stretch. A few of the people I'd worked with over the years should have been institutionalized but they had enough other people managing their lives to keep them out of the asylum most of the time. There were few limits to what a person with enough money and fame could do.

"What if Lisette wants to see you?"

"She won't."

"What if she does?"

"She won't. It's over." I didn't know this for sure, but I wasn't going to admit it. I was already mourning Lisette and hoped that I wouldn't feel this way for long. I did not like being the villain. My behavior had created unhappiness, disturbances in the field, more often than I cared to admit. I realized that others I knew had done much worse, but this wasn't particularly reassuring.

Elsa was different in America, less confident, more childlike, and I tried to comfort her by spoiling her. If she asked for something material, I said yes. My wallet flew open and the money disappeared into clanging cash registers all over town. *Old fool*, I could hear a voice in my head sneer. Lily in particular gave me a hard time after she found out about Elsa. "What about Lisette?" she said. "I *liked* Lisette. You're a jerk,

Dad. Don't complain to me when things get weird. How do you know you can even trust this person?"

"She's a sweetheart, Lily. When you meet her, you'll see. She's not taking advantage of me."

She made a harsh sound. "I've heard that one before. Note to Dad, I don't want to meet her, so don't bother sending me a plane ticket."

Patrick had nothing to say about Lisette or Elsa when he found out. "Whatever" was his stock response. Dad has a new girlfriend, so what. I thought that if he met Elsa, his attitude would change. Something that is more obvious in L.A. than in most other places is that men hate each other. Aging men especially hate younger men because the most coveted girls like the younger guys more, even if they have less money. The gorgeous girl with the old man? It's his money, the security he offers, not some asinine Freudian thing.

Elsa was so beautiful that worry over losing her crouched in my gut like a venomous toad. She was dependent on me for everything, but it didn't matter. I constantly imagined another man snatching her away, knocking on the front door while I was off hustling for my next big paycheck, Elsa left on her own, sleeping in and watching television, sunbathing, reading magazines, passing the time until my return, when we'd go out to dinner or down into L.A. to sightsee. I took her to Chinatown, the Griffith Observatory, and the Walk of Fame, to shop on Melrose and in the Grove, and I'd notice people looking at her. In a city where no one wanted to be caught looking at anyone else, especially if they weren't famous, people were looking at her. They were probably wondering if she was someone they should know. I felt both proud and viciously possessive. I was glad I had found her but a pit had opened in my stomach and I stood on its edge, trying not to look down. I knew at least three or four other guys who would have tried to take her from me without a second thought.

I hadn't read her as well as I thought either, because she was, in fact, sentimental. She missed her family and called her mother every few days and I'd hear her crying sometimes, but she swore that she didn't want to go back. This was it, the center of the world—Los Angeles de los Estados Unidos. The land of myth and money and movie stars. We had shade to go with our sun. Manicured lawns, clear water shooting out of fountains and golf-course sprinklers. Polite dark-skinned men in white suits parking fancy cars. Starving people were mostly out of sight in the places we visited. I had a swimming pool, four bedrooms, a dishwasher, a lawn service, a house-keeper who came three mornings a week and made our lunches and dinners if I wanted her to. I bought Elsa clothes and shoes and had her hair trimmed at a good salon. In her loneliness, she was nonetheless dazzled. She was still saying that she loved me.

My housekeeper, Lucía, was from Guatemala, and I paid her pretty well. She and Elsa didn't talk to each other very much; Lucía had liked Lisette too, who often gave her perfectly fine castoffs from her wardrobe. Elsa wanted to know what she earned. "Fifteen an hour," I said. "Plus an extra two-hundred and fifty a month for health insurance."

"That's so much," she said. "The kitchen is still dirty when she leaves, and she turned your *chones* blue last week."

I didn't care about the underwear. I had dozens of pairs, and Lucía was very embarrassed and apologetic when she showed them to me. "She's never done that before," I said.

"She takes advantage. She brings food home with her. Did you know that?"

"I told her she could. It's really not a big deal, Elsa. She's worked here for three years and I've never had a problem with her. Some people I know have gone through ten housekeepers in eight months."

"You're too nice to her."

"No, I'm only being fair." Lucía was loyal, reliable, and had four kids back in Guatemala that her older sister had stayed behind to help take care of. Neither woman had a husband anymore. One had died in a farming accident; the other had walked out.

I suspected that Elsa was jealous of my bond with Lucía, innocent as it was, but I didn't want to cast Lucía into the street, despite wanting Elsa in my bed each night, her slender, warm body pressed against my hairier, fatter, older one. I'd forget then about the steak knife, the tearful phone calls, the age and class differences, the future with its inevitable violent collisions. Other times, I'd look at her and realize that I couldn't possibly be what she wanted.

"Do you know Brad and Angelina?" she'd ask. "George ClooneyJuliaRobertsJenniferAnistonNicolasCageStevenSpielberg AdamSandlerBenAffleckMattDamonJenniferGarnerScarlett JohanssonSalmaHayekClintEastwood?"

The list went on, long, tiresome, unsurprising. I did know some of them, not very well, but we had worked together. I could have said quite a few things about a number of actors, but I didn't. I was jealous. I would be fifty in three years and she would be twenty-four. The birth date on her Mexican identity card showed that she was twenty-one; she had only added two years to her age when we met. I'm not sure why, but it didn't make much of a difference. She was over eighteen.

A month went by. I took her out whenever I had the time, to the beach, to the shops, to the studio that employed me, where Elsa hoped George Clooney or some other big star would be hanging around in the halls, waiting to sign an autograph for her, one she would send to her mother and her friends, though she suspected that her little brother would try to sell it on eBay, as he apparently had done with a few of the things her mother cherished in the house.

Aside from a couple of short visits to the studio, I avoided most of my industry friends, anyone who might have been a rival for Elsa's affections. But almost as bad as my jealous paranoia was the morning when I caught her and Lucía arguing, their Spanish so rapid that I could only make out that they were fighting about the kitchen floor, Lucía's face closed, her mouth a grim line of reproach. "Please," I said to Elsa. "The floor's fine."

Both women turned on me, one furious, the other red-faced and tight-lipped. "It's dirty. I can see dirt everywhere," Elsa snapped.

I looked down but didn't see anything. "Please don't make trouble, Elsa."

"You're not my father," she said.

Lucía said nothing and turned back to the carrots she was peeling.

"I know that, but I really wish you wouldn't fight with Lucía."

"You are so blind," Elsa hissed before stalking out of the room.

My face had gone hot, as much from embarrassment as anger, and Lucía still wasn't saying anything. Her shoulders were hunched, her head tilted at a mulish angle.

"I'm sorry about that, Lucía," I said quietly. "I'll do my best to make sure it doesn't happen again."

She glanced at me, her face unreadable. "None of my business," she said, lowering her eyes. "No apology, Mr. Tonelli."

I had to go back on location the next day, and it was almost a relief. I took Elsa with me, and as we drove to Las Vegas for my next job, *Schmitt's Alibi*, I tried to tell her as gently as I could that I was disappointed in the way she had treated Lucía. I hadn't slept much the night before, my thoughts fixated on the scene in the kitchen, and how subsequently Elsa ignored me all afternoon. She didn't speak to me until dinner, when she said that I'd embarrassed her, made her look like a fool, even though it was Lucía's fault that my house was such a pigsty.

But the house wasn't dirty. She was only making trouble, as far as I could tell, and I didn't understand why.

"She's not a bad person," I said. "Her life isn't easy. Her family is far away and she can't come and go from Guatemala like I could if I wanted to."

"You're too nice. No one ever helped me when I got yelled at by customers."

Before her great-aunt's booth at the ceramics market, she'd worked in a clothing store. She'd told me more than once that it had been awful. Sometimes men would come on to her, and their jealous wives would tell the manager that it was she who'd flirted with them. Eventually she was fired, accused of shoplifting, but she swore that she hadn't stolen a thing.

"I pay Lucía's salary," I said, "and unless you want to start paying it, I'd appreciate it if you'd leave her alone."

"Fine," she said, hands clenched in her lap. She stared out the window at the blinding desert where nothing but scrub grew.

"Please don't be like that. I don't want to fight."

She snorted. "Yes, you do."

"You'll like Vegas," I said.

She didn't reply, and it wasn't until we were standing at the hotel reception desk that she spoke to me again. "You're right," she said. "It is nice here." She did not apologize for the way she'd treated Lucía, but I let it go. I was tired. We would be away for several weeks and I wanted us to get along.

We stayed with the rest of the crew at a Tuscan-themed place just off the Strip. The actors were lodged in a block of rooms at the Flamingo, except for the two who owned condos in town. My workday was ten to twelve hours on some days, eighteen to twenty on others. The film's star, the guy playing the title character, Carlton Schmitt, was a big-haired, loud, alcoholic thirty-year-old named Barclay Dunston. His real name was Matt Dusseldorfer, but he'd been convinced by an agent years earlier that he'd never make it with such a clunky name. Not surprisingly, Elsa was captivated by the possibility of meeting Dunston, but for the first week, I didn't bring her to the set—we had an explosion to stage, a car chase, two sex scenes with only the director, the actors, and the essential crew allowed in.

I knew that Dunston had his hands full with a wife, a baby, and probably a girlfriend or two, but that didn't really matter. Nothing was sacred. Some of those guys slept with a dozen different women a week, probably more. It was part of the whole gold-dusted deal—fame, ungodly amounts of money, endless pussy. It could go on like that until they died, and for some of the most famous actors, I'm sure it did.

"I won't bother no one on the set," she begged. "I promise."

"Anyone," I said. "'I won't bother anyone.'"

"Anyone, no one, no everyone," she said. "The casinos are so boring. I never win and people blow their smoke in my face. *Lo odio*. Let me come with you. Please, please, please."

Unless I was close by, she was too shy to talk to anyone on the set. For the first few days, she shrank into the corners, trying not to trip on all the cords. But then the director, a scrawny Welshman named Kel Williams, who ate uppers three meals a day and spoke with a lisp when he got riled up, spotted her and said that he wanted her in the nightclub scene we were shooting later in the day. She didn't even glance in my direction before she went to the wardrobe trailer, where she was decorated in silver platform boots and a black minidress by the wardrobe mistress.

When I saw her come out in that dress, more heart-stopping than the five-million-dollar female lead, my first desperate thought was that she wasn't in love with me, and in a year or two, she would have forgotten me.

"You like my dress?" she whispered, passing me on her way to the floor where the other extras were already being ordered around.

I managed to smile. "You're the most beautiful woman here."

"Really?" It looked like she might cry.

I could feel myself sweating. "You're gorgeous, Elsa. You know that."

"I'm so happy," she said, her voice trembling. "My life is finally here."

The assistant director was watching us and motioned for Elsa to hurry it up. I stood back, my heart seizing. Okay, I thought. Okay okay. Let go. Adios.

I found a grip I had known for several years and took a pale blue pill that he sold me for ten bucks. He had a lot of pills but didn't advertise. Like me, he'd worked in the industry for a long time. He knew that word traveled no matter what, and that it was best for everyone if it traveled quietly.

"Is she your girlfriend?" he asked when he slipped me the pill. "The one in the silver boots?"

I nodded.

"Where'd you find her?"

"In Mexico."

"Jesus," he said, his brown eyes a little glassy. "If she's got a cousin or a sister, let me know."

The pill softened the ache in my gut, straightened out my head, calmed the stupid bloody fist in my chest that was the source of so many of my problems. In twenty minutes, I was a better, happier man. I could probably have watched Barclay or Kel grope Elsa for an hour and not have felt like someone was punching me repeatedly in the stomach.

I don't think Barclay really noticed her though. He was too worried about how he would look in the scene, and if he was saying his lines like an automaton. His wife was also in town to keep an eye on him, coming and going on the set as if she were the governor of Nevada. I didn't see Kel do much of anything to Elsa either, aside from leer at her and call her sweetheart and put his bony hands on her hips and ass to show her where and how to stand, but he did this with a number of the other girls in the scene, including the lead, Kate Walters, a blonde-haired, born-and-bred Hollywood sweetheart who hated Barclay Dunston and looked like she wanted to murder someone after finishing their two closed-set sex scenes, which had required both her and Barclay to be completely naked, one of the shoots taking almost seven hours to get right.

The big stars might make a pile of money, but sometimes they earn it. What they do on camera, as many as fifty or sixty times before the director is satisfied, can be excruciating. Some of the things I've seen them do for a shoot—hauling bundles of bricks back and forth across a sweltering parking lot all afternoon or hanging upside down while someone sprayed them in the face with a garden hose for five hours—I would have walked off the set from after three takes. But the best actors will do it over and over, like well-programmed machines, their bodies not responding in any obvious way to discomfort or exhaustion. When the cameras roll, they become almost supernatural. They'll look at you and not recognize who you are, despite working with you for ten years. They probably wouldn't recognize their own name if their mother showed up and shouted it at them a dozen times.

"Was I good?" Elsa asked after we wrapped and she'd changed back into her own clothes. She was all adrenaline, not having eaten in at least eight hours. She hadn't said a word during the scene, had only swung her hips and jiggled her ass and made sure not to look at Barclay and Kate as they danced and pretended to fall in love at first sight. This was the opening scene—movies rarely ever shoot in sequence, which often surprises people when I tell them.

"You were terrible," I said.

She was crestfallen. "What?"

"I'm kidding. You did a great job."

"You're so mean," she cried. "I hate you! Why did you say that? It's not funny."

"I'm sorry. It was a joke."

She hit my arm hard and wouldn't talk to me on the way back to the hotel. The blue pill had worn off and my tongue felt swollen. I had a headache too, not having eaten in several hours either.

"Let's order room service," I said.

"I want to go out. Aren't there parties? Not everyone goes home and does nothing."

"People are tired after fifteen hours on the set, Elsa. Of course they go home. We can go out tomorrow. I have to be back at work again in six hours. We're doing a sunrise shoot."

She shook her head, grimacing. I still felt lacerated from the sight of her in the nightclub scene, of everyone's eyes on her. "I want to go out tonight," she said, her voice rising toward tears and hysteria.

It was almost ten. We weren't going anywhere. "Tomorrow," I said. "I promise. I need at least five hours of sleep or I'll be worthless."

She went into the bathroom and slammed the door. I heard the water running after a few seconds and picked up the phone and ordered two steaks medium-rare and two baked potatoes, a bottle of champagne and a couple of pieces of chocolate cake. In her current mood, she would pick at her food, if she touched it at all, and I would end up eating half her plate. I was about fifteen pounds overweight and wasn't supposed to eat red meat or butter or sour cream. My father had died of a heart attack at fifty-one. His father had had the same bad luck at forty-eight. I wasn't supposed to be taking the grip's pills either, but I didn't do it very often.

After a few minutes, I heard her voice. She was on her cell phone, one I had given her with the account charged for calls to Mexico. From her tone, it sounded like she was talking to her mother. I stood by the door and listened to her say that she was going to be a movie star, the director loved her, she might soon have enough money to bring over her mother and two younger siblings and buy a house in Hollywood or Pasadena. It wasn't hard to understand her; she had said these things before, but without the same conviction. I heard my name once, and she said that I was the same— *lo mismo que siempre*, then another few words I didn't catch.

I knocked once but she ignored me. I wanted to wash my face; it felt gritty and hot, as if sand were lodged in the lines around my eyes and mouth. I knocked again and she paused before saying that there were a lot of very pretty girls on the set, but she might have been the prettiest. "*Sí, es posible, Mamá,*" she said.

She didn't deserve them, but I didn't want the night to be a complete bust, so I called down to the concierge's desk and ordered some roses, paying quite a bit to have them delivered with dinner. When room service showed up fifteen minutes later, she was still in the tub. I knocked a third time and told her that it was time to eat, but she didn't come out for ten more minutes. By then it was eleven and I needed to go to bed soon but wasn't looking forward to doing it on a full stomach. I could tell that I would probably have to take another one of the grip's pills in the morning.

She finally emerged from the bathroom in her lavender robe, hair slicked back from her flawless face. The robe was short, barely covering her ass. I wanted her despite how tired I felt but she wouldn't look at me until she spotted the roses, her face instantly softening. "For me?" she asked, her cheeks flushed.

"Congratulations on your first shoot in America."

She came over and kissed me, pressing close, feeling my erection against her stomach. In a second we were on the bed and I opened her robe and pulled down my shorts and didn't stop, her warm, elastic wetness taking me in, my eyes damp with grief and lust. I buried my face in her hair, smelled her warm, clean scent, and knew that I adored her in spite of her prejudices and ignorance and selfishness. I also knew that she couldn't possibly love me.

Right afterward, I fell asleep, sweaty and sticky but too exhausted to do anything about it, my half-eaten dinner congealing on the tray. When I woke, all the lights were off. I squinted at the clock by the bedside, suddenly panicked that I was late for work, but its red face glowed 3:17, and I saw then that Elsa wasn't next to me. I called her name but she wasn't in the room. The hall was empty too, a jaundiced light shining on its yawning vacancy. She had taken her handbag, her phone, her new spring coat purchased from Saks just a few days before we left California. One piece of cake on our dinner tray was missing, nothing else. I could smell her perfume and knew that she must not have left too long ago.

When the crowds thin after one or two in the morning, Vegas's Strip looks barren, postapocalyptic, despite the uninterrupted line of hotels and tourist traps, the casinos still lit as if for primetime. The Luxor, the enormous Egyptian pyramid next to the gaudy Excalibur castle, is probably the most strange and otherworldly of the big casinos in deep night, my skin prickling as I passed it, knowing that I wouldn't find her because she was in a hotel suite with someone else, Barclay or one of the other flashy, idiotic young actors who couldn't yet utter a line without smirking, her skimpy clothes in a pile on his floor, her nervous laugh silenced when he kissed her with his thick, ugly tongue. I wanted to shout at her that when a woman gets into bed with a famous man, she's fucking his fame, not the man and his average body. There is no real connection, no love or respect or sympathy. She's fucking nothing but an idea and it won't last beyond the time it takes him to roll onto his stomach and fall asleep. My eyes were blurry as I drove back and forth, my pulse leaping the two times I saw a woman with long dark hair, but it wasn't her. The few people on the street sometimes glanced toward my car as I glared out at them, two drunk guys in jeans and L.A. Dodgers jerseys laughing and giving me the finger as I passed. I understood why some of us turn into murderous animals, why O. J. and the Columbine kids had done those cruel, depraved things.

She wasn't in our room when I got back at four fifty, after I'd driven up and down the Strip a dozen times, all the way from the Tropicana to the Golden Nugget in the old part of Vegas where casinos are less cartoonish, less coy about taking every cent you're willing to gamble away. When I got back, furious and bereft, only twenty-five minutes remained before I was due on the set. I took a three-minute shower, washing off the film of sex from a few hours earlier, my skin gray in the mirror, my gut looking like a deflated punching bag as it sagged over my jeans before I pulled on a rumpled red shirt.

I tried not to look at myself, didn't want to see my own face because I realized then that I was upset for the wrong reasons: I hadn't lost her. She would come back. She would keep sneaking off and coming back until I kicked her out for good or else did something worse to her. I didn't yet know what I was capable of. Most of us, either because we're lucky or we're cowards, never find out. She was too young for me, too certain that she deserved the things the women she admired most already had. She saw no difference between herself and them. She was no less beautiful and no less ambitious.

THE FUNCTIONARY

THE MEN SMOKED IN the room where they gathered to discuss the changes they would have to make, most involving strangers in places few of them had ever visited. Some of the older men smoked cigars, the younger ones cigarettes. They wore dark suits and sober ties, their shoes polished to a prosperous sheen, and many things were implied rather than said. This was how it had long been done, which Marcus Smith understood before becoming an aide to one of the members of the inner circle of smokers, though their duties were never precisely defined, just as the circle's enemies were never given names—instead they were labeled and categorized, discussed as the islanders, the rebels, the dissidents. The men, Marcus assumed, found it easier to work with a concept; human individuals with discrete identities implied organic life, something tractable and hard to dismiss.

Marcus Smith was his professional alias, his real name unwieldy and foreign-sounding. He did not smoke, because the airborne grit of burning tobacco dried out his eyes and cauterized his nose; he was, however, taller and more cheaply dressed than most of the men in this private room, which was underground and could be reached only after keying in three numeric sequences, submitting to a palm scan, and passing a voice prompt. The authorization process had taken him five weeks to complete, and after the phone call arrived with the news of his clearance, he had felt a witless, animal pride—as if he were already deep into the work of helping to ensure that dissidents everywhere would soon find themselves submitting to a greater, more lethal power than their own.

The smokers' work, and his own by extension, was dire and necessary, though he was not fearless and did not like fighting, whether it was wrestling or boxing or warfare. He preferred basketball to blood sports and the idea of a gun rather than one's actual heft. After a month of access to the underground room—some of its meetings only forty minutes; others, fourteen hours—something he had not anticipated began to happen: images arrived unbidden in his head, along with questions and misgivings pornographic in their ability to make him sweat and salivate. They were problems that he knew he was being paid not to mention, each problem a link in a long chain, one telegraphed from year to year, from one cigar-smoking man to another. This chain, however, was never acknowledged by any of the men underground, all of whom seemed to live in large homes behind locked gates and to own magnificent wooden boats they did not know how to sail properly. They drank in great quantities too, except for the Undersecretary and the General who were religious men and grimly averted their eyes to the drinkers' excesses and went home before eight most nights to their wives and small house pets and maids and landscaped gardens.

Most of the seasoned men wore their bellies like body armor. They were mighty, these corporeal badges of wealth and power and a long procession of rich meals, but Marcus's boss, the Secretary, had not acquired an imposing belly. He was thin and taut-muscled, and despite the cigars ran five miles every morning, with or without a hangover, through the park that sprawled along the northern border of the capital. He liked Marcus to accompany him on Mondays and Thursdays and Marcus did so without argument because anything that the Secretary asked, he was required to execute without complaint. At his third and final interview with the Secretary's staff, six months before he was allowed access to the underground room, it became clear that he would have to be ready to serve his superiors in any capacity they declared necessary, for the greater good, obviously, *not for them specifically!* This was slavery, Marcus realized after he had accepted the Secretary's offer. Nonetheless, the dark possibilities of this slavishness had titillated him. He would also earn twice what he had earned at his last job as a junior speechwriter for a senator who was an old law school friend of the Secretary's. The senator had liked Marcus, had told him that he saw promise in his stoic bearing, his patriotism and work ethic. Was he willing to put his country's needs before his own? Yes? Splendid!

The beginning of his own dissidence, as he later came to think of it, occurred in the underground room on the day when the General suggested that the women who had begun to turn up dead and dismembered on the edge of one of their main allies' borders be blamed on pimps and drug dealers, not infidels, the last having long been his favorite label, as far as Marcus could tell from the newspaper blurbs he had read about the General for years before he was allowed into the underground room. These murdered women were not their responsibility, the General argued, despite their self-conferred role as the planet's conscience.

"If we make it a religious issue, we'll have to go after them," said the General, who had the distracting habit of smoothing his eyebrows when emphasizing a point. "I don't think I need to prove that to any of you. I also don't think I need to tell you that if we wait long enough, those pimps and drug dealers will take care of their own needs."

This last utterance was code for annihilation, as so many of the underground room's phrases were: "address all contingencies," "overcome obstacles," "confront a foreign presence," and, in a few of the more specialized cases, "meet and greet." As Marcus soon realized, the underground room was a morgue, with the world's dead hidden in words rather than on rolling metal planks concealed behind a stainless-steel wall.

How had he not known what he was getting into when he'd accepted the job with the Secretary? D., a trustworthy college friend, asked. D. was not in the same business as Marcus; he sold German luxury cars with other unhappy salesmen who did not appreciate his advanced degree in philosophy. He didn't know for sure what Marcus did for a living, not anymore, but Marcus could see that his friend understood what his cryptic comments alluded to. D. recognized that men who met in secret rooms and later drank to excess were not usually upstanding citizens, despite the charitable donations, the pictures taken with orphans, and, of course, the impeccable suits.

"Those guys you work with don't sleep much, I'll bet," said D. "There's no way, unless they take pills. Or else that's what all the gin martinis are for."

"You can't talk about this stuff with anyone else."

D. looked at him. "Why would I? It's not like we don't already know how little those dead dark women matter to the rich white guys you work with."

"I didn't say they were dark."

"You didn't have to."

"Let's not talk about this anymore," Marcus whispered. He was sure that he was being followed. All of the men from the underground room thought they were being followed. At least this was what the outgoing aide had whispered to him on the last day of his intensive training period. This paranoia had, according to the trainer-aide, become such a natural phenomenon among higher-level government officials that a Naval Academy psychiatrist had recently coined a term for it: the Shadow Syndrome.

"You brought it up," said D.

The Secretary would have fired him, or else have him arrested, if he'd known about this security breach. Marcus had signed a confidentiality agreement on the same day he was offered the job—*no unauthorized communication, written or oral, with any unauthorized personnel . . . an actionable offense . . . treason . . . imprisonment . . .*

death and dismemberment . . .

Something he had discovered after a few weeks of silent watchfulness in the underground room, of note-taking for the Secretary, notes that were destroyed soon after each meeting: there was almost no laughter in this private chamber. The jokes came later, at the bar, ones about women or scorned foreigners or rival politicians, especially those whose careers had ended in public disgrace.

"Just tell me one thing," said D. "Do you have trouble sleeping too?"

"Not very often," said Marcus, thinking the lie was necessary.

"When do you start traveling with this guy?"

"I'm not sure if I'll have to."

"You'd better hope not."

Marcus hesitated. "What do you mean by that?"

"He'll have you carrying his luggage and arranging his rendezvous with prostitutes. He'll call them business contacts, but you'll both know what that means."

"You're being ridiculous."

"You'd never tell me if you did have to do those things, but you'd still know that I know."

Marcus said nothing.

D. gave him a gloomy smile. "Come on, man. Can't you tell when I'm teasing you?"

D. and his friendship, ailing since Marcus had started working for the Secretary, receded after this conversation. D. called a couple of days later, but Marcus did not call him back. He called a few more times before giving up. The dead women, however, were relentless, his constant companions, a mute audience to his frequent restless nights and the proceedings in the underground room. On the days when the Secretary did not have to go to the room, Marcus stayed with him in the office, with its smokeless air and pretty girls in tailored dresses, and read international affairs articles and op-ed pieces from fifteen newspapers that he culled and summarized for the Secretary.

Dead men turned up too, in dozens of cities local and foreign, but this was not as troubling. The women were more poignant, more possible—any one of them, if they had entered his life, might have become his lover, a girlfriend, perhaps even an exotic, grateful wife. Dead men were different because he did not worry that he could have loved them, and many times he found himself thinking that these dead guys were guilty, having done something stupid and criminal to bring about their premature deaths. The women, however, remained blameless. They were romantic, forsaken figures, tragic ghosts. He was too soft to be with the Secretary (a lifelong champion of firmness, of stiffness, ideally), something he was surprised hadn't come through to him or anyone else after the innumerable questions in the two psychological profiles he had submitted to during the interview process, or during the meeting with the government shrinks, or the sleep lab observation, or the brain scan, the MRI, the stress tests.

In his eighth month with the Secretary, as D. had tauntingly predicted, a trip was planned: the Secretary ordered Marcus to accompany him on a fact-finding mission to the country of the dead women. The public was restive, tired of the unrelenting bad news, the sexual violence an abstraction but still, somehow, terrifying. No one wanted to hear about innocent victims, often naked, sometimes missing their legs or arms or heads. Fact-finding missions for the Secretary and his associates were high theater, orchestrated for the international media and would-be campaign donors. Nonetheless, Marcus could not see himself leaving the Secretary's office, even if he was no longer dazzled by the spectacle of the household names who smoked and coughed together far below the capital's congested streets. He was too afraid to quit; he had no idea where he would go if he did. No one would want him. He would be ruined, as tainted as a raped woman in a country where victims were blamed for the crimes they suffered.

The Secretary would be accompanied to the land of the dead women by two bureaucrats who sat high in the national security tree, three bodyguards, his beautiful personal assistant, and Marcus, whose role was to do as he was told; in this case, he was charged with drafting the official remarks the Secretary would make to the public.

"I know we'll be able to stop this," the Secretary confided to him as they flew over the final vast stretch of desert between home and the foreign land. "Just setting foot on their turf will deter these reprobates. It'll work. Mark my words, Marc."

"No pun intended," the Secretary added with a snicker.

"What if it doesn't deter them," said Marcus, his voice quiet.

The Secretary shook his head. "Don't waste your energy on doubt, my friend. It's a zero-sum game."

"Yes," he agreed. "Probably so." He had no idea what the Secretary meant. On some days, few words made sense to him, especially after a bad night's sleep. Sentences were little more than screens filled with vague shapes.

Jennifer, the Secretary's personal assistant, gave him an irritated look. She had never warmed to him, and Marcus wondered if this was because the Secretary appeared to like him quite a bit. With her disapproving glances, Jennifer chipped away at Marcus's confidence every day. She wasn't overly warm to anyone in the office but wasn't ever openly rude or condescending, and few seemed to realize that she disliked them. Marcus suspected that the Secretary wanted to do alarming things to her body, and possibly, she was letting him. She was a lovely, sheathed dagger, flawlessly groomed, and Marcus had never, not once, seen her smiling with unfeigned joy. She was all rigor and veiled menace.

"Marcus looks tired," she said to the Secretary.

"I guess I am," said Marcus.

"No, you're not," said the Secretary.

Marcus looked down at his chapped hands. He needed nail clippers, lanolin, a manicure, but could never bring himself to make an appointment for one.

"What you are is too uptight," said the Secretary, squeezing his shoulder with a knobby paternal hand.

Jennifer was staring at Marcus. "You need to do something about your sleep-deprivation problem. You can't compromise this mission."

"Don't be such a pessimist, Jenny," said the Secretary. "I'm sure Marcus is in good form." For a moment it looked like he would squeeze her shoulder too, but she shrank into her seat.

The bodyguards were playing Yahtzee for money in the front of the plane, a few rows up. The bureaucrats from the national security tree were staring at the newspaper and chewing on ice cubes left over from their orange juice. It was early, not yet eight A.M., and Marcus was so tired that he felt dizzy. He was being haunted and had no brotherly feelings toward any of the people with whom he was flying to the dead women's land. Something unfortunate was happening to him and he did not know when or how it would end.

When the plane's wheels met the runway, two hundred miles an hour reduced to a sudden crawl after the terrifying clash of speed and gravity, Marcus found that his body would not move. His exhaustion had overtaken his brain's insistence that his legs walk, his eyes see.

"It would help if you drank coffee," Jennifer muttered, pinching his forearm. "Time to get up."

"I can't digest the caffeine," he said, his eyelids too heavy to raise.

"I've never heard of that."

"Do you want a doctor's note?" he said, eyes still closed. His stomach felt heavy too, as if he'd swallowed a bag of stones instead of toast at breakfast.

She didn't reply.

When he forced his eyes open, the Secretary was peering down at him, trying not to look worried. "Maybe you should rest before we meet with the Premier. You can take ten minutes after we get to the hotel."

"Thank you."

"Are you ill?" said the Secretary.

"No. I'm fine. Just tired."

"Good. We need you at your sharpest."

Marcus managed to smile. The Secretary looked almost guileless, the face of the wheat-farming boy he had once been briefly visible. The flashes of his boss's past innocence unbalanced him. In these moments, it was hard not to like him.

Marcus's room was on the eightieth floor of a glass hotel that overlooked the desert, its sands the color of a rotting peach. On the southern horizon, the ocean was the faintest smear of gray-blue. He wished he could leave, go out to walk the land of the dead women on his own, no Secretary, no Jennifer with her high heels and muscular ass and long legs. He wondered if she was afraid of becoming a dead woman too. No, she couldn't be; she did not seem afraid of anything. She had never been in the underground room, as far as he knew. But she would have liked it, found it exciting and poignantly serious, all of the smoke transformed to her eye into a sexy, masculine mist. If he took her there, the Secretary would probably have been allowed to see her naked. Marcus wondered whom she did sleep with, if not the Secretary. Maybe no one. He did not want to care.

He set his bag down on a chair next to the southern windows, dropped onto the bed, unbuckled his belt, and fell asleep.

Someone was knocking furiously. He lay immobilized, stupefied by the sound. "Time to go, Marcus." The voice was Jennifer's. "Your ten minutes are up."

"Okay," he croaked.

She didn't reply, but he knew she was still out there, shifting her weight from one hip to the other, her head tilted in annoyance.

His own head was full of wet sand. In his mouth, a taste like dirt. He needed a shower and wished he could stomach a cup of vicious black coffee. He staggered to the door and jerked it open. Jennifer stood looking at him under the surgical brightness of the corridor lights. She wore red lipstick, several shades wilder than her usual color.

"Mr. Secretary and the others are in the lobby waiting for us," she said. "Before we meet with the Premier, we're taking a tour of the area where they disinterred the sixty-three bodies last week."

"Great."

She blinked, her face briefly showing uncertainty, but she said nothing. He turned around and rebuckled his belt.

"You're not nervous?" he asked when they were in the hall moving toward the elevator.

"About what?" She didn't stop and look at him as she spoke.

"Seeing where all those women were killed?"

"We don't know if they were killed there. It's just where they were buried. I don't see why I should be nervous."

"It makes me a little nervous," he said.

She called the elevator. When it arrived a few seconds later with its reassuring, universal ding, they stepped into the empty car; he moved to the back but she stayed by the doors. It was disconcerting to see her so privately and close, her lean, feminine body available to him as it was to no other man at that moment, as the murdered women had at one time been available to their killers. If he had been like those men, he could have closed the gap between Jennifer and himself in less than a second, leapt upon her, fastened his hands to her neck and squeezed so hard she would have been dead in little more than the time it took to plummet from the eightieth floor to the first.

He was shivering when they emerged into the lobby and met the others. The Secretary had changed his red striped tie to a solid navy blue one and had combed his dark hair straight back from his forehead, as if he were a playboy. He was a handsome enough man, but his cheeks sagged a little and his nose had the broken blood vessels of a heavy drinker.

In the car, the Secretary smiled at him warily. "Have you ever been to this country before?"

Marcus shook his head. "No."

"It's too bad that your first visit has to be such a somber occasion. It's a beautiful place."

"I'm sure it must be." He could feel Jennifer dismissing him with a look of disdain. He stared out the window, trying not to detest her. Soon this trip would be over. They planned to leave early the next morning. As they had discussed before their departure from the capital, the Secretary's strategy, with such a brief visit, was to promise a return trip. But it was doubtful that he would make one, at least not for the dead women.

Their two-car caravan took them past men selling bags of oranges and unshelled nuts, bouquets of dyed flowers, bundles of sticks and what looked like wheat. They passed children playing soccer and others who stood by side of the road, waving as the strangers' cars passed. There were skinny dogs and skinny chickens loitering in front of tents and tin-roofed shacks and colorful tattered shirts and trousers hanging on clotheslines, old shoes dangling from power lines. He looked for flashy, feral men, the supposed drug dealers and pimps, but saw no one who fit the description. He was afraid he would see ghosts but only a few long shadows flitted before his tired eyes.

At the place in the wind-scoured desert where sixty-three mangled female bodies had been discovered a week earlier, they found five of the Premier's henchmen and a dozen soldiers with rifles upright at their sides. The soldiers raised their hands in salute when the Secretary emerged from one of the two Mercedes that had been employed to ferry him from luxury hotel to scene of sixty-three unceremonious burials. Marcus wondered if there had been more bodies, ones the Premier had decided not to count.

"This is a sad day for all democracy-loving people," the Secretary proclaimed to the Premier an hour and a half later, after they had arrived at the Premier's gilded offices. Both men nodded soberly at each other. Two state-sanctioned photographers were there, snapping pictures of the Premier shaking the Secretary's hand. No reporters had been allowed into the meeting room. "What I have seen this morning deeply troubles me," the Secretary continued, his face a mask of pious grief.

What he had seen was nothing. All evidence of the dead women had been spirited away, taken to a federal morgue where their bodies had been packaged in plastic after tags were attached to their toes, if any toes were available. At least as Marcus imagined it. He had no idea what had been done to the dead women's remains—had grieving, dread-filled relatives come forward to identify them? Many of the women, however, apparently were immigrants, here only to work in the vast, thriving factories that their own home countries did not yet feature in such large numbers. They had come to make a little money and send it home to their sprawling families, to stay out of trouble with men and boys and avoid, for now, marriage and indefinite servitude to husbands and children.

The site featured nothing but crude wooden stakes and roped-off rectangles of sand and scrub to demarcate where the bodies had been disinterred. Marcus and the others had stood gawking at the mass grave and then had been herded into their cars and driven back to the city to meet with the Premier. Marcus composed the perfect headline for the Secretary's first press release: SITE VISIT = FOOL'S ERRAND. But instead it would have to be SITE VISIT PROVIDES PERSPECTIVE ON UNSOLVED MURDERS, or DIPLOMATIC METHODS USED TO ADDRESS TRAGIC MURDERS. The morgue or wherever the remains had been taken would have been a better place to visit, but the Premier would never have let them see it. An actual corpse was gratuitous. It was ugly and real, too expensive and inconvenient to consider. *Bad feelings all around*, as Marcus had once heard the Secretary say. *And what use are they?*

He stared out the window on the drive back to the city, Jennifer and the Secretary talking intermittently, though both were subdued, his boss addressing him only once to say that he hoped Marcus had enough to work with for that evening's press conference. Marcus nodded. "It won't be a problem," he said.

The Secretary smiled, his eyes brutal. "Good, good."

He wasn't so tired now, but he had a headache, one that hung on during the meeting with the Premier. Marcus filled a page of his notebook with doodles rather than quotes, drawing the Premier's sharp nose and his small hands with their disturbing fingernails. This short muscular man, ruler of forty-one million poor people, reminded him of a bird of prey. Only once did the Premier make eye contact with him. When they were introduced, the statesman repeated Marcus's name in his throaty, accented voice and smiled at the wall behind Marcus's head, but a half an hour into the meeting, when Marcus glanced up at the ceiling and noticed the water stains shaped like the Great Lakes before returning his eyes to ground level, the Premier gave him a hostile look that he did not try to decipher.

His notebook had almost suffered an interdiction anyway, the Premier and his advisers not wanting any of their remarks taken out of context. The Secretary had assured them that they could review his prepared comments for the press conference before it aired. Marcus had already written the script before flying to the Premier's country, but the

Secretary did not know this. The common phrases were startlingly interchangeable: *We are cooperating/working hard/ conferring with our allies on this matter . . . We are making progress . . .*

It is with regret . . . Any enemy of our democratic ideals will be vanquished . . . The voice of reason has spoken and it is our duty to respond . . .

As with oil and water, or throats and knives, candid disclosure and dead women did not easily mix.

In his hotel room before the press conference, Marcus printed out the script and fell asleep on his bed a second time. Again it was Jennifer who used his door and her fists as an alarm clock. She had brought along a bottle of pills this time. "Take one," she commanded.

"What are they?" asked Marcus, looking at the blue pills inside the green bottle.

"They'll help keep you awake for a few more hours."

He shook his head. "No thanks."

"Don't think of it as a drug. It's like food. A sugar pill."

He blinked. "Call it whatever you want but I'm not taking it."

She put the bottle back in her handbag with an irritated sigh. Perhaps she did want to help him. Or else she was trying to poison him.

"You're not going to last if you don't learn to be more flexible," she said.

"Thanks. I'll keep that in mind."

"All of this is a test," she said. "Every second."

He had already assumed this. "Who's being tested?"

"Who do you think? You and me, for starters."

He shrugged on his suit coat and straightened his tie, saying nothing. He had fallen asleep with his shoes on and traces of sand were now at the foot of the bed. He brushed them onto the beige carpet and went into the hall, Jennifer following him.

The press conference, staged in a ballroom at the hotel with dozens of the Premier's frightened loyalists, was later pronounced a success. The Secretary addressed reporters for five minutes using Marcus's prewritten speech, answering questions for ten more, before the Premier took the podium to address the reporters and answer the same questions. Almost nothing said would be remembered a month or even a week later, not until it was time for re-election and the past was mined for the most egregious claims and promises. The next morning, however, as Marcus and the others were flying home, seven men were arrested in conjunction with the murders. Whether these men had anything to do with the dead women could not be determined by the human rights activists who arrived within the week to investigate the arrests, but along with everyone else, they had only two options: to believe what they were told or to hope that the real murderers would eventually be apprehended if they were not among these seven drifters and petty thieves.

Dead women kept appearing, but in less malicious numbers. Marcus read the news in the papers that he reviewed for the Secretary and dutifully summarized and submitted by three thirty on many afternoons. A cold, coursing stream of questions arrived in his head: Did the women weep when the men killed them or were they silent with disbelief and horror? Had some of them dreamt that their lives would end this way? What was the last thing they had eaten before they were murdered? Had anyone ever written a love poem for them? Had they ever learned how to swim? What were the songs that played repeatedly in their heads? Had they had any money to spend on movie tickets when they weren't working? Were they always worrying about their weight or were they starving? Did they plead with their murderers to tell their families that they loved them, that they were good girls?

When he went home at night, he still could not sleep and began to look at the objects in his apartment with disgust. Why did he need seven pairs of shoes, five pairs of running shorts, eleven neckties? He no longer understood the point of the TV shows he had watched and laughed at for years. He hadn't been on a date or made love to a woman since the first month he'd started working for the Secretary. His job had taken over his life, as predicted, but at the time he had not expected to mind so much.

He tried to put his insomnia to better use and studied the two cookbooks in his cupboard, *A Treasury of Great Recipes* and *The Joy of Cooking*, with the dim hope that he could teach himself to become a chef and begin a new career, but he quickly discovered that he did not have the patience to retry a failed recipe multiple times. He thought about learning graphology so that he might study handwriting samples and solve crimes; then he checked out a book on tax accounting before moving to portraiture and musical composition, but he knew he would never master any of these arts and sciences without years of intensive study and practice. His neglected friend D. called once during the week after his trip to visit the bogus gravesite of the dead women but hung up before leaving a message. Marcus's widowed mother called regularly on weekends. Sometimes she worried aloud that she was responsible for his unhappiness, which she had begun to speak of long before he realized that he was unhappy.

In the underground room, talks focused on new weapons technology and assassination plots, both at home and abroad, and the Secretary invited him to go down with him among the important smokers less often than usual. Apparently he was needed in the office, where he was instructed to spend less time on the newspapers in favor of writing notes and sketches related to the major world events of the past several years, ones that the Secretary said he would use as the basis for his memoirs.

After several days of writing detailed notes about earthquakes, hurricanes, genocide, suicide bombings, tsunamis, typhoons, school shootings, military coups, famine, water shortages, oil crises, mudslides, vote recounts, earthquakes, domestic terrorism, and prison riots, Marcus thought he could see ghosts in the middle of the night, faceless wraiths that collected at his bedroom window and looked on while he lay in bed and tried not to see them. He began to leave the lights on and covered his face with a pillow but could rarely sleep for more than an hour at a time. At work, his eyes dark and baleful, Jennifer and the other office staff eyed him warily but said nothing. Few appeared better off.

Instead of sketches, he began to write lists. At first they were practical—old movies he wanted to see, cities he hoped to visit—but soon his lists became flippant and indulgent: actresses he planned to seduce, sports cars he would drive off cliffs if ever told to do so. Sweaty-palmed and with a queer feeling of victory, he left one of these lists on the Secretary's desk, but it was briskly intercepted by Jennifer, who brought it back to him, holding the yellow legal paper in front of her chest like a squalid rag. Her shoulders were small and shapely, her waist tiny in her cinched shirtdress. He wondered if she, too, watched pointless comedies and hated herself for it. The current state of the union: catatonia, drug- and food-induced obliviousness.

"Are you trying to get yourself arrested?" she said, eyes wide behind her decorative eyeglasses.

He blinked. "Arrested?"

"They can do whatever they want to you. You know that as well as anyone."

"Why do you care what happens to me?"

"I care what happens to *me*," she said. "For all I know, I could be implicated in this."

The list was "What I Did at Work Today," ghostwritten by Marcus for the Secretary, who would not have liked it, not at all, but Marcus doubted that he would have suspected Jennifer of collusion.

1. Took call from Premier S——; assured him we would keep backing arrests
2. Named some of the dead women after famous actresses in report: Jane, Marilyn, Joan, Barbara, Jodie I, Jodie II, Brooke, Claire, Stephanie, Rita, Katharine, Julia, Jill, Amy, Faye, Sarah, Helena, Julianne, Courtney, Liz, Jean, Karen, Annie, Jenna, Zoe
3. Looked at three favorite skin sites
4. Had lunch with the Reverend, the General, and the VP to discuss monitoring of human rights activists
5. Gave all-clear for air strike on market district in insurgents' triangle of influence
6. Had J. make appointment for teeth cleaning and checkup, 4/23, 8 A.M.

"I don't think he looks at porn while he's in the office," Jennifer whispered. "I've never seen anything like that."

He thought that she was only pretending to be obtuse. He also doubted that she needed to whisper. The bug would pick up their voices no matter what. It seemed likely that the Secretary had the budget for the most sophisticated in-house surveillance available.

"I'd like to get to know you better," he said. "Outside of the office. Would you like to have dinner with me tonight?"

"Is that what this is about?" She shook the paper at him. "Do you think this kind of thing impresses me?"

"I have no idea what impresses you."

"Not this," she said. "That's for sure."

"We could go wherever you want, but I know a good Mexican place a few blocks from here."

She paused and looked at him for a second before ripping up the list and throwing it into his wastebasket. "I don't usually date people from work."

"Usually?" he said. "So you'll make an exception for me?"

She regarded him. "If I go out with you, Marcus, I want you to stop writing lists. I've seen the others you've written."

"Have you seen *Rashomon*? If you haven't, maybe we could watch it together."

"I haven't seen it."

"Do you want to watch it with me later?"

She shook her head. "I'll go to dinner with you, but that's all. Eight o'clock. Let's meet at J. Paul's in Georgetown. Do you know it?"

"Of course I do."

She rolled her eyes. "Of course you do."

He was at the restaurant before she was, his palms damp, his face tender from having been shaved twice in one day. He could not quite believe that she'd said yes and that she would not stand him up, but at last she appeared, twenty minutes late. He noticed other men's eyes following her as she walked toward him. Her long, dark hair was loose, liquid and edible-looking, the first time he had seen it out of its constraints. At the office, she kept it subdued in a tight twist at the nape of her neck. He could not stop staring at her. "You look great," he blurted, then took a big swallow of his beer, nearly choking on it.

"You know, Marcus," she said when they were seated at a table next to windows that overlooked tourist-congested M Street. "You shouldn't trust anyone we work with, even me."

He laughed a little, which made her frown. "What?" she said, incensed. "You think I'll fall so hard for you that I'll compromise my career if you get caught doing something stupid and ask me to come to your defense?"

He shook his head. "No, I would never think that. For one, you're not going to fall for me."

"You need more confidence," she said. "How did you end up here?"

"At this restaurant? Or do you mean how did I end up a sheep in wolf's clothing?"

"You're a weirdo, Marcus," she said, unable to suppress a small smile as she looked down at her menu. "Just relax. Not everyone is as bad as you seem to think."

He had never before spoken so flippantly to a woman he was attracted to. Sleep deprivation had turned him cavalier at the same time that it was draining him of every molecule of energy and good judgment. There was, however, the chance that Jennifer was attracted to him too.

Or else she was their boss's spy: a sexy, merciless woman the Secretary used to identify and flush out the weakest of his staff members. Marcus knew that he should be wary, but he was too tired, too weighed down with forebodings and long-entrenched misery, to care very much that Jennifer might be the kind of message it was best to send back unread.

They didn't talk about the office or the Secretary for the rest of the meal; she spoke at length about a college friend who had just moved to Rome to live with a man as old as her father, "a sugar daddy," Jennifer said with contempt, but Marcus could hear envy in her tone too. When they finished dinner—salmon for her, steak for him—she smiled at him across the table, took a sip from the cup of black coffee that she'd ordered instead of dessert, and announced, "If I go home with you, I'm not going to stay the whole night."

He stared at her, both flustered and thrilled. "Okay," he said, his voice faltering. "That's fine. I'm just a couple of miles from here. Up in Dupont Circle."

She laughed. "I knew that had to be where you lived. It's where all the soulful types live."

"And the drag queens. Don't forget them."

"Yes, them too. You're in good company. Better than I am in boring Arlington."

"I like Arlington," he said.

"Actually, I do too."

She let him guide her by the elbow out of the restaurant and into a cab, her long, gleaming hair so tantalizing that he gently pressed his face to it when she had turned to look out the window as the taxi driver sped north on Wisconsin Avenue, away from the melee on M Street. "We'll have fun," she said with a smirk. "I've wondered for a while what it would be like with you."

"I've wondered about you too," he said.

"I'm sure you have. There aren't many women in our office a guy your age would wonder about."

"That's true," he said, "but even if there were, you'd be the one I'd want."

"That's very sweet," she said. "But hardly necessary."

Despite her earlier declaration, she did stay the night. After she took off her clothes and climbed into his bed, her pride in her slender body obvious, after she used her mouth on him, twice—her generosity startling him, along with her aggressive appetites, her almost masculine predilections—she fell asleep. Sex with her was like stumbling upon something treasured but long believed lost, and he was very happy that she did not wake again until six A.M., an hour and a half before she usually appeared at the office. With her in his bed, he'd managed to sleep for five hours without interruption, the first time in weeks that he hadn't woken at two A.M. to stare despondently at his alarm clock, sensing the dead women's ghosts, aware that he'd allowed his job to consume his life.

When Jennifer awoke and peered at his bedside clock, morning light slipping past the window blinds, she was suddenly, irrevocably awake. Marcus knew that he would not be able to convince her to stay a little longer, to open her body's closed doors to him once more. "I had fun," she said a minute later, fully dressed, slipping on her heels. "You did too."

"Yes, I did."

"We'll do this again soon," she said, running a hand through her beautiful hair.

"I'm going to hold you to that," he said.

She smiled and nodded a little. "Sure, that's fine."

At the door leading to the outside hallway, one that would take her to the street and back to their coldly impersonal professional lives, she gave him a measuring look. "If you're still obsessed with those dead girls, Marcus, you'd better figure out how to get over them. There are bigger problems out there."

You don't mean that, he thought, but he could see that she did. "I don't know," he said noncommittally. "Maybe, maybe not."

"It's true. Just get over them. Why waste your time obsessing? What can you possibly do about it now? Save yourself, not some ideal or daydream or whatever you want to call it."

"A nightmare is more accurate."

She shook her head. "See? You've got to stop that." She leaned closer to him. "At the office, just so you know, I'm not going to flirt with you. Business as usual. No offense."

After she was gone, her scent remained with him, the feel of her skin on his hands. She was a live woman, the only kind that could do him any good.

He still did not understand any of it, though—her, his job, the underground room where men gathered to eat other men alive. But this was the way the world functioned, according to the textbooks he'd read in grade school. He was supposed to know how to dismiss cruelty and distant catastrophe, to not take them personally, because with time, they would go away and be replaced by newer versions, refined variations, which at first would not appear to be the same things. He would be replaced by a newer version of himself if he quit. He had learned long ago that if he stood before one mirror with another mirror behind him, his image would endlessly repeat itself.

WORDS THAT ONCE
SHOCKED US

AT THE CALL CENTER lodged within Clean n' Soft's sales
and marketing department, five of us earn our liveli-
hoods working twenty-five to forty hours per week. We have
no windows in our workspace, but we do have a functioning
coffee machine and an eerily glowing man-size box that, if fed
the right coins, will disgorge fattening snacks like Snickers
bars and Lorna Doone cookies during good weeks, waxen
donuts and filling-ruining peanut chews during bad. The
youngest among us is twenty-one, the oldest seventy-two. It
is the two people in the middle, Sam and myself, who refuse
to reveal our ages, but Cassie, who is twenty-one, and Britt,
who is seventy-two, happily answer any co-worker's questions
about their ages, love lives, driving records, and weight-loss
anxiety. Rachel, who started just two days before I did, is
thirty-two. I turned forty a week ago, but even when bribed
with cake and Pepsi and a few thoughtful presents—a gift
card for movie tickets, an electronic poker game, and a clover-
green scarf that Britt knitted for me after work while watching
episodes of *Days of Our Lives* that she TiVos during the
day—I refused to tell them that I was turning forty. It seems a

strange thing to be—so far removed from childhood and adolescence, some of which is still so vivid in memory, and also past the safest era for bearing children. Forty is more likely than not the midpoint of my life, if I am lucky enough, that is, to live for another four decades.

Employee turnover in the call center of Clean n' Soft is high, considering the not-generous pay and benefits, and the data entry we're required to do when not performing the often thankless task of taking calls from rude or distraught strangers, but Sam has worked here for a whopping five years and Britt is closing in on eighteen months. Rachel and I have been here for almost six months, Britt's birthday scarf possibly begun before I was even hired, but she has said that she plans ahead, stockpiling gifts in her closet for last-minute birthday and hostess gifts. She plays bridge with seven other women she has been meeting on Tuesday mornings for thirty years. She always brings a gift for that week's hostess, though not everyone in the group does, something she knows is reasonable enough, but it is not her way. More than I have at past jobs, I feel close to my four co-workers at Clean n' Soft, even if we aren't all together eight hours a day. Rachel and I arrive at eight thirty on weekday mornings and work until five, and Sam comes in at noon and stays until eight thirty at night, with Cassie and Britt working part-time, their hours different on different days, but usually three of us are here to answer the call center phones and reply to the twenty or thirty daily emails that come in through the address included on most of Clean n' Soft's products.

Within our first week of working the WATS line for our soap- and shampoo-company employer, Rachel and I identified four main kinds of callers: the know-it-alls, the neurotics (mostly parents of small children), the kooks, and the lonely hearts. It is this last category that is sometimes hardest to respond to both affably and professionally, in part because they keep us on the phone for as much time as we will give them. They'll start with a common question, the same kind the neurotics often ask: "Are there any known carcinogens in Quick Clean shampoo?" Or "I got a rash when I used Powerhouse soap the other day, and it won't go away. What do you advise?" The answer to the first question is no; the answer to the second is "Please discontinue use for now and call your doctor if the rash persists beyond a few days." Straightforward questions with equally straightforward answers.

But then the lonely heart will often let out a small, self-conscious laugh and say, "What I really wanted to ask is, how did you get started doing this job? Do you like it? Do you get calls from a lot of wackos? I'd think that you would."

Our training manual has tips for abbreviating calls from the lonely hearts, which cost Clean n' Soft money because someone has to pay for our toll-free line, though I'm not sure if we even need a toll-free number. Most people have cell phones now with unlimited minutes, but maybe the bigwigs here are thinking of the customers with landlines. Whatever the reason, we do what we can to keep calls to a maximum of ten minutes. This can be difficult, though, because for one, some callers actually have quite a few legitimate questions. When a caller feels rushed or slighted, our previously cordial conversation can get a little unpleasant, and it's not like I can remind them that the call center is a courtesy to customers, not a central pillar of the Clean n' Soft business model. It would probably be the first thing to go, along with free soft drinks and fruit juices on Fridays, if we ever fall on harder times. It is relatively expensive to maintain, and Clean n' Soft is not a freewheeling company, not one that hands out generous annual bonuses to the lesser lights among its staff.

And "customer comfort specialists" are indeed among the lesser lights.

Customer comfort. I just love this. Especially when someone calls to say, "Comfort? Who do you think you're fooling? You call this chemical burn comfortable?"

As for the best way to abbreviate a call when we're faced with a lonely heart's small talk, our training manual prescribes a number of responses. One is that we ask the caller to hold the line for a moment and then leave him in limbo until the blinking red light dedicated to his line goes dim. Another is that we simply hang up on him (while we are in midsentence so that it will seem a true accident), and if he calls back, we apologize and tell him that currently we are having technical difficulties and then, midsentence, we cut the line again. A third is that we answer his non-product-related questions with a question of our own, repeated until the lonely heart gets the message: "Do you have any other questions about Powerhouse soap/Clean n' Soft laundry detergent/Quick Clean shampoo (or conditioner)/Tub n' Tile Taskforce/ Sunshine dish liquid . . . ?"

There is one other last-ditch tactic in the manual, this one for the chronic repeat-offender lonely heart: "Sir/Madam, I'm sorry, but I now need to speak with another valued customer because there are a number of callers patiently waiting in my queue. But please feel free to call us again if you have a *specific* question about one of our products."

Rachel and I haven't yet found the nerve to use these hard-hearted tactics. We are hostages to our sympathetic natures, or else just foolishly patient, rarely cutting off lonely hearts unless they say something obscene, which, thankfully, does not happen very often. Still, it does happen, and when it does, we laugh over it, but sometimes I think about what was said for days afterward.

In the past month and a half, Rachel has acquired an ardent lonely heart fan, Jack, who says he is in his early fifties and already retired from a career as a stockbroker in Chicago. He also says that he has been a widower for three years and has two grown children. A few days after my birthday, not long before Halloween, Rachel and I are alone in the office when Jack calls. She gives me a sly smile and puts him on the speakerphone, something she doesn't do too regularly because Sam is often with us, but today he called in sick with food poisoning, an excuse so overused that Rachel and I are sure it's a fib. Jack's voice is deeper than I expect, and there's the hint of an accent I can't place. German maybe, or Italian.

"How are you today, Ms. Rafferty?" he says. "I tried the new Spring Fresh Powerhouse scent like you suggested and it's very nice," he says. "I also want to tell you that my ankle is healing just fine. The doctor says that I can start skateboarding again in a couple of weeks." He laughs and so does Rachel. It looks to me like she's blushing a little too.

"Do you have a crush on him?" I mouth, raising my eyebrows. Even before now, I had a feeling that she might, but when most of Jack's previous calls came in, I was busy with my own callers or in the bathroom or else loitering in front of the vending machine, trying not to let Flamin' Hot Cheetos win out over the more boring but less fattening Rold Gold pretzel twists.

She waves an impatient hand, silencing me.

"I'm glad to hear that," she tells Jack. "I was a little worried that you went waterskiing with your daughter last weekend. But if you're only skateboarding, that's just fine." She laughs again.

"Listen," he says, lowering his voice. "I want to ask you something. But it sounds like you have me on the loudspeaker. Is somebody else there with you right now?"

She clicks him back over to the regular line. "You're not on the speakerphone," she says. "The line's just been a little tinny today."

I make a face but she ignores me. He's twenty years older than you, I want to say, feeling vaguely betrayed. The lonely hearts are the ones we pity, not fall for. Also, she's married.

And only recently—she and her husband, Ben, were married a little over a year ago. Ben is adorable, someone I would have noticed too if I'd been lucky enough to meet him at a friend's birthday party like she did. I've seen him a few times when he has come to pick her up, shyly saying hello and waving when I walk with Rachel out to their red Corolla. They only have one car and sometimes she gets to use it, sometimes not.

"Yes," she says to Jack. "I think I can do that. This Saturday? At the Olive Garden in Coralville? You're sure that's not too far out of your way?"

Right before she hangs up a minute later, my line rings. I answer it, annoyed by the interruption, but as always, I use my nice-lady voice. "Yes," I tell the neurotic on the other line. "You can use Quick Clean conditioner with any shampoo. It doesn't have to be Quick Clean shampoo, but we do recommend that you use them together."

To the neurotic's next question, I reply, "It shouldn't give you dandruff if you mix and match shampoos and conditioners, but you'll get the best results if you use the Quick Clean hair products together. We recommend Quick Clean conditioning spray too. It's excellent for getting out tangles."

Rachel is on another call when I finish with the neurotic, someone who might have been a twelve-year-old crank caller rather than a real neurotic; there was a lot of muffled giggling and rustling in the background during our conversation, but I ignored it. I can hardly accuse a caller of cranking me, even when it's clear that's what the person is doing. "Would you recommend using Quick Clean detangler on my pubes?" "What if I stick a bar of Powerhouse soap up my uncle's tailpipe? Would his car backfire?" One week not long after I started, there were so many ridiculous questions that I complained to our boss, Mr. Lambert, who sits in an office with four big windows three floors above our workspace and looks at sales reports when he's not checking up on us. He gave me a strange look and said, "Well, Marcie, I'm sure you can handle it. That's what we hired you for, after all."

For a number of reasons, it was not a good idea to complain. Sam and Britt were certain that the call center would be shut down if Mr. Lambert or anyone else started to keep track of how many pranksters and how many legitimate callers we have each week. There really aren't too many crank calls, but we do have outbreaks from time to time, as if the whole graduating class at Coralville's high school is pulling a senior stunt before they go on to college or jobs at the mall.

It's several minutes before both Rachel and I are off the phone and I can grill her about what happened with Jack. "Is he coming to see you?" I ask.

For a long second, she doesn't look at me, but when she finally does, I can see that she's embarrassed. "Yes, he is. He's coming to visit his son who's a professor at the university and he asked if I wanted to meet for lunch."

I feel sort of strange when I hear this. I'm worried for her but also, I suppose, a little jealous. "Does he know you're married?"

She looks down at the notepad she's doodling on. "It's only lunch," she says. "It's not a date."

"So he doesn't know about your husband."

She shakes her head. "No, but does he need to? I just thought it'd be fun to hang out with him for a little while. Everyone needs a new friend, don't they?"

"Oh, Rachel," I say, trying to keep my voice light. "That's how it always starts."

"I've never been unfaithful to Ben."

"I would hope so. You've only been married for a year."

She hesitates. "We almost never have sex anymore."

When I open my mouth, no words come out, only a little croak of surprise.

"We used to do it every day," she says, blushing. "But now it's like twice a week. Maybe three if I'm lucky."

I almost laugh but I can see that she isn't kidding. "That's not so bad," I say, falsely cheerful. "Before Tim and I got divorced, we probably did it once a month. Which I suppose is one reason he started having sex with someone else. If you took a poll, I bet you'd find that a lot of married people would say that twice a week is very good. Even exceptional."

This is the first time in the six months we've known each other that she has spoken so openly about her sex life. Any complaints about Ben have always been more or less G-rated: his mother calls too often and he's afraid to tell her to give it a rest for a while; he won't let Rachel kill flies or spiders—they all have to be taken outside and released behind their apartment building. She also wishes that he made more money as a music teacher at an elementary school here in Iowa City, enough so that they could start thinking about having a baby, because she turned thirty-two this year, and she worries that her ovaries won't cooperate for too much longer. I've told her that she has at least ten more years, maybe thirteen or fourteen, but she doesn't want to use hormone treatments. "I've heard they make you fat and grouchy. No drugs. I want to get knocked up the old-fashioned way."

"When's the last time you had fun with a guy?" she asks.

"What kind of fun?" I ask, although I'm pretty sure I know what she means.

"You know." She rolls her eyes suggestively.

"It's been a while."

In fact, it has been a couple of years, since Tim left me, back when I was fifteen pounds lighter and still in my thirties and using my degree in accounting to earn a living. When they closed the tax auditing service I worked for, I couldn't get another accounting position no matter how hard I tried. Every job that I interviewed for had at least fifty applicants, some much more experienced than I was, which is how I ended up in my current circumstances: living on the top floor of my great-aunt Judy's creaky old house and talking to kooks and lonely hearts and neurotics for $11.65 an hour, telling them that they shouldn't gargle Sunshine dish liquid when they're out of mouthwash because it will make them sick. "Yes, sick sick," I told the kook who asked me this. "Like you might need your stomach pumped sick." His reply: "Is this stuff actually safe for me to wash my dishes with? Because it sounds dangerous." Not a bad question at all, but I could give him only one answer.

"Maybe Jack has a friend I can introduce you to," says Rachel. "Maybe I should call and ask him to bring his friend along. Do you like older men?"

"I do, but please don't ask him to bring anyone." I look at her flushed face, her dark eyes still avoiding mine if I try to hold her gaze for more than a second or two. "Are you really thinking of running around on Ben? Wouldn't it just be easier to tell him that you want to have sex more often?"

"I'm not going to sleep with Jack. I just want to flirt a little. That's all."

Rachel, you're heading for divorce, I almost say. Don't you see? If you want to stay with Ben, you shouldn't be courting trouble like this.

What I do say is, "You've never been married to anyone but Ben?"

She gives me a funny look. "No, of course not. You knew that."

A moment later, she says, "I'm not a tramp. You shouldn't think that about me."

"I don't."

She regards me. "But you don't approve of me meeting Jack."

"It's none of my business. You should do whatever you'd like. But I do think you're inviting trouble into your life. What if this Jack guy is dangerous?"

"He's not. I Googled him. He has a website. He uses it mostly to write about his beagles, Georgia and Otis." She laughs self-consciously. "He takes them to dog shows. Since he left the Board of Trade, he's been traveling all over with them."

"Lucky dogs, I guess," I say. "What does his son teach?"

"Environmental science. I Googled him too. He's there, like Jack said. His name is Mace Taggart."

"That sounds like a fake name."

"It does, but I guess it's real. He got his Ph.D. from the University of Colorado, which is where I wanted to go but I had to settle for Iowa because it was a lot cheaper than Boulder. Maybe I'll get to meet him at some point. Maybe you'll get to meet him and he'll be the perfect man for you."

"He's probably married. Or else he's gay."

"No, he's probably divorced."

I look at her and we both laugh. "Probably," I say.

A couple of things happen on Saturday, the day Rachel is meeting Jack. Cassie reports to Mr. Lambert that she has contracted mono and can't work her Saturday-morning shift and probably none of her other hours for the next couple of weeks. Even though I'm supposed to take my aunt to play bingo at the Elks (her favorite thing in the world, along with George Clooney movies), I agree to cover the shift because Rachel won't be able to do it, Britt is already scheduled, and Sam isn't answering his phone, being smart enough, unlike me, to know better. Mr. Lambert, in the rare emergency, will cover a few hours, but he is probably off playing golf or visiting his mistress or buying silk socks in Chicago. I have to call and beg seven different friends, some mine, some my aunt's, before one of them agrees to take her to bingo in my stead, and then when I show up at the call center, the coffee pot is filthy, crumbs are scattered all over our work area from either Sam or Cassie, who both regularly eat Twinkies and Cheetos from the vending machine like they are the purest health food, and Britt is also sick, but she tells me that she only has a cold and didn't think that it warranted calling in sick. I try not to touch my eyes and nose, and also try to apply hand sanitizer every half hour without her noticing, but eventually she smiles at me and says, "I'm sure you won't catch my cold. You're hearty as a horse, Marcie. Didn't you once tell me that you take that—what's it called? Ekphrasia?"

"Echinacea. I do, yes, when I remember to."

"You'll be just fine," she says, reaching across the table to pat my hand, which I just put hand sanitizer on. She laughs a little, seeing my face. "Sorry," she murmurs, trying to suppress her smile. She is a pretty older woman, often in good spirits, and frets needlessly about her figure. She's more fit than I am from frequent two-stepping with her longtime boyfriend, Wayne, a man she says she doesn't plan to marry, mostly because they both have houses, ones they've paid off, and the fuss of selling and moving is just too exhausting to consider. There are also his three children, a boy and two girls who don't like her and think she's a gold digger, which she isn't, but she says that someday she might marry Wayne just to spite his greedy kids.

The second thing that happens on Saturday is Rachel calls around five thirty, a few hours after I get home from work, and tells me that Jack stood her up and she ate too many garlic breadsticks and got drunk on white zinfandel at the Olive Garden. Ben had to come pick her up too, which wasn't so easy to do because she had their car.

"What did Ben say about you being drunk at the Olive Garden by yourself on a Saturday afternoon?" I ask. "Did you even tell him you were going there?"

"I told him I was doing some shopping and that I might have lunch afterward. So, no, he wasn't surprised when I called from there but he didn't like that I was kind of drunk. I still feel a little tipsy."

"Where are you?"

"At home. Ben's out jogging. He wants to run a marathon in the spring."

She wants to fool around on this gorgeous, athletic man? I really don't understand her.

"Has Jack called you?" I ask.

"No, but I was wondering if he called work. I thought maybe he'd lost my cell number."

"No, he didn't call," I say, irritated.

"I wonder if he's all right."

"I'm sure he is."

"I almost called his son. His email address and office phone are on his department's website."

"I think it's good that you didn't."

"I was so sad that he stood me up. That's never happened before. Has it ever happened to you?"

"Yes. Once."

"Were you crushed?"

"I suppose I was."

"What happened?"

"It was Tim. I should have known then that he'd be the wrong man to marry. It was our second date. He told me the next day that he'd called and left a message on my machine the night before saying we'd have to reschedule, but there was no message. He stood me up to go to a Bulls game with some buddies who called at the last minute and said that they had an extra ticket."

"What an asshole."

"I know, but at the time, I refused to believe it."

"Do you want to come over and have dinner with us tonight? It might help put Ben in a better mood. He thinks you're cute."

How nice she is to say this, whether or not it's true. "I don't know," I say. "Wouldn't another night be better?"

"Oh, come on. Ben's fine. He's not mad at me anymore. I'll make hamburgers and cook up some hash browns. The way I make them, they're pretty amazing."

My aunt is already ensconced in her easy chair in front of the TV, watching some old movie with white guys in face paint playing the Indians; she's eating pickled herring from a jar and carrot sticks for dinner. I was planning to read and watch a movie too, or maybe go out to one by myself. Most of my friends in town are married with kids, or else they travel on weekends to other cities to see their lovers (or else host them here). I'm from suburban Chicago, not Iowa City, but I went to college here and eventually met Tim here, and I haven't left, not even for a little while, despite the divorce and faltering job market. I want to go to Rachel and Ben's place, but I also know that it's unlikely Ben will be in the right mood to entertain me or anyone else.

Even so, my boredom or loneliness, or maybe it's fear of becoming a woman much like my solitary aunt (who is kind-hearted but sits home most days and watches too much television and has never traveled beyond the Midwest except for two trips to San Francisco with a man who didn't end up proposing in 1965), wins out over reason. "I'm on a diet," I tell Rachel, "but all right, I'll come over. I can only eat salad though. I'll bring it."

"Okay," she says. "If you insist. This'll be fun, Marcie. I promise."

They live about two miles from me, in a brick apartment complex with a dozen units. Theirs is on the second floor, and when Rachel buzzes me in, the first thing I notice in the hallway is the overwhelming smell of buttered popcorn. My stomach leaps, always hopeful, and I know then, salad or no, that I'm going to eat everything they put in front of me, and seconds too. I feel more defiance than dread, even as I notice my thighs chafing against the seams of my jeans. Still, I could probably run a marathon too. I could be like Ben and start training and burn down the fat cells my body doggedly persists in carrying from one day to the next. And maybe I will. Maybe if I change my routines and the way I look, my life will be better. I will find a new job and a nicer man than Tim, one who will not stop for pizza on his way home from work when he knows that I'm making us something special for dinner, one who will not sleep with his much younger co-worker and leave me for her before leaving her for one of her even more-dimwitted friends. Maybe I will run and run and it will clear my mind of all the self-doubt and angry grudges and petty fears, and I will become a better judge of character and also find the guts to tell the crank callers just where to stick it when they ask if I've ever tried soaping my "boobs and beaver" with Sunshine dish liquid. Maybe I will become so healthy and cute that a promoter for an energy bar formulated specifically for middle-aged women will see me at a race and ask if I want to be their new spokesmodel.

These things happen. Apparently they do.

Ben answers the door in khaki shorts and a Cubs T-shirt, his dark blond hair falling in his eyes. He is so good-looking that I feel nervous and sweaty-palmed the second I see him. He smiles and leans in close, but I pull back until I realize that he's trying to kiss my cheek, both of us laughing a little. He smells wonderfully of mint-scented shaving cream; it has been so long since I've gotten close enough to a man to smell his freshly shaven face that I have to stop myself from asking him to stay where he is for a few seconds longer. "Thanks for coming, Marcie," he says after he manages to kiss my cheek. "I hope you're not allergic to cats. Did Rachel tell you that we have two?"

"I'm not allergic at all. I love cats."

"Good, because they're not like most cats. They're actually friendly and will demand that you pet them."

"What are their names?"

"June and Myra."

"That's so cute," I say.

"They're my grandmothers' names. I think the lazy beasts are on the couch in the living room. You can go in and join them if you don't mind. Rachel's finishing up in the kitchen."

"Does she need any help?"

He shakes his head. "No, we're almost ready."

I give him the salad I've brought, and with a dimpled smile, he takes it and disappears into the kitchen. The cats are both curled up on a forest green couch that dominates the living room, right where Ben said they would be. The living room also appears to be the dining room; a card table has been set up a few feet from the sofa, with plates and forks already arranged on it. I stand for a moment and look at June and Myra, both of them peering back at me impassively. They are pretty cats with thick, healthy-looking fur, one gray-striped, the other solid black. The black one yawns and squeaks adorably as she does, then closes her eyes, having decided that I don't need further monitoring.

"Marcie," Rachel calls from the kitchen. "What do you want to drink? We have Rolling Rock and Coke."

"Coke," I say. "Diet if you have it."

"There's only regular."

"That's fine."

She brings the Coke half a minute later and whispers, "He called. He said one of his dogs was sick and he had to take her to the vet. He wants us to meet tomorrow instead."

"He does? Do you believe his excuse?"

"I don't know if I do, but I told him that I thought I'd be able to meet him."

"Do you really want to give him another chance to stand you up?" I set the Coke on the table. "I don't know why you want to risk losing Ben for some stranger who called to ask if he could use Powerhouse soap to spot-clean his sofa."

"Are the hash browns done?" Ben calls from the kitchen. "They look like they're starting to burn."

"Take them off the stove," Rachel yells. "They're done." She looks at me and whispers, "I'm not sure if I'm going yet. Ben wants to drive up to Cedar Rapids for a concert at Coe College tomorrow afternoon. I told him last week that I'd go."

"You should. Jack can stick it."

"Ben will need the car, but I could take the bus or ride my bike to meet him."

"That's hardly the issue."

"I know. I'm still thinking it over."

Ben comes in with a platter of hash browns and my salad bowl and sets them on the table next to my Coke. Both cats jump down from the sofa and run over to him, the black one leaping up to paw his leg. "This isn't for you, Junie," he says.

"You little glutton. You already ate." June meows and Myra stands mutely, tail swishing, staring up at him with her glowing green eyes. My aunt had a cat for a while but he was a foul-tempered codger named Dragonfly who hissed if you got within ten feet of him. When she had to put him down last spring, I felt bad for her, but not so much for him.

"Stop it, you two," Rachel says, shooing the cats back to the sofa. They actually listen, but while we eat, I can feel them staring at us, an occasional pitiful meow escaping their furry throats.

Rachel chatters about a night class in basic photography that she's thinking of taking at the high school, and Ben tells us about his plan to make a CD of the songs he's been working on for the last couple of years and his attempts to get second graders to play the recorder without one of them hitting an ear-splitting note for an entire round of "Mary Had a Little Lamb." The age difference between us is only eight years, but I feel a lot older and much more tired than they seem to. I don't know if either of them has any idea of the disappointments coming their way—ones they will suffer as a couple, as aspiring artists, and maybe as parents, if they make it that far. I look at Rachel, at her animated, pretty face, no wrinkles yet that I can see. I look at Ben, too, his surfer beauty so rare for our small Midwestern city, and before I can stop myself, I glance at Rachel again and say, "Don't go tomorrow. Just don't."

She stares at me, alarmed. Her eyes widen in a silent plea.

Ben is bewildered. "Don't go where? To Coe College? Did Rachel tell you we were planning to see a concert up there?"

My face is burning. "No," I croak. "I mean, don't go in to work if Mr. Lambert calls and asks you to fill in for Cassie like I did today."

Rachel is still staring at me, but Ben laughs and says, "No, she won't go in if he calls. I won't let her."

"We could use the money," she says, recovering herself. "If he calls, I should go in."

I realize then that I have just inadvertently given her an alibi—she can tell Ben that she is going to work to cover for Cassie and even have him drop her off before he goes to his concert in Cedar Rapids, and then she can have Jack the lonely-heart beagle lover pick her up and take her to the Olive Garden or the Motel 6 or wherever it is he plans to take her.

"I thought we'd already made up our minds to go to Cedar Rapids and have dinner up there too," says Ben.

"We'll see, okay? If Mr. Lambert calls, I'll probably have to say yes."

"Don't answer the phone," he says.

Rachel shakes her head. "Maybe he won't call."

"But maybe he will," he says, distraught.

The hamburger I'm chewing loses its flavor, and it's all I can do to get it down. Rachel's appetite doesn't seem to have suffered, though, and Ben is managing to eat a second heap of hash browns. He glances up from his plate and says, "When Rachel first started at the call center, I loved hearing what kinds of calls she'd get each day. We have this list called 'Words That Once Shocked Us,' and we can only put words on it that we've heard at work. I don't hear too many at the school, because I'm not a recess monitor, but I do hear some. What about you, Marcie? Are there any words you can think of for our list?"

"Don't bother her with that, Ben. It's boring," says Rachel.

"It is *not* boring," he says. "It's awesome."

"What words are on your list?" I ask, very curious.

"Pussy," says Rachel, drinking from her Rolling Rock.

"That word still kind of shocks me," I say. "It's so, it's so vivid." I laugh. "I mean, it just sounds nasty."

"I like it," she says. "Always have."

"Me too," says Ben.

"A lot of people probably do," I say. "What are some of the others?"

"'Faggot,'" says Ben. "'Cocksucker.' Those are both from my school. I heard a third grader using them on a second grader in the hall outside my classroom. She got a two-day after-school detention and the principal called her parents."

"Jesus H," I say. "Rough crowd."

He laughs a little. "I know. A few of them are pretty hard-core."

"Someone asked me about my beaver the other day," I say, blushing for what feels like the hundredth time in the past hour.

"Really?" Rachel gasps. "You didn't tell me that."

"You were on break when it happened, and Sam was there, so I didn't want to say anything when you got back."

"'Beaver' is such a strange-sounding word," says Ben. "It's kind of charming, though."

"For months after Tim told me he wanted a divorce, the word 'adultery' kept ricocheting through my brain," I say. "But it's not really shocking, I suppose."

"'Adultery' is shocking," says Ben. "But if you didn't hear it at work, it doesn't qualify for our list."

Rachel looks toward the sofa, staring at the staring cats, but I can see that her face is pinker now than it was a moment ago.

"No, I guess it doesn't," I say.

"'Fuckwad,'" says Rachel. "That's another one."

"That's also from my school," says Ben. "I guess I've heard more shocking words there than I thought."

"Time to get out the bar of soap," I say. "Tell those miscreants to line up."

Ben laughs. "I wish we could get away with it. Some of those kids could definitely use it."

"Let me get dessert," Rachel says abruptly and stands up. "We've got chocolate chip cookies and vanilla ice cream. You'll have some, won't you, Marcie?"

We don't exactly linger over dessert. Rachel eats hers fast and takes her bowl back into the kitchen before Ben and I are halfway done with ours. When she returns, there is no offer of coffee or tea, and it's clear that she's ready for me to be on my way, whereas Ben seems in no rush to bring the evening to a close. It's not yet nine o'clock, but she yawns and says how tired she is, though I can hardly blame her. I have done her no favors tonight, except for the accidental alibi, which makes me a little sick to my stomach to think about. She will use it, I'm sure, if she decides that she really does want to meet this Jack character with the college-professor son and the show-dog beagles.

"Do you want to play Scattergories?" Ben asks after we've finished dessert, ignoring his wife's fake fatigue. "I love that game, but it's not as much fun when it's only the two of us."

I don't plan to stay, but I look at my friend to see her reaction. She shakes her head. "No," she says. "Count me out. I'm going to bed, and maybe I'll be the one to get up to go running at six thirty while you sleep in."

"I'm getting up then too," says Ben.

"I should probably go home," I say. "I like to check on my aunt before ten to see if she needs anything before she goes to bed."

"That's so nice of you," he says.

"I don't know," I say. "You think so? She's the one who's nice. She lets me rent the top floor of her house for half of what she could charge."

"I'll walk you out," says Rachel.

"Where's the fire?" says Ben. "Relax, baby. You don't need to go to bed this second, do you?"

"It's fine," I say. "I should head home. Thanks so much for dinner. It was delicious."

"Do you like to run too, Marcie?" he asks. "You could go with us sometime if you do."

"Thanks. Maybe I will."

He gets up from the table to hug me good-bye, but I feel awkward because Rachel is watching us and I know she's mad at me.

"Thanks for coming over," he calls after us. "It was fun."

The hallway still smells like popcorn, and I also notice that Rachel is furious with me. "What were you trying to do?" she hisses as soon as we're alone, the door to her apartment closed behind us. "I haven't even cheated on Ben and you're acting like I made a deal with the devil or something. You're my friend, remember? Not my husband's. Ben has his own friends."

Before I realize what's happening, I've started to cry. Rachel stares at me, confused and annoyed, before worry softens her face. She puts a hand tentatively on my shoulder. "I'm sorry, Marcie. I didn't mean to yell at you."

"I'm sorry," I say, wiping roughly at my cheeks. "Just ignore me. I'd better go." I turn away, but she tightens her grip.

"I was just a little surprised when you mentioned adultery," she says. "Do you have a crush on Ben? Do you want him to divorce me?"

I shake my head, vehement. "No, of course not! I want you both to be happy. I wish you'd never given that Jack guy the time of day. I'm sure he's a creep."

She sighs. "I understand your concern, but it's really not any of your business."

"You're right," I say. "It isn't."

"Don't take this the wrong way," she says, "but you shouldn't take your unhappiness out on other people. I know your husband cheated on you and he's an asshole, but I'm not like him, and Ben's not you."

I look at her but say nothing. Of course he's not, I could say. But despite what you think, you are like my husband. He had excuses too. He didn't think he was doing anything wrong until he had done so many things wrong that no one with half an ounce of sanity would have said that he was blameless. There are always excuses. We will never suffer a shortage.

"Thanks for dinner," I say. "I'll let you get to bed."

"You're welcome," she says, uncertain now. "Don't be mad at me. I'm just tired and I only want to have a little fun. That's all."

"You should do whatever you want. I won't say anything about it anymore. Goodnight."

"Goodnight, Marcie." She hugs me and then I go down the hall and out to my car with its ailing muffler. On the drive home, I notice a lot of students walking in groups of three or four, many of them in red and white, the university's colors. I haven't been a student in eighteen years, but I'm still here. I have been married and divorced here. I have become an adult here, whatever that really means. I feel hollowed out and very tired as I drive slowly back to my rented rooms and elderly aunt, to the clothes that don't fit me so well anymore, to the hairbrush on the dresser with all of its fine graying hairs. I will use it before bed. There are routines that bring me comfort. There are people I have loved without them knowing it. So many more people than seems sane or worthwhile. What do you do with so much heartfelt but unessential affection, I wonder. Because I doubt there is a remedy.

FIVE ROOMS

TWO QUESTIONS YOU DON'T ask a blind person: Aren't black-and-white movies boring? Is that cop car following me? Another thing you have to keep in mind when you're with a blind person is that if you move anything like the paper towels and the soap that usually sit to the right of the kitchen sink, you can bet you're going to get chewed out for it later. No matter that you are sometimes an idiot and didn't mean anything by it at all—you're still going to get in trouble.

What I don't like about making a mistake is that no one gives you the chance to explain yourself. You're supposed to sit there and let everyone yell at you, even Mr. Rasmussen, who when he's annoyed, looks like he's staring at a spot above my head, which I don't think he knows he's doing. Sometimes he wears sunglasses, but mostly he doesn't. His eyes look like a person's who can see, which is a little strange because I start to wonder if he's faking it, but if he is, I doubt he'd want me hanging around his house messing things up.

Wednesdays, we go grocery shopping. Thursdays, I do his laundry so that I'll learn to be a good person. Supposedly I don't know what that means, like most kids of my "ingrate generation" who would trample a nun on crutches if one got in the way on our headlong dash to the store to buy the latest piece of technological garbage.

Something my mom probably wouldn't like is that Mr. Rasmussen pays me a little for helping him. For the first month or so I tried to give him back the money, but he wouldn't let me. He'd shake his head and smile toward the floor when I tried to hand it back. I know that some people would say it should be easy not to take his money because I could leave fast and he wouldn't be able to catch me, but I wouldn't want to slam the door in his face, or worse, slam it on his foot and make him fall over if he tried to go after me without his cane. When he pays me, he always gives me five singles. Every Thursday it's the same thing, five of them folded over into a little wad, and I wonder how he knows for sure they're singles, not twenties, which I wish they were even if this makes me greedy. If he did pull out some twenties, I'd give them back, all but one of them, because that last one would be my reward for not keeping a hundred dollars when he only meant to give me five.

He used to work with my mom at the school where she's the principal's secretary. He took care of the computers there, including the ones with all of the grades and IQ scores, but then his eyesight got so bad that he had to quit and go on disability. He told me once that he knew for months that he was going blind and it was like knowing someone you loved more than anything was going to die very soon but there was nothing in the world you could do to stop it. The doctors had told him it would happen, but he had hoped someone would be able to cure him. He went blind nine years ago, when I was seven, but I didn't meet him until last year, because before then, Mom hadn't yet had the great idea that I needed to be a compassionate dork.

During this whole time he hasn't been able to see, he's been doing things that are a little strange for a guy, like learning how to knit and taking piano lessons and carving sheep and dogs and cows out of bars of soap and selling them at a Christmas craft fair that the Catholic church on Fir Street holds the weekend after Thanksgiving. I'm not sure how the piano lessons work, because he has to learn everything by ear and by feel, but when he practices while I'm over, it sounds like he knows exactly what he's doing. The pieces he plays are long and soft and remind me of someone turning slow cartwheels. I suppose it's kind of impressive that he isn't sitting around feeling sorry for himself and turning into a grouchy old man. Technically he isn't that old, being only fifty-something, and he has a girlfriend named Ellen who lives in another state, which is pretty damn convenient for her. From what I can tell, when she breezes into town once or twice a month, all they do is eat and get naked, which I don't really want to think about, but like the piano lessons, I suppose that having sex with Ellen keeps him from turning into a crab. She's a professor at a college three hundred miles away in Minneapolis and teaches political science, which means that she is obsessed with things that are mostly pointless—no matter which person gets elected, nothing changes, at least not in my town. Since I was a little kid, there have always been the same unemployed weirdos standing around the same corners laughing and talking with their friends at the top of their voices about nothing.

Mr. Rasmussen's name is Forest, a name no one else I know has. He once had a son named Apollo (he swears this is true), who died when he was fourteen because he fell out of a big tree at summer camp. I know this must make Mr. Rasmussen very sad and probably angry too, but we don't talk about it. My mom is the one who told me. His son died a few years before he went blind, but Mr. Rasmussen and the boy's mother had been divorced for a while before any of these things happened. If he gets mad at me because I moved something in the kitchen, I try to remember that he has had it pretty bad—if I couldn't see and had a dead kid too, I'd probably be a lot more moody than he is.

I've been helping him out for about five and a half months when Ellen calls and dumps him. She does it when I'm over on a Thursday afternoon doing the laundry and I'm sure she planned it this way—she has to know my schedule as well as her own, because she seems like the type of person who keeps track. The two times I've seen her, she's looked me up and down like I'm the competition or something, which is so ridiculous because, for one, I'm not interested in Mr. Rasmussen and never would be, and two, it wouldn't matter if I looked like a supermodel or a drooling troll because Mr. Rasmussen is friggin' blind. He and I don't flirt, and we definitely don't touch, except when I take his elbow to help him through the door or down the stairs or he takes my elbow for the same reason.

After he gets off the phone with her, he tells me that I can go. His voice is so quiet that he has to say it twice. I've been at his house for only an hour and a half, but he wants me to leave. He says he'll put the second load of clothes in the dryer; he'll fold them and put them away himself this week. Then he reaches into his pocket and pulls out some money and hands me a ten.

"That's okay, Mr. Rasmussen. I really don't need it. Ten is too much anyway."

"Take it," he says, mad. "Just take it, Josephine."

I still don't want to. It feels too strange, like he's bribing me not to tell anyone that I saw him so upset, which I wouldn't do anyway. I know what his conversation was about because from the other room where I was watching *Jeopardy!* and waiting for the dryer to stop, I heard him begging her, "Can't we talk about this in person?" "Are you sure you really feel that way?" "Can't you come down here this weekend so I can at least see you one more time?" She knew what he meant, because obviously he isn't going to see her or anyone else ever again unless there's a miracle, but he still says things like this all the time: "I'll see about that," or "I'd like to see you here at four o'clock, not four thirty." Talking to her, he sounded so hurt and beaten down that I got a little choked up for him. If I hadn't had the laundry to worry about, I would have sneaked out before he could remember I was there.

"I really don't need it, Mr. Rasmussen, honestly."

"Take the fucking money, Josephine. I don't want to discuss this right now."

I take the ten and get my book bag and go. His face is all red and his wavy gray-black hair is a mess, like he was trying to pull it out while he was on the phone, getting his heart stomped on. I walk out to my car (which is really my mom's car but she lets me use it when I help Mr. Rasmussen) and the air is filled with an enormous lilac smell. It is a beautiful day, but for Mr. Rasmussen, it is shit on the bottom of his shoe, tracked through the whole house.

The reason my mom thinks I need to learn compassion is because my friend Gina and I used to go to the Lakeside Mall and drop pennies on old people from the second floor. It wasn't because we were mean; it was only because we were bored and it was the funniest thing we had ever seen. Whenever a penny would land in front of an old guy, he would start wildly looking all over the place, as if someone had thrown a rotten tomato at him instead of a little penny. He'd open his mouth and lean his head back as far as it would go and it just looked so funny we nearly peed our pants every time.

But then we got busted by a security guard on break at the Starbucks and that was the end of our fun. He took our names and called our parents and they bitched us out and it was so dumb. It's not like we were stealing or hurting anyone, but we still got in trouble because no one was supposed to be throwing anything, nothing whatsoever, not even hundred-dollar bills, from the second floor down to the first. We could have injured babies—had we thought of that? Or we might have blinded one of the old people if the penny had landed on their eye, which seemed pretty impossible to me, especially with the huge glasses some of them wear, but no one had asked my opinion. When I told Mr. Rasmussen why my mom had made me help him, he started laughing and said that he had done a lot worse when he was a teenage punk, but girls weren't supposed to be interested in practical jokes, so he suspected the guard had come down on us extra hard because he was sexist. That was the first time I'd ever heard a guy accuse another guy of being sexist. I liked it.

When I get home an hour early from Mr. Rasmussen's, Mom gives me a funny look. "Laundry takes three hours, unless he didn't want you to dry his clothes, but I'm sure he did."

"He wanted me to leave."

Her face gets that bunched-up look, which means she's about to yell at me. "What did you—"

"I didn't do anything. He got a call from Ellen and then he told me he'd finish the laundry himself."

Mom is quiet after this, and I start down the hall to my bedroom, which, incidentally, is "an abominable pigsty," according to Mom, who is the foremost authority on any and all things I am supposed to be doing with my life.

"Hold on, Josie. Is he all right? You didn't leave him in a state, did you?"

"No, I did not leave him in a state. Ellen left him in a state, and he didn't want me in any part of it."

"Did she break up with him?"

I feel like I shouldn't tell on him, but I don't want to lie. It's not something I usually do, even if I'm guilty of doing other boneheaded things sometimes. "I guess so."

"You guess so?"

"I'm not sure. He didn't lie down on the couch and ask me to get out my notepad so he could bare his soul to me."

"You're not so grown up that I won't slap your face if you keep talking smart to me."

I look at her. Her lipstick is chewed to a thin ring and her eyeliner is a smear under her lower lashes, but she is still pretty, prettier than I am, and we both know it.

I sigh noisily. "Sorry."

"I'm not convinced you mean it."

"Sorry, Mom. Really."

The thing I'm not going to tell her is that Mr. Rasmussen looked like he was crying when I left. I didn't hear the lock turn in the front door either, not like I usually do when I leave because he knows that a blind guy is not exactly the hardest person to rob, and plenty of people in town, the rejects and the morons included, know about him, how he lives alone because his parents are both dead and his son is dead too. He has one brother who lives in Wyoming or somewhere way out west who I guess once asked him to come live with him, but Mr. Rasmussen didn't want to leave Tulip Lake because it's where he's lived for the past thirty years. No matter that he can't see it anymore—it's still his home. "It has its own smell," he said once, "and that's one of the things I know I couldn't live without."

"What does it smell like?" I had to ask him. There have never been any good smells here, except in the spring with the flowers blooming everywhere, like the lilacs are right now. Usually it's just a dead-fish stench from the lake and exhaust fumes from the diesel trucks that load up at the industrial bakery a block from my house every night around eleven o'clock.

"Sometimes it's a cold smell like snow; other times it's hot green plants. Once in a while, it's like a mountain—all minerals and wild grass."

I have never smelled a mountain in Tulip Lake. It's pretty flat around here. And whatever kind of grass he meant, I can only guess. He doesn't act like a hippie, but maybe he and Ellen smoke together. She could have been his girlfriend and his pot dealer for all I know.

That night after dinner, Mom comes in and tells me it looks to her like I've lost a few pounds and she's proud of me and if I keep at it, before I know it, I'll probably be prom queen. I roll my eyes, but she can't see it because my face is behind a dirty romance novel, *The Pirate Lord's Mistress*, a book that's hiding inside my world history textbook. "I haven't lost any weight, Mom. Nice try."

"Josie," she says.

"What."

"Put that book down when I'm talking to you."

I stuff the books under the comforter. I probably don't have to hide the trashy one, but it seems best not to give her another reason to be pissed at me.

"Do you think I should go over and check on Forest?" she asks.

"Forest?"

"Mr. Rasmussen."

"I know who you mean. No, I don't think so. He's probably fine. Maybe he's even back together with Ellen by now."

"What's so sad is that he can't get in a car and drive himself up to Minneapolis. He'd have to hire a cab and that would cost him a fortune. Maybe you could drive him up there after school tomorrow if I offer to have you take him?"

This is basically the last way, aside from cleaning out every litter box in town, that I want to spend my Friday night. Mr. Rasmussen is fine for a few hours a week, but it wouldn't be my idea of a good time to drive him up to his skanky girlfriend's house and try not to watch him beg her to take him back and then have to wait if she invited him inside for one last boink before dumping him again. "Why don't you offer to drive him?" I say. "Why do I have to do it? He could take the bus."

"I have another obligation tomorrow night. We're not putting him on a bus either."

"You mean you have a date with Ron."

She just barely blinks, which is enough for me to know I've hit the right nerve. "Yes, I have a date with Ron."

"Oh great, that dickweed."

"He is not a dickweed. And I don't want to hear you use that word ever again in this house."

"Who's going to pay for gas? For my time? For the wear and tear on the car?"

This last bit is her favorite excuse whenever I ask to borrow the car and she doesn't want me to. I've only had my license for seven months and she barely lets me drive down the street, let alone to another state. But I know what she's up to—she wants to have Ron over and have sex with him in her bed, instead of in his nasty waterbed that upsets her stomach if she does too much sloshing around on it with him. She has never said why she gets upset stomachs after seeing him, but I think that must be the reason. I've been on a waterbed myself, with Brent Boliona, who is not my boyfriend, but for two weeks right before tenth grade, when I was twelve pounds skinnier and had used a lot of Sun-In on my hair that summer, he sort of was.

"This would be a good deed," she says. "I'm not worried about the expense."

What I could say is, You just want me out of the house so you can get laid by that slimeball Ron Dilworth, who would screw a knothole in a tree if it were greased up enough.

But all I say is, "He'll be mad if you ask him because he'll know you know about Ellen."

"Then you ask him. Tell him you'll check with me but you think it'll be fine. Once you offer, I'm sure he'll want to do it."

"He'll think I'm nosy. I can't call him and say I know his girlfriend dumped him."

"Yes, you can. Because I know this is the right thing to do."

She's using the voice that means I have to do whatever she says or she'll pout all weekend and not talk to me and not let me borrow the car to go out to the movies or wherever with Gina. It's the voice that probably drove Dad out of the house when I was ten and now he only sets foot in it once a year because he lives in Arizona with a different wife. He calls me once a month, on the last Sunday night, and sends me emails sometimes, but mostly they are lame forwards with prayers that I delete without reading. He is religious because of his second wife, Shari, who is a born-again dipshit, and basically Dad is so far away now that it's almost like he's dead. Mom won't let me go down to Arizona to visit him either; she says it's too far for me to travel by myself, especially on a plane. She'll let me drive up to Minneapolis with a blind guy, but no way will she let me fly to Arizona to see my own damn father.

I don't hate her though. I never have. I've seen her cry too many times, her eyes so swollen and red that I can't help feeling sorry for her. I do hate Ron Dilworth, but to be honest, she has dated worse guys. Five years ago, it was the government teacher from the high school, Mr. White, who didn't even try to talk to me because I know he thought I was ugly.

Then there was Phil Sarcobi, who owns the pizza parlor on Tripp Avenue and used to sit in the living room and stare at the TV and crack his knuckles while he waited for Mom to come out in her tight blouses and huge, pathetic smiles that I couldn't look at without feeling sick to my stomach. Then for a year or so, there was no guy at all, and I thought I'd like this much better, but every weekend she would sit in front of the TV with a big jar of dill gherkins and a smaller jar of green olives and a bag of Ruffles and eat them slowly in the same order—first a pickle, then an olive, then a potato chip. She would drink a two-liter bottle of Diet Dr Pepper and get up to pee every hour because she drank so much; she was trying not to get bloated from all the salt in this disgusting crap.

Despite the crap she eats and keeps in the house, she probably isn't the reason I'm not skinny. I've always been kind of big. Dad is big, six foot three and two-hundred-some pounds, and I got his bones, so he's the one I blame. There are bigger girls at school, and I'm not really that ugly, even if I feel like it sometimes. Gina tells me once in a while that I have the prettiest face and if I could get from a size 14 down to a 4, I could have any guy I wanted. Yeah right, but I doubt I'll ever find out. I'm not going to puke, and I'm not even close to understanding how some girls can turn anorexic. Food, air, and water—there's a reason why they say you can't live without these things.

It's a little after nine o'clock when I call Mr. Rasmussen, after Mom has stopped nagging me and gone back to the living room. He answers before the second ring. But it's a little hard for me to spit out why I'll take him up to Ellen's without first making it clear that I know he got dumped. After he hears me say we can go to Minneapolis if he wants, there's only silence.

I wonder if he's hung up on me, but then I hear him breathe out and it's a sound like a balloon going dead.

"Are you sure you're willing to do that? Will your mom let you? You realize that it'll probably take us about five hours to get up there."

"I know. That's okay. I'm sure my mom will say it's fine."

"If you really are sure, I could pay for you to stay in your own motel room for the night. Driving there and back in the same day is too much for anyone."

A motel room all to myself. I've never slept anywhere alone before, and it actually sounds kind of exciting, but if Mom lets me, she's more of a wackjob than usual to think this trip is a good idea. "Are you going to stay with Ellen?"

"I hope to, but with my luck, she might not even be there when we arrive."

Great, I think. Just great. Almost six hundred miles round-trip with a sad blind man, for nothing, just some crappy highway food no one in their right mind should ever eat. I have no idea if Mom realized that I'd probably have to stay the night up there. I suppose she must have and is already planning to have Ron sleep over without me on the other side of the bedroom wall trying not to hear their nauseating sex moans.

"We can give it a shot if you want to," I say, so compassionate I'd probably make Gandhi throw up if he were still alive.

"I'd really appreciate it. Before you called, I was thinking of getting on a bus."

Why do you like that ho? I want to ask. Is it because she's the only woman who's bothered since you went blind? This isn't the first time I've thought of questions like these. I once made the mistake of asking Mom why she was going out with potbellied, knuckle-cracking Phil Sarcobi, and she slapped my face.

I tell him I'll stop by at three thirty tomorrow and his voice is already happier. He suggests that, to save time, I fill up the car before picking him up and he'll pay me back. If I do the driving, he'll cover all of the expenses.

He says one other thing before I hang up: "You can probably imagine that this is a little embarrassing for me. Normally I wouldn't dream of making you drive me up there, but the two friends here who could do it wouldn't want to, for reasons I won't go into."

I want to ask him to tell me why, but I don't. I bet it's because they aren't big fans of Ellen's. "It's okay, Mr. Rasmussen. At least you have someone to chase after. I'm not even blind and I still can't get someone to go out with me."

Shit. Stupid comment of the year.

But he doesn't seem mad. "Boys your age are usually idiots. Give them a little more time. Things will improve soon enough, and then you'll have the rest of your life to wish you were still single."

Sure, I almost say. As if that will ever happen!

Even so, a sneaky little part of me wants to believe him.

At school the next day, Gina can't believe I'm taking Mr. Rasmussen on a booty call. "That's what you're doing," she practically screams. "You realize that, don't you? Can I come?"

It would probably take the pressure off if she did come. It's not like Mr. Rasmussen and I are going to tell jokes and play slug-bug or I Spy the whole time. "Okay, but I'll have to check with him first."

"You have to ask him? Can't you just tell him? Say your mom wants me to go in case you need someone to help with the driving."

"I don't think you're the one she'd pick if she did." Gina has only had her license a month longer than me, and she's already gotten into an accident because she hit a patch of ice and drove into a parked car.

She scrunches up her face. "Wait, I can't go anyway. I have to babysit Sean. My parents are going to a party tonight and there's no way they'll hire a sitter."

"I suppose I wouldn't want to pay someone either if I were them, but that sucks."

She rolls her big brown eyes at me. She's wearing fake eyelashes and they look a little like spider legs, but she's still cute. I tried to wear them once but screwed up the glue and ripped out half my lashes and it took a month for them to grow back. "Yeah, they have me, their slave. You're so lucky you're an only child."

I'm ten minutes late picking him up because, halfway to his house, I had to turn around and go back for my inhaler in case my asthma acts up, which it hasn't done in a long time, but I don't want to risk it. It's three forty when I get to his house and he's standing outside the front door, a red duffel bag in one hand. He looks like a great big advertisement for the burglars in the neighborhood: *Guess what! Now it'll be even easier to rob me!* I've wondered how he would know what was missing if he ever did get robbed. He's very good at finding things with his hands, because I've watched him take the cereal out of the cupboard and the milk out of the fridge and pour a bowl without a splash hitting the counter, but how would he know if someone sneaked in and stole some of his CDs or a few of the shirts in the back of his closet? If the burglar didn't get too greedy, it could be months before Mr. Rasmussen figured out anything was missing. It might seem like I've spent a little too much time thinking about this— maybe it seems like I want to rob him myself, but it's just a puzzle for me, one I doubt I'll ever make sense of. When I try to keep my eyes shut for two minutes to see what it's like for him, I can't do it. After thirty seconds, I'm already cheating, afraid of whacking my shins on the edge of the coffee table or knocking some of Mom's ceramic raccoons and giraffes off the bookshelf. How he puts up with it all after being able to see for the first forty-five or so years of his life, I can't even imagine. It makes me want to yell or maybe cry.

"I was wondering if you'd changed your mind," he says as soon as I've got him settled in the front seat.

I tell him about the inhaler. "I did get gas, though."

"Good." He reaches into a green cloth bag he pulled out of the duffel before I put it in the backseat. Out comes a handful of CDs, ones so old their jewel cases are cracked. My heart takes a dive. "I brought some of my favorites," he says. "If you don't object, we could switch off. You play one of yours, then I'll play one of mine."

Maybe he needs to get pumped up for the big confrontation, but it's still a pain in the ass to have to listen to his music. I look over to see what he's got and it's not as bad as I thought—two Rolling Stones, one Pink Floyd, two Bob Dylans. He can keep them straight because they have little braille sticky tags on them, which is something he learned to read when he was going blind. He took classes from a guy at the community college in Whitefield so he would know braille after he realized the doctors weren't going to find a way to make him see again. He has a bunch of huge books on his bookcase now. I hadn't realized before I met him that books for blind people were so thick because the pages have all those little raised dots on them.

After I put *Sticky Fingers* in the CD player, he fumbles something else out of the bag—a little white box that turns out to be the home of a soap turtle so insanely cute that I want it for myself. I can tell by the scent that he's carved it out of Irish Spring, my favorite guy soap.

"It's for Ellen," he says. "He's my newest little critter. Do you think she'll like him?"

"If she doesn't, then she doesn't deserve him."

"You're right," he says. "You're absolutely right." He turns toward me and looks almost happy, as if he really thinks I know what I'm talking about. His face is clean-shaven except for some whiskers in the chin crease, which is pretty normal for him, but I'm surprised he hasn't done anything about them this time.

"Haven't you given her any of your other animals?"

"No. This will be the first. I'm not really sure if she likes them. She says she does but they're probably not her style."

"If she has half a heart, she'll love him."

He laughs a little but says nothing. His face is turned toward the window and I hope he's not getting weepy. It's good that I have to keep my eyes on the road because I really don't want to know.

I drive us to the highway and he hums along with "Brown Sugar," and then the next song, which I don't recognize but it's mellow and sounds pretty good. I mapped out the route from Tulip Lake to Shoreview, the suburb where Ellen lives, with Gina helping me during lunch because I knew I couldn't ask Mr. Rasmussen to navigate. This is the first time I've gone on such a long drive as something other than a passenger. It makes me wonder what kind of perverted shit Mom is up to with Ron if she's letting me take her precious VW Golf to Minnesota. It makes my stomach turn to think about it.

When we get on 94, I ask, "How did you meet Ellen?" Before now, we've never talked about anything too personal, at least not on his side.

"Her mother was my piano teacher. She died two years ago, and I met Ellen when she came down for the funeral."

"You've been dating her for that long?"

"No, just since last year. But let's not talk about her. I'm starting to wonder if this is a stupid idea."

It's about time! I want to say, but I'm not a jerk.

"I'm sure it'll go fine," I say, not believing it for one second. The dread stays with me the whole way up there too, when we stop for dinner at Burger King, when we stop at the rest area near the Minnesota-Wisconsin border and he asks me to make sure he doesn't have any food on his face or in his teeth or down the front of his shirt and pants. He looks nice, actually. His hair is combed down and he's wearing a blue button-down shirt, and if Ellen kicks him out, she's a heartless bitch.

But the feeling of doom is not going anywhere. I'm pretty sure that this trip is a bad idea. Even though I think Mr. Rasmussen is a nice person, with some cool talents, like the soap carving and piano playing, I know that it can't be easy to have a blind guy for a boyfriend, especially one who lives five hours away. You'd always have to be the one to drive, you'd always be worrying that he's fallen down the stairs and is dying at the bottom in a pool of his own blood. You'd worry about him pulling out the twenties instead of the singles and getting shafted by greedy people. You'd also wish that he could see your new hairstyle or dress once in a while, but there's no way.

When we're about to cross the Mississippi, he knows it. He can smell it coming. The window is down a few inches and he says he smells the muddy water, which turns out to be a grayish brown, not even close to the blue-green like the ocean that I'd thought it would be. He inhales and holds his breath for a few seconds before exhaling in a long gust. "I love that smell," he says and sighs. "I haven't smelled it in more than twenty years. Not since Apollo was a little boy."

For a few seconds we're quiet, hearing the tires go over the metal bridge, the sound telling us that we're doing something important, that we're like other people going happily about their business—ones who have no real problems and aren't fat or blind or worried that no one likes them enough, if at all.

"Don't be mad, Mr. Rasmussen, but why did you name him Apollo?"

He laughs, a great big explosion that is all nerves and hot air. "His mother was responsible. She was a classics major in college and always wanted to name her children after Greek gods and goddesses. If Apollo had been a girl, he would have been called Athena."

"That's nice. She's probably my favorite goddess."

"His mother was a romantic," he says. "To her detriment and mine, as it turned out." He unrolls his window all the way and sticks his face in the wind. "That smells marvelous. Heaven must smell like this, if it exists."

"It probably does," I say, but I don't think I believe it.

"We'll all find out someday. That's one thing I don't doubt."

"What does it look like?" he asks when I tell him a little later that we've pulled onto Ellen's street, after I got us lost coming off the highway and had to stop at a gas station to ask directions. "Can you describe her house for me too? She's told me about her neighborhood, but I wonder how someone else would see it. For all I know, she's made it sound much nicer than it actually is."

I say that it's not a very long street and the houses are small, some brick, most with postage-stamp front yards and military-style hedges, all stiff and proper. The cars in the driveways aren't flashy either—just Oldsmobiles, Fords, a couple of Toyotas. Ellen's car is an Audi, but she probably keeps it in the garage. It's definitely not in the driveway when we pull in. It's after sunset and the lights in her front room are on and my stomach drops and I know we have to go through with this, after driving all this way on a Friday night when I could have been hanging out at Gina's, looking for new pictures of Channing Tatum online and eating sugar cookie dough out of a tube.

"Her house has white aluminum siding," I say. "It's just one story, with green shutters. She's got flowers in the front, some little rosebushes by the door that are pink and red and white, none of those uptight hedges. Her yard looks pretty good, Mr. Rasmussen. The grass is green and it must have been cut a day or two ago."

"So it is a one-story house. I thought maybe she had a second floor but didn't want me going up there the few times I've been here."

"She was telling the truth."

He breathes out and clenches his hands in his lap. "I don't know if I should do this. Do you think I should? Am I being a fool?"

He's sweating. I can smell it, but for some reason, it smells more like wet dirt than b.o.

Yes, you are! I want to shout, but all I say is, "If you don't go knock on her door, you'll probably feel worse about chickening out. I can go with you if you want."

How I got so damn compassionate is one of the world's great mysteries, but despite what my mom thinks, I've always been like this. At least I think I have, except for the pennies and the old people.

He doesn't say anything.

"Do you want me to go with you?" I ask again. "I don't mind."

"Maybe you could walk me up but go back to the car before I ring the doorbell."

We get out of the car and I go over to his side and put my hand on his elbow when he and his cane are ready. I'm looking hard at the curtains in the front window, wondering if Ellen is standing behind them, watching us, but everything is so still it doesn't seem like she's even home.

"Are you sure you're okay?" I say once we're standing at the door. He has his cane in his right hand and is standing so rigidly that he looks like a soldier, which he never has been. He told me once that he would have gone to Canada to avoid the draft if he'd been old enough for Vietnam. I don't blame him one bit for not wanting to go and get his ass shot off in the jungle with a bunch of other scared people on both sides. "Everyone's scared," my history teacher said to us when we were talking about a bunch of wars last fall. "Don't think that the so-called enemy isn't scared too."

"I'm all right," he said. "You can go."

I run back to the car and get inside and he rings the doorbell and waits. Then he rings it a second time and waits some more. I'm about to go up to get him, but then the door opens and it's Ellen in a pink bathrobe, even though it's not quite nine o'clock. She looks annoyed, but also sad. Her hair is in two long braids, like she's trying to be Pocahontas, and I don't think she's wearing any makeup, but Mr. Rasmussen wouldn't know if she looked crappy anyway. Then the door shuts and he's inside and I'm not sure what I'm supposed to do. He hasn't rented me a motel room yet and didn't tell me if I should hang out at McDonald's or somewhere while he talks to her. I have my pirate lord book but don't feel like reading. It's too dark now to do it without turning on the light and that would drain the car battery and then we'd really be stuck.

After an hour of sitting there and calling Gina and a couple of other friends on my cell, none of them bothering to pick up, Mr. Rasmussen is still inside and I have to pee. It's gotten to the point where I either have to squat by the side of the house or knock on the door and ask Ellen if I can use her bathroom, but I don't feel like it because (a) she's a wench, and (b) they might be doing it.

Things are getting pretty bad after fifteen more minutes, so I get out of the car and go to the back of the house, but there are lights from the neighbors' backyards on all three sides, and if I tried to pee by the little vegetable garden Ellen has growing back there, I'd probably get spotted by some goody two-shoes who would call the cops and then I'd get arrested for indecent exposure or peeing on someone's lawn without permission. It's now past the point where I could drive somewhere and find a bathroom, which means I have to knock on the damn door. I'm starting to get really mad at Mr. Rasmussen too—he could have thought to check on me instead of leaving me in some kind of shitty limbo in his girlfriend's driveway while he begs her to take his blind ass back.

Ellen answers the door and this time she isn't so slow about it. "Can I use your bathroom?" I say, not bothering with hello. "Sorry to interrupt you."

"Yes, of course, Josephine. Think nothing of it." She opens the door wider. "It's down the hall on the right."

Her house smells like chocolate brownies and my stomach growls, loud enough for half of Minnesota to hear, but we both pretend to ignore it. I don't see Mr. Rasmussen anywhere, and Ellen is still wearing the pink bathrobe but her braids look messier, like someone's been pulling the hairs loose.

The bathroom is painted a light purple and has loads of matching hand towels in a basket on the toilet tank. There are about sixty-five million little bottles of hand cream in a second basket, and I put three of them in my handbag—lemon meringue, cranberry, and ginger. When I come out, she's waiting for me. I wonder if she has all of the lotions marked and will know later that I swiped some, but her expression is friendlier than usual. She doesn't look like a crazy woman on a soap opera anymore, the kind who sizes up the new girl because she plans to stab her in the back with her extra-long fake nails.

"I'm sorry you've been sitting out there by yourself this whole time," she says. "Why don't you go into the living room and watch TV? I don't think Forest and I will be too much longer."

This is good news for me, cruddy news for him.

"Thanks," I say. "But I'll just wait in the car." If they're going to be doing any yelling or crying, I don't want to hear it.

It's forty more minutes before he comes out. I've been sitting there, calling Gina every five minutes and bitching to her voicemail for not picking up. Sometimes she doesn't answer because she's playing online Scrabble like a total nerd or else has her headphones on, listening to crappy seventies music and going deaf.

The look on Mr. Rasmussen's face when he walks out of Ellen's front door makes it pretty clear that there isn't going to be a room of my own at the Holiday Inn tonight. I wonder if I should call Mom and warn her that she and Ron had better not be having an orgy in the living room when I get there or else I'm going to call his ex-wife, who I think is actually still his wife but I don't know for sure. Mom says he isn't married anymore, but I would not be surprised if he's lying to her. It would hardly be the first time.

Mr. Rasmussen has something in his hands that he passes to me before I help him into the car. You'd think Ellen would have helped him this one last time, but she's nowhere to be seen. Or maybe he told her not to do it. "These are for our ride back," he says. "You can have all of them."

I look down and see that she's packed us a bag of brownies. They're still warm, and she's left the bag unsealed so they won't get soggy. It's so sad, one of the saddest things I've ever seen. She's cut the brownies in such perfect squares for a guy who doesn't want them at all because he just got dumped a second time. Mr. Rasmussen is so gloomy and closed up right now; it's like he's covered over every single window with bricks.

After we get on the highway, I say that I'm sorry.

He doesn't say anything.

We cross the Mississippi for the second time that night, the window down on my side but not on his. It does smell good, and it's weird how it makes me feel hopeful, despite how depressing the night has been. "Should I drive us all the way home?" I ask when we're a mile or so past the bridge.

"If you think you can," he says.

I'm not that tired but I'm starving, and I can't help it I have to reach into the bag and grab one of Ellen's breakup brownies. Then I eat it so fast I'm almost dizzy. It is the most insanely delicious piece of junk I've ever had. She's added chocolate chips and the walnuts are big and meaty and it's better than anything I can imagine right then aside from being home in my bed reading and this night never happening. If Mr. Rasmussen were to eat one, he might feel better. He's said that tastes are more intense than when he could see. Sounds are louder too, and textures are smoother and harder or softer and slipperier. But he's told me that he lives in four rooms now instead of five—the fifth room, his sight, is like a forbidden chamber at the top of the stairs that he'll never be able to go into again, unless something magic happens, like the princess getting her enchanted kiss, but instead of a kiss, he'd get a new pair of eyeballs from a doctor.

I'm dying to know what happened with Ellen but I don't have the nerve to ask. He's put in one of the Dylan CDs, and when I look over at Mr. Rasmussen, his eyes are shut but he must sense me looking at him because he opens them and says, "She's got someone else. That's all there is to it. He lives nearby, he's not blind, he's got more money too, I'm sure. There's no way I can compete. No way in hell."

"You have to compete, Mr. Rasmussen. Write her love poems. Send her soap flowers every day for a month. I'm sure she still loves you."

He shakes his head. "She wants a guy who won't trip over a seam in the linoleum when he's trying to walk from the kitchen to the bathroom. She wants someone who can drive a car and isn't as needy as an infant."

"You're not like that."

"I'm not? That's news to me."

"You're not, Mr. Rasmussen. You can do so many things that other people can't. Did you give her the turtle?"

"That stupid fucking turtle. I'm such a fucking idiot."

"No, you're not."

He snorts.

"You're not."

"I'm sorry I made you drive all this way for nothing."

"It wasn't for nothing. I think it's good that you came up here to see her. I bet she'll change her mind. Tomorrow she'll call you and tell you she made a mistake."

"Nope. Won't happen." He laughs, an angry sound, and reaches out a hand to grope the buttons on the stereo, turning it up loud enough that I know I'm going to get a headache pretty soon, but I don't say anything.

We stop only once, for gas and the bathroom, a few miles past the Dells. By now it's after midnight and I'm exhausted, but I'm not going to stop. Mr. Rasmussen takes a long time to come out of the men's room and I have to stand outside the door and wait for him, like some gas-station hooker hoping to snag a trick. When he finally appears, he has streaks of soap lather on his face. I tell him, and he asks if I can rub them off.

I feel strange touching him in a way that I've never touched any guy before, but I do it, and when I'm done, he puts his arms around me and hugs me hard. Then he's crying onto the top of my head, and no one, thank God, is there to see us. I feel bad for him, but weird too, and pull away after a few seconds and take him back to the car. When we're turning onto the highway, I tell him we'll be home soon, that he's just tired and will feel better in the morning.

"That's not true," he says. "But I realize you don't know what else to say to me."

I look over at him but he's facing the window. His hands are gripping his knees so hard that I can feel my own hands start to cramp up. He keeps staring out at the road, but I know he doesn't see anything, not even in his head. There's not much out there anyway, only other speeding cars and faded billboards that advertise $3.99 breakfasts and high-stakes bingo every Wednesday afternoon. I want to tell him he's not missing a thing, that soon he's going to forget about tonight, but I know he doesn't want to hear another lie.

ROGER WEBER WOULD
LIKE TO STAY

How it happened isn't clear to her. Roger Weber is possibly the product of a dream that made the leap from her subconscious into waking life, but his habits are human enough in their predictability. He sticks to a strict schedule, disappearing during the daylight hours into the walls or the cedar chest at the foot of her bed, an heirloom that was a wedding gift from her grandfather to his second wife and had once held lacy, confining undergarments, Irish linen, family snapshots, and picture books he purchased in France, the sort that true gentlemen were not supposed to spend time examining.

Roger's presence doesn't scare her, though she isn't sure why. Maybe it's because if he were still alive, he would probably be the handsomest man Merilee has ever seen. His hair is black, his deep-set eyes sapphire, though she cannot know for certain because he appears before her solely in shades of gray. He knows many of her secrets and seems unconcerned that she once used the opera glasses her great-aunt Anna Maria willed to her to spy on the next-door neighbors while they ate dinner in the nude, their long-haired dachshund sitting obediently at their feet. He does not care that her elbows are covered with sandpapery skin, or that she rubs her right knee obsessively when she is nervous, or that sometimes she has trouble concentrating on her job and on her pleasant-enough lover, Brian, because she is more intrigued by Roger, who claims he is a concert pianist resembling Glenn Gould, though of course even more handsome and less prone to ingesting dozens of prescription drugs for real or imagined ailments. Her ghost is not a hypochondriac or in the habit of eating one meal a day, usually of scrambled eggs submerged in ketchup.

Roger seems not to have been flashy and vain while still alive, despite his public career. He says that he did not spend frivolously or waste time on gossip, nor did he grumble about his neighbors when they failed to mow the front lawn before its dandelions turned to puffballs or forgot to take in their garbage cans from the curb. He wasn't particularly concerned with what others thought of him when he questioned the ruling class's habit of prescribing strenuous work for everyone but themselves either. Even now he does not seem to bear any serious grudges, unlike Brian, who often complains bitterly about noisy children, his richer younger brother, and the clerks at the bank who continue to ask for his ID when he makes a withdrawal, despite the fact he has been a customer there for six and a half goddamn years!

Unlike Roger, Brian also frequently forgets to ask about her day. Though Brian is only forty-three, four years older than Merilee, he is affably absentminded, as if he were an aging uncle who can't remember what his nieces and nephews do for a living, or whether they went to college. As for herself, she no longer remembers if it was she or Brian who made the first move on the back porch at a mutual friend's New Year's party, if it was she who leaned close for an awkward kiss that quickly became heated. Afterward, his skin looked mottled, almost angry.

Her ghost friend, for one, never assumes that she will always end up in bed with him because she has done so in the past. After his first few appearances, he begins to confide in her, explaining that during his adolescence, he preferred cloudy days to sunny because he would rather have spent the morning at the piano without feeling guilty that he wasn't outside, making studious use of the warm air and bright light. The circumstances of his death remain unclear, though she imagines it involved a betrayal of some kind, an ungrateful lover, a violent end. Not suicide, but nonetheless not a death most would wish for.

He has told her this much.

* He never learned to drive, fearing that he would fly off a cliff, a scenario that often appeared in his nightmares.
* More than once he has walked through a movie screen, straight into the picture.
* He has discovered that criminals prefer to bury evidence rather than burn it and has never understood why this is the case.
* If he wishes, he can see behind his life into the distant past, before airplanes or the great massacre of the western buffalo; everything in these depths is blue or green or scarlet.
* His brother is still alive in Bellingham, Washington, working as a high school drama teacher; the brother never tries to speak to Roger.

There is always this problem, this lack of meaningful communication—the dead to the living, the living to the dead, the living to the living. Merilee thinks she understands what he means when he tells her that no earthly minute escapes the sorrowful confusion induced by what is never said or else is cried out as a feverish jumble of imperatives and pleas.

To show him she's worthy of these perplexing confidences, she says, "When I wear red three days in a row, people always think it means something other than the fact that I like red. They want me to be a freak, but I'm not, not really."

"*Ma chère*, Merilee," he says in the very soft voice he uses to flirt with her, reaching out to touch her shoulder, but his hand, as it always sadly does, dissolves into her flesh. She feels nothing, not the faintest shiver or tingle, and it depresses her. She hopes that at some point they'll figure out a way for him to reach through his dimension into hers. Or else the opposite, though she worries that to enter his sphere, she would have to die, and though she adores him, she loves her life more. "All you can do is suffer fools. That's the worst of it. You know what Sartre said, *L'enfer, c'est* . . . and all of that bad news. He's right, and he certainly likes to lord it over the rest of us hapless souls." Roger chuckles. "Kind of ironic, isn't it, fulfilling his own most dire prophecy. Blowhard ghosts like him keep me loitering around here as much as possible, if you want to know the truth."

This disappoints her and he sees it. "Don't worry," he says hastily. "I really do want to be here with you. Out of all of the others I could be with, it's you who's most kind and welcoming."

On a different night, she confesses, "I feel a little embarrassed about having Brian come here after our dates, but his place is so dusty that I never sleep well there." She pauses, turning red. "I hate to think of you having to see us. I don't want to make you uncomfortable."

Roger shakes his head. "You have your needs. Don't cheat yourself on my account. Once you're dead, that's it, so take all you can now. I wish I'd done more of that when I was still alive. Gather ye rosebuds, et cetera, et cetera. The poets were right." He smiles. "You don't have an audience when Mr. Dunn is here anyway. I can go back through those walls, easy as shoo-fly pie." He smiles, touching and not touching her again. "There is one thing though. Forgive me, but the times I have seen your friend, I've wondered why he doesn't put a little more effort into his wardrobe. His shoes are so scuffed and his pants could stand to be at least an inch or two longer. I would think that he might try a little harder for someone like you."

Brian does not know about Roger Weber. Merilee tells no one about him except for her journal. Roger thinks it's best that way too, not wanting her to be laughed at or scorned and labeled a lunatic or, worst of all, taken to a mental hospital, a place he has no interest in setting his proverbial foot in, he has made clear, all apologies but nonetheless earnest. He realizes that being in such close contact with a ghost is not necessarily good for her grasp on the material realm in which she so capably dwells, despite her recent feelings of dissatisfaction. They have been friends for close to two months when he begins his commentary on Brian's shortcomings. His opinion matters to her, more than anyone else's, she immediately realizes.

She finds herself passing on his advice to her boyfriend, who listens patiently but then goes on to ignore most everything she says. His pants stay flood-length and are sometimes appallingly wrinkled; his hair is still cut by the same inept barber; he often lets her split the check, but worst of all is that he keeps a photo of his ex-wife tucked behind the obsolete business cards in his wallet—something Merilee isn't aware of until Roger fills her in one evening after Brian has stepped out to buy them a quart of vanilla ice cream to eat with the chocolate cake she has made for his forty-fourth birthday. The evening is one of their best until Roger slips soundlessly through the wall with his disappointing revelation only a minute or two after Brian has driven off to the all-night grocery store two miles away.

"Please don't be so upset, Meri, darling," he murmurs, giving her a contrite look. "I shouldn't have opened my mouth, especially because I know better than anyone that we all have our pasts. Maybe Brian doesn't remember that he's carrying around this picture. We can agree that he isn't the tidiest fellow on earth."

Leave me alone, she wants to say, this unfriendly thought startling her. If Roger can read her mind, he hasn't yet let on. She feels so tired now and would like to close her eyes for a catnap while Brian is at the store. "Maybe we shouldn't talk about him anymore," she finally says. "It doesn't seem fair since he's not here to defend himself."

Roger hesitates but then nods. "You're a better person than I am," he says mildly, passing a long-fingered hand over his brow. "I'm sorry for being so tactless. I'll leave you to your evening now." He drifts backward in his pressed pin-striped suit, his luxurious dark hair perfectly combed, and dissolves into the same wall he has just sprung from, his handsome, sheepish face the last part of him to disappear.

She knows there is no logical way for Brian to compete with him. In her case, the unfortunate clichés are true—"You're seeing ghosts . . . dreaming of someone who isn't there . . . chasing after phantoms." How preposterous but sad: she has become an heir to Mrs. Muir's peculiar romantic angst.

For the next few nights Roger doesn't appear, lamentable timing because Brian is out of town for business, leaving her with plenty of nighttime hours to lavish on her dashing specter-guest who seems to be punishing her for her loyalty to a flesh-and-blood suitor, his carpe diem speech from the other day an obvious load of hooey. She glumly tries to read, to watch television, to exercise, but feels only boredom along with the chill of his absence. He once tried to describe for her where he sometimes goes when he isn't with her, explaining it as a simple state of nonbeing, a suspension of thought and all of the senses.

"Like sleep?" she asked, this the only thing she could imagine, other than the white clouds and harps of heaven or the voracious demons and bonfires of hell.

"No, not really," he said, shaking his head. "Just death, the eleventh dimension. The biggest black hole of any out there, but no living thing has discovered it yet, and I daresay, no living thing ever will. You have the enlightened people of Hollywood to imagine everything for you, and I suppose they do come close but I have a hard time seeing what good it does. Two world wars and others on the way, if you have to know."

She has begun to worry that he is a trick she won't ever understand, his lucidity and good advice and unpredictable disappearances a projection of some bizarre, buried trauma from her past. But the real mystery is why he bothers with her at all when presumably he can go anywhere—to her mind, a destination that becomes truly abstract when applied to ghosts. Why doesn't he want to hobnob with Sartre, even if the famed existentialist really is a boor? And if Roger used to be a pianist, why doesn't he listen to Bach or Gershwin or Beethoven or Liszt play a few new compositions, since they must be doing something with all of their free time? Why not discuss the largest conceivable Whys with the likes of Hegel or Kierkegaard or even Nietzsche if his mind was put back in its proper place when he died? To have the possibilities of this world and the next wide open to you is indeed a stunning, intoxicating notion, the very richest material of the movie-makers he professes to disdain.

The answer is obvious when he tells her: "I have forever to do those things. I'd rather be here right now. The earth is even better than you can guess, corny as it sounds. I love all of the water, for one—that wonderful buoyancy you don't have on land or even in space. And the coral reefs off of Australia, I'm enjoying them while I can. Spirits really are attracted to water, like the clairvoyants have long been claiming. It's the only place where we can hope to find our reflection, believe it or not."

"I want you to tell me how you died," she says snappishly when he returns from his three-night snit over Brian's birthday bash *à deux*, as Roger calls it with a slight but wounding trace of scorn. "You know everything about me, probably even things I don't know, but I'm glad you're not telling them to me."

He gives her a strange look, hollow-eyed, possibly looking through her. She wonders if he can take his eyeballs out like the ghouls in B movies and still see with them, but doesn't dare to ask. She is turning her beautiful ghost-visitor into a clown with these ridiculous thoughts. If he can read her mind, he must be very insulted. "Do you mean like when you're going to die? Or how it'll happen?"

His words send a bruising shudder through her body, all mutinous thoughts fleeing. "Don't say things like that," she says quietly. "To you it might be nothing, but that's the last thing I want to know. You won't talk about your own death, so you should know how I feel about mine."

"A car," he says. "I was hit by a car. But you'll die in your sleep. One of the very lucky ones, so to speak."

"Stop," she cries, putting her hands over her ears. "I don't want to know! How would you even know that?"

His mouth twitches. "Actually I don't, it's just a hunch, but I'm often right. You should just be glad that you don't have to be afraid of flying anymore or riding in trains and cars. The speed of life is what kills most of us, one way or another."

"Do you know who was driving the car that killed you?"

"My wife," he murmurs, smiling morosely. "The neighbors saw everything, though they usually did. She went to prison and they gave her the chair eight years later. As you can imagine, we avoid each other now."

Merilee stares. "She's not in hell?" But as soon as she says it, she knows it's a naive question; still, the severe and bug-eyed Miss O'Malley and her catechism classes from thirty years ago have not yet lost their hold over Merilee.

He shakes his head, his expression wry. "I've told you there isn't any hell. Not the kind you're picturing. As I've said, that weaselly Frenchman was right." He gives her a plaintive look. "May I stay with you tonight? I barely rested while I was away."

She looks at him. "You didn't have to run off like that. We would have had the house all to ourselves. Brian's been out of town, but he comes back tomorrow morning."

"I know," he says, avoiding her eyes.

In this terse response, she immediately senses his guilt, followed by a colossal jealous force of hot, anxious air that she had no idea before now that he could become. It is suddenly clear to her that Roger the ghost has been tailing Brian the human being, playing the private eye she had no desire or reason to hire. Brian Leonard Dunn, her boyfriend of thirteen and a half months—a good accountant, a decent tennis player, a divorced father of a grown son who lives in San Diego and works the midnight-to-seven A.M. shift at a gym that never closes, even on Christmas. Her lover may be a bit grouchy at times but he is still a likable man: well-meaning on the whole, prone to telling corny jokes about golfers and talking frogs, a little thick in the waist in his early-middle age, reliable and frugal but not to a fault, a circumspect driver and investor, a person who tries more than most people she knows (though in her opinion, he tends to get much too embarrassed about eating bananas in public). She is lucky to have him, she recognizes, to share his bed and a part of his life.

"You're actually in love with him?" says Roger, disbelieving.

So, he can read her mind. She winces, hoping he can't see her thoughts too, the pornographic imaginings that sometimes flood in. She does have a libido, but of course there's no shame in that; it's the coal that keeps the furnace glowing, provided it doesn't get out of hand.

"I don't know," she says, her tone sarcastic. "Am I?"

His face is somber. "It seems so."

"Have you been you spying on him in Phoenix?"

"I don't spy," he says, offended. "I observe, and that's my peculiar curse. I'd rather not have to be on watch for all of eternity, but it's one of the few choices available to a ghost."

"No one asked you to observe him. Aren't there at least seven billion other people you could be keeping an eye on instead?"

He is quiet for a long second; he hovers in front of her, arms akimbo. "Then you don't want to know what I found out."

She sighs, tempted to run out of the house where he can't effectively follow her. Outdoors, he can't stay in a recognizable form. The night air envelops him, makes him its hostage, as it does all spirits, he claims. It is the afterlife's truest form of anarchy, he has told her—the outside world has none of the defined edges and boundaries of human rooms, and so each cell of his otherworldly energy is sucked into the overwhelming nothingness of the universe. ("I'm writing a book about this," he once confided. "*Being in Nothingness*. That old French egomaniac might try to sue me over the title, but one of the perks of being dead is that there are no courts anymore.")

She does want to know if Brian behaved himself in Phoenix, but she also feels a sudden ferocious anger at being offered this perverse opportunity. Along with his earthly form, Roger seems to have shed in death any previous concerns about behaving ethically.

He takes no notice of this unvoiced criticism. "Your paramour was a saint," he mutters. "You have no reason to doubt his devotion. Early to bed, early to rise. He ate salads at lunch and dinner and permitted himself only two margaritas at happy hour. He woke up at six every morning and went for a swim in the hotel pool, pleasured himself in the shower afterward, and then went to his meetings like a very proper adult boy."

This is exactly what Brian told her over the phone, except for the shower part. She tries not to look relieved, but Roger knows and is miffed.

"I wonder how he can stand himself," he whines. "Sure, my wife murdered me, but while I had the chance, I knew enough to enjoy the world's sweets. Sometime I'll tell you about them." He pauses, noticing her look of distaste. "Most men in my position were no better. The majority were much worse. Celebrity and wealth are the strongest aphrodisiacs, make no mistake. I chose carefully and was always respectful of my lovers. They adored me and I them, as much as I was capable. The stories I might tell you . . . my goodness," he breathes. "If you were a screenwriter, you'd have enough material for fifty films."

X-rated ones, she thinks huffily.

"I heard that," he says, smiling.

"Why do you think I'd be interested in hearing about your escapades?" she says.

"You're only human."

"Very funny."

"Well, it's true, my dear."

"I really don't think I want to know about all of the people you slept with."

His gaze is piercing but she wills her brain to empty itself, a wave of fatigue and hopelessness overwhelming her.

"As you wish," he finally says, "but if you change your mind, I'd be happy to oblige."

"I need to get some rest now," she says, wanting to sob over how bizarre and possessive this once-gallant and very dear ghost friend has become. "Maybe we should say our goodnights."

"I'm sorry about Brian and his trip," he says gloomily. "But at least I was honest about his good behavior. I could have lied, but I won't lie to you, I promise."

"Fine, but you shouldn't have been spying on him in the first place. Please don't do it again."

"As you wish, Merilee." He nods and dissolves into the wall without saying goodnight. She feels a tremor of remorse for chasing him off so soon, but for all she knows, he's still lurking about, spying on her now, biding his time before turning menacing like real ghosts are supposed to be. These thoughts are enough to keep her awake for most of the night, her anxiety and irritation not helped by the fact that the hairbrush and perfume bottles on her bureau twice start to rattle for no obvious reason. The south wall of her bedroom also seems to take on a waterfall effect when she opens her eyes somewhere around three A.M., so annoyed by Roger's antics and her insomnia that the two sleeping pills she took at one A.M.

haven't had a chance. She takes two more at three thirty and sleeps through her seven o'clock alarm, not waking until nine fifteen, when she is already forty-five minutes late for work.

Throughout the day, the grisly thought plagues her: she is going crazy. She has survived these same doubts on other occasions, especially when Roger first began his nightly visits from the eleventh dimension to her bedroom at 314 Myrtle Lane, but this time her misgivings are fierce. She knows that if she were to see a doctor, he would probably want to lock her up and medicate her for schizophrenia. And who's to say she isn't schizophrenic? This is the real problem! She has no idea anymore if she is, in fact, a sane human being. All of her years as the smart and sturdy (but rather spinsterish, in some people's ignorant estimation) Merilee Crowley are perhaps about to end because of one jealous, slippery ghost whose womanizing tendencies were not snuffed out by death. Who knew how many other vulnerable women he haunted? Who knew where he spent his daylight hours? On the other side of the world where it is night—maybe in Japan—he might have a favorite geisha girl or a houseful of concubines. She can't put it past him now.

Roger Weber, dead concert pianist and inveterate Romeo, murdered by his wife for breaking her heart a few too many times, must be banished from her home. She wants her sanity and freedom restored as soon as possible. At lunch over her turkey-and-cheese sandwich, she decides that she might even tell him that she will hire a priest to exorcise him if he refuses to go. This is a lie, but she spends the lunch hour convincing herself it isn't so that Roger will not be able to read the truth in her thoughts.

That evening she does not return home until almost eight thirty but Roger is there as usual, patiently waiting for her when she comes through the back door, hovering next to the kitchen table, where an untidy heap of objects has been dumped. She feels cross, wondering why he is cluttering up her house, but he beams at her, very pleased with his mess.

"Do you recognize this?" he says, pointing to a golden earring in the shape of a dolphin on the pile's fringe.

She sets down her grocery bags and peers at the earring. "No," she says. "I don't think so."

"Sixth grade," he says. "You lost it when you got on the bus on May twelfth, nineteen eighty-five. The back was loose and the earring fell to the street. How about this?" His finger pokes through a tattered notebook with a paper cover meant to resemble pink denim.

This she remembers. Her diary from seventh grade to ninth. She worried that a classmate had stolen it but prayed that it had fallen down a strom drain or into a garbage can or had somehow been devoured by a wild dog.

"Someone did steal it," Roger confirms. "Reese Spiffen? Or was it Reggie Spinner . . . something along those lines? The name's a little foggy."

"Oh my God," she says, dumbfounded. "Where on earth did you find it?" She sees now what this pile is—lost objects, many of them items that had caused her something close to heartbreak when she discovered they were missing. A marble fountain pen given to her by her father on her fourteenth birthday; a rusted house key (her grandmother's); a shinier car key (her ex-boyfriend's—a loss that had nearly brought about a breakup); a wrinkled fifty-dollar bill; her autograph book containing the signatures of none other than Mark Hamill, Carrie Fisher, and Rick Springfield; her social security card; a brand-new leather wallet purchased in Florence on her senior-year trip to Europe and lost somewhere on the way to Paris for her flight home; a cassette tape of the *Grease* soundtrack; a crucifix necklace from her first communion; a soiled Chicago Cubs jersey that had belonged to her friend Mike Kreski, who had never forgiven her; a long, porno-graphic love letter from the scandalous and gorgeous Austin Lepadien, her most searing college fling.

"I didn't find any of this on earth, Meri. Everything was in our lost and found," Roger says. "I had to get special author-ization to claim your things, but it wasn't much of a problem. Normally you don't get your lost goods until you can claim them yourself. But I pulled a few strings, called in a favor." He chuckled. "The wheeling and dealing continues after death, I'm sorry to say."

"I can't believe this," she says, collapsing into a chair, picking up the still-immaculate wallet and fumbling it open. Inside are several thousand liu and a receipt for a half-dozen chocolate bars her now-almost-unknown younger self stashed there over twenty-one years ago.

"Your wish is my command, dearest one."

She stares up at him, his benign, sorrowful face begging her to adore him again. "But I didn't ask for these things, Roger. I wouldn't even have known to ask for them. I'm happy they're here, but it's a shock to see them after so many years."

He waves his elegant pianist's hand. "I had to make it up to you. I want you to know how much I care for you. There aren't any geisha girls, by the way. Don't worry. One woman at a time. Those are the rules out here. A bit stodgy, but it works, I suppose."

"Brian's coming over at nine thirty," she says, "and I need a shower before he gets here. I hate to say it, but maybe we should think about cutting it short again tonight." Despite the hangdog look and the otherworldly loot on the table, she absolutely needs to be alone. All is not forgiven. In fact, she is very creeped out by the sudden reappearance of the diary and the earring and the rest of her old forsaken things.

They look so strange to her, some of them faded and possibly tainted by the dust of some spooky alternate universe.

"Couldn't you call and tell him you're too tired tonight? Just this one time?"

"I want to see him, Roger. He's a man with all of his parts intact, and as we both know, you're not. I'm sorry to put it so bluntly, but it's true."

"Fine," he says, wounded. "I'm off again then. Banished to the frigid nothing of the eleventh dimension or wherever else I listlessly wander. I'll see you tomorrow, unless you want to put me in quarantine for another day or two."

She takes a breath, her stomach leaping queasily. "I really think we should consider seeing less of each other. Maybe only once a week. Or even once a month."

He stares at her. "Once a month. I see. You want to call it off. I'm not a fool, Merilee. If you want to break up with me, you only have to say so and I'll leave you alone for good."

"This isn't a breakup," she says, alarmed.

He snorts. "Call it whatever you'd like."

"We haven't been dating."

"I love you, Merilee. We're in a relationship, whether you call it that or not." He lunges toward her and tries fruitlessly to hug her.

"Oh God," she says, feeling his grief in their failed embrace. "Please don't say that."

"But I do love you. I'm a dead man without you." He has started to cry, his tears falling into thin air and vanishing before they reach the table.

"You're a dead man with me too."

"I'm even more of a dead man without you," he sobs.

She feels terribly guilty but does not want to back down, even if he is now so pliable and not the least bit scary. How easily he might turn into a horrible ghoul, she thinks, suppressing a shudder. (Before meeting him, she thought ghosts and ghouls were the same, but ghouls, she has learned, are much less civilized, the ids of the afterlife, the party crashers.) "You'll find another girlfriend," she assures him. "You're very handsome and giving, though if you start spying on people again, you'll get into the same trouble you did with me."

"My wife was right," he snuffles. "She used to say that I made it impossible for anyone to love me. She told me all the time to go straight to hell. I suppose I had the last laugh because she thought the fire-and-brimstone hell actually existed. But it's not like the afterlife without Satan has done me much good either."

"Maybe you should take a break from here and finally go to Washington to visit your brother. I bet he'd be happy to see you."

"No, he wouldn't, but his wife would, and that's the main problem."

Merilee blinks, not wanting to look surprised. Even when she has the upper hand, Roger can still make her feel like such a rube. She knows that she shouldn't be surprised, but she has met so few playboys in her life. "Well, perhaps he's forgiven you by now," she mumbles.

He shakes his head. "Garrett doesn't believe in ghosts, so I'm out of luck on two counts. The only people who see me are the ones who want to. Let me stay with you," he begs. "I can tell you almost anything you want to know about life and death. I can chase the ghosts out of all of your machines so you'll never have trouble with your car or electric toothbrush or stereo or blender again. I know how you hate to waste time on all of the piddly things that consume most people's lives without them being aware of it. You've been so kind to me; you've cared for me when I thought that no one ever would again. This Brian character has no idea what a treasure you are. I don't know if he ever will and I suppose that's the reason I followed him to Phoenix. I wanted to see if there was anything about him that I hadn't yet pegged."

"Was there?" she asks, dreading the answer.

He sighs noisily. "I suppose so. There's always the C factor. Chaos. He's as prone to it as anyone else, but it so rarely interrupts his steady trudge forward. It did once when his dog got run over by a tow truck and then in college when he caught his girlfriend cheating on him with her roommate. Both times he made some uncharacteristic decisions afterward. It'll strike again, I'm sure, but I don't know exactly when."

"I have to get in the shower now, Roger. He'll be here in twenty minutes. As you know, he's always on time."

"I could change that for you tonight, if you let me."

She gives him a stricken look. "Don't you dare."

He raises both of his hands in false surrender. "I hate goodbyes, Merilee. Life is full of them. It's ridiculous that death should be too." With this, he abruptly disappears.

She does not try to stop him, nor will she admit that with his absence, her house feels oddly bereft. When her toaster burns out a week later, she doesn't give in and summon him. When her car dies on the highway the next week, she still won't give in. When her microwave inexplicably fries itself into dereliction while she heats up a package of frozen lasagna, she knows he's toying with her but she refuses to succumb to his bullying.

Brian very kindly buys her a new toaster and gives her the microwave he won the previous year in the raffle at his company's annual picnic and has had sitting in his crawl space since then. Brian is exhilaratingly real with his teeth-grinding at night and callused hands and badly tailored trousers. She sees now that it is Roger who cannot possibly compete, even with his knowledge of death, the scariest secrets of the universe made mundane, and his legendary, curmudgeonly French consorts. She is gloriously alive, as boring and unromantic as it sometimes is.

When she tells Brian on their first camping vacation that she had a ghost friend for several months not too long ago, he gives her a long, funny look but finally shrugs and says that a lot of people probably see ghosts. She really shouldn't worry about it. There are much more frightening things, in his view. He gives her a tolerant smile and says he'd rather take on a ghost any day than a grizzly bear in the woods a few feet to the south of where they've pitched their tent. "Or some maniac with a machete," he adds. "Or the Unabomber. Or those Columbian drug lords who cut off the testicles and toes of the poor fools who try to cheat them. Or some hack surgeon who forgets his sponge inside my large intestine. Or Hitler, who I hope is dead, but I do wonder sometimes if he found the fountain of youth and is still alive down in Peru or some place like that. Don't you ever worry about this too?"

Anyone with half a brain must, she agrees, hearing in that instant a whisper behind her, *What a nitwit*, before insect racket engulfs it. She knows that she won't be left alone until Roger loses interest. "The poor old masochist," she accidentally says aloud, Brian giving her a puzzled look but knowing enough (Bless his heart, she thinks, squeezing his hand) not to ask. The night around them is alive with the buzz-saw symphony of a billion hungry insects, all of them fierce with the desire to live.

WHATSHISNAME

You have a mice problem was the first thing he said to me. Then he said, "No, no. I mean, I have a mice problem." He confused *I* and *you* sometimes. Once in a while he also confused stoplights with streetlights and this had caused him a couple of worse problems than mixing up his pronouns. As for his mouse hang-up, he had to have known that I'd be curious. What normal person wouldn't be? I considered myself normal and had for a long time. But if your switchboard wasn't in full working order, one thing you might do is take detours that end with you knocking on the door to some stranger's toolshed or the padlocked entrance to the movie house that closed down three years ago, though faded boxes of Good & Fruity and Goobers still sit inside its display case. Josh had taken a detour like this at least once that I knew of: on his way to the store one afternoon, he got it into his head to drive to his old elementary school and sit in the parking lot playing his leg like a piano until someone came out and made him leave.

He might have been a little off, but he didn't say cruel things to people, not on purpose, and his pronoun dyslexia had started after he was whacked in the head with a baseball bat in gym during his last year in high school, which had scrambled up more than his pronouns for a while. He went colorblind for a couple of months, and a few times he had to be stopped from chewing on kitchen sponges and tinfoil. He also couldn't stop calling his mother Robert for several weeks, which was the name of the kid who almost accidentally broke his skull. She didn't like this because she thought it was his way of saying that he blamed her for the accident, even though she hadn't been anywhere near the school when it happened. As usual, she'd been at home, where she worked in a little room off the kitchen, sewing placemats and tablecloths and kitchen aprons for sale in gift shops for rich people who couldn't or didn't want to sew their own.

As for the mouse problem, it wasn't even close to what I expected. Along with the other side effects, the head injury sometimes made him blurt things out, but not like people with Tourette's did. It wasn't dirty words or angry yelling, nothing that would have gotten him in trouble with his teachers or his boss if he'd had one at the time. He just didn't know how to put his thoughts in the right order and it took a couple of years for most of the kinks to straighten out again. He was still recovering from his messed-up brain when we started going out, and I finally realized what he meant by the mice. He'd confused them with cats. The truth was, he had a cat problem: he was allergic to them. I was so relieved when I figured this out because what I thought he meant was that he had a thing for mice, like some guys have a thing for feet, or for girls who dress up in leather bras and get paid to whip them.

Two other things Josh said that I know I won't forget for a long time: "It's so weird to have a tongue. Think about it. This big pink thing in your mouth that's like a rug made out of muscle."

And: "I hate bingo. You're one square away and then someone else wins. I don't get why more people who play it aren't mass murderers."

When we met, I was in my third semester of community college, studying landscape design, which I didn't like as much as some of the other students in the program did, freaks who spent their free time having contests of who could build the best diorama of Central Park. I changed to restaurant and hotel management before my fourth semester; it was much better because, for one, you could wear decent clothes to work and not have to worry about stepping in cow manure, or as it was called by landscape professionals, "organic fertilizer." Josh was at the college too, taking classes in accounting and falling asleep in them. I had a big crush on him right away and paid forty dollars to a witch to put a love spell on him, but I found out later that he already liked me anyway.

What happened to him, to us, probably happened because some people can't be counted on to say the right things at the right time. Or do the right things when they're required, like giving a sympathy card to your boss when his brother dies or letting your friend pick the movie that night because her car was totaled at lunchtime in the mall parking lot.

I was in love with him and we'd been together for eight months when he told me that he wanted to open an orphanage for kids who had lost their parents in the wars in Africa. He thought he could actually do this because a week earlier, by some miracle that I'm still not sure turned out to be a good thing, he won the lottery. Not *the* lottery, but the Little Lotto, which wasn't so little—$401,000—though the state wanted to dole it out $40,100 at a time for ten years. After taxes it would be about $24,055, unless Josh could figure out a way to get more by donating some of it to charity, which was maybe how the orphanage idea came about, but he never admitted this. As it turned out, charity or no, he still had to hand almost all the tax money over—we realized then that the state had a lottery only because it could make money off of poor dopes who kept thinking they'd win, and if somehow they did, they still had to give half of it back so that the bosses in the government offices could have their free coffee and donuts and fancy luncheons whenever they felt like it.

Josh did buy me a gold bracelet and paid for new struts for my car, which weren't cheap, and he bought me a big pile of groceries: rib eyes and shrimp and Asian pear apples—the kinds of things I didn't normally buy for myself because they were special-occasion food—tossed in the cart with the store-brand Kleenex and bread and laundry soap. I had never had a special-occasion life, not for more than a day or two at a time, at least not until Josh came along and picked the right numbers because he saw them written on some guy's forehead in a dream.

What I wanted him to do with the money, as any idiot would know, didn't have anything to do with African orphans. It wasn't that I wanted orphans to starve and be miserable for their whole lives, but I did think that someone else could be in charge of them. Josh had enough to worry about—he was barely passing Spanish, which was supposed to be his easy elective, and he didn't want to study accounting anymore but wouldn't change his major to something else because he was stubborn. He kept going to his classes after he had the orphanage idea but didn't do enough homework because he was looking for the right orphan house to buy and figuring out how he could find a bunch of kids in Zimbabwe or Sudan who wanted to come to America, and then have them shipped over, but there were so many problems with this idea, as anyone who had not been cracked on the side of his skull by the pothead Robert Skipkus would have realized right away.

We talked about his orphanage idea, hundreds of times it seemed, but he never wanted to hear anything I said because I was too negative for him. "You could help me," he complained. "Instead of telling me what a dumbshit I am." This was on the day he found a house that he thought would be right for the orphans, but it was way too small and looked like it was stuck between two crack houses.

"I never said you're a dumbshit."

"You don't have to, Kim. I can tell by your expression."

"I just think you could find a better house if you're really going to do this."

"The price is good and it's not far from where I live. What, do I want you to wear a Kick Me sign?"

I looked at him. Sometimes I didn't get him. Not even close. His pronouns again, I thought.

He'd found a house in Mundelein, a town about eight or nine miles from the college, where lots of people from Poland and Russia and Wisconsin lived but not too many people from Africa, as far as I knew. Besides its crack-house neighbors with their peeling paint and yards full of deflated inner tubes, the house looked like someone had stolen it from the cover of a book of ghost stories. Its black shutters and four chimneys, or whatever they were coming out of the roof, screamed *Nightmare on Elm Street* and no way would I want to be a kid who had just lost my parents to a bunch of crazed heroin addicts running around with machetes and have to come live in a house like this one, with neighbors next door that, for fun, grill up huge bratwursts and baloney rings on weekends and beat the crap out of paper donkeys filled with candy and Super Balls on their birthdays. It had five bedrooms and three dinky bathrooms and was not really that big of a place at all, not for an orphanage, but Josh thought that he could put three sets of bunk beds in two of the rooms, and two sets in each of the other three. I didn't see how. The kids would have to climb over one another to get in and out of the room. I said this to Josh, who scowled at me. "They're little kids," he said. "The beds can be shorter than the ones I'd have to get for adults."

"I don't know who you're going to get these kids from. You can't just put in an order for them like they're mail-order brides. And who else is going to work at the orphanage? How are you going to pay them?"

"If you don't want to be a part of this, you don't have to. You should just say it."

"You can't buy that house. It's too spooky. The kids you order from Africa will take one look at it and beg you to put them on the next plane back to Darfur."

"I don't see why you have to make a joke out of this. That's fucked up."

"I don't think it's a joke at all. That house is scary. I would never want to live in it."

"You don't have to."

"Thanks, I won't."

Maybe I was jealous and wished the idea had been mine instead. Maybe I wanted to be the sort of person who lived for saving orphans and actually did it instead of just talking about it. Anyone can tell you how noble and great they'd be if only they had the money or the time. It's like someone you meet at a party saying she was adopted, but her real parents, who'd been killed by an insane dictator who liked to hunt rhinos and grizzlies in his spare time, had been a prince and princess back in the Old World. How could you tell that girl she was full of shit?

"I'll help you, Josh. I promise."

"If you want to help me, you have to stop pissing on everything I say."

I don't know. Maybe his friends were telling him that I was a gold digger and he was starting to believe them. Money does change you, even if you plan to give most of it away.

His mother, whose name was Cindy, not Robert, was on my side. She worried that Josh only wanted to start the orphanage because his brains were still goofed up. "Why not save the money for your future?" she said. "You could put it away and retire early."

"From what?" he said.

"From your accounting business."

Hearing this, he rolled his eyes. "You don't know if you want to be an accountant." He paused, his eyes working back and forth from her face to mine. "I mean, I don't know if I want to be accountant."

Her face went a little pale. "You don't?"

"What I want to do is run an orphanage for kids from Africa," he said.

His poor mother—besides being called Robert, the things she had to put up with after the accident! He'd tell her that he'd cut his fingers off when what he meant was that it was time to mow the lawn. Sometimes he went outside and climbed the crabapple tree in the backyard and called out that he had never been to such a good museum before. These episodes didn't happen often, but when they did, they were usually in the middle of the night. He was very cute, though, and tall, which meant that people thought he was in charge, or could have been if he wanted to be. The neighbors also liked him because in the winter he would use his mom's snowblower on their driveways without them having to ask. His dad wasn't around to do the snowblowing anymore. I was told that he'd been on a sailboat in the Caribbean during a storm and had not come back. Josh was five when he disappeared and the next day washed up on St. Thomas missing some of his parts because something had gotten to him, but not a shark, because there probably wouldn't have been anything left if it had been a shark that ate him. Josh told me that he still remembered his dad pretty well—he used to put on his father's big black dress shoes and shuffle around the house and they would laugh, until one night Josh tripped and landed on his mom's ficus, which sat in a big clay pot. This irritated her because the pot cracked when he fell on it and he got dirt all over his face and the rug next to it.

His mother told him that if he was really serious about helping orphans, he needed to get other people involved, those who worked with refugees or people in countries with real problems and knew what channels to go through if he wanted to start his own charity. "Call those Doctors Without Borders and see what they have to say for themselves. You probably have to get some kind of license from the state too. I don't think this is something you can do overnight, Josh. It could take years."

"Fine," he said. "There will always be orphans."

As it turned out, Doctors Without Borders did not have much to say once he got someone to answer the phone in their dusty office with shirtless little kids running around playing soccer outside with a ball made from an old wig, wadded newspaper, and a few rubber bands to hold it all together (this was how I pictured it) and listen to what Josh was planning to do in Mundelein, Illinois, in his haunted house with the piñata-smashing, baloney-ring-noshing next-door neighbors. After the first four or five times, they stopped answering his calls. They said they were doctors who dispensed medicine and treated things like tapeworms and malaria, not orphanage administrators. Wherever they were, in Liberia or India or Brazil with the wig soccer ball, they must have had caller ID, because they stopped picking up, and after another week or so of trying to get through and convince someone to come and help him get things going, Josh moved on to bugging the Red Cross people. He said that the last he'd heard, the Red Cross was based in Switzerland, and that meant they must have a decent office with free chocolate bars up for grabs by the entrance, and more than one person to give kids vaccinations and file paperwork and answer the phone.

The Red Cross person told him to get his local government involved and maybe a church or a school too; that was really the only way to get permission to start an orphanage. He would need synergy between local political people and a tough nun and some kind of consultant person who would know how to start an orphanage. "Synergy," Josh repeated to me later, over and over. "Synergy synergy synergy. That's a stupid-sounding word, like taco. Taco sounds dumb, doesn't it. Taco taco taco."

"If you say any word over and over, it's eventually going to sound dumb," I said.

"How do you know?"

"I just do."

"Maybe we should try it sometime sometime sometime," he said, very depressed and tired that no one wanted to help him start the orphanage.

"Sometime is a nice word," I said.

"I need a vacation vacation vacation, I think think think," he said.

"You have to stop that," I said, already annoyed.

"Okay, okay."

"Stop," I said again, trying not to yell. "I think you should open a dog or cat shelter instead. That'd probably be easier."

"No," he said. "Orphans. Human ones. Not orphan cats or pit bulls. But you know, that's not a bad idea. Maybe after I start the orphanage, I'll start an animal shelter. I know a veterinarian. Maybe she would donate some of her time, or I guess I could pay her too. I did win the lottery."

"The Little Lotto," I said.

"Yeah, I know, thanks."

The haunted house, by some miracle, or maybe it was black magic spells cast by the real estate agent, sold before Josh had a chance to put in a bid because he was wasting time trying to get help from the Red Cross and those heartless Doctors Without Borders. He got more depressed and nearly flunked Spanish and he started eating nothing but popcorn, but several different kinds: kettle corn, white cheddar cheese corn, lightly salted with rosemary and parmesan corn (my favorite), extra-salty corn, caramel corn, air-popped and no-salt corn, and that neon orange kind they sell in huge bags for a dollar and a half but it tastes like greasy Styrofoam and turns your hands into Day-Glo monster claws.

I told Josh that he should give some of his lottery money to his mother, so that she didn't have to sew oven mitts twelve hours a day. He looked at me strangely when I suggested this and I asked him what was the matter with helping her out?

"Let me see. For one, you can't stop her from doing what she wants. She loves to sew as much as you should love helping orphans. And I already give her two hundred dollars a week to live with her. I thought I knew that. Wait, you thought I knew that. I mean—"

"I got it," I said. "You really give her two hundred bucks a week? That's a lot of money."

He nodded. "I know."

"That's good. She really shouldn't shop at Bargain Barn anymore then. Their paper towels are—"

"Like I said, I can't stop her from doing what she wants."

That was when I had the idea that made Josh fall for me forever, or at least that's what he said later when he gave me a bunch of daisies and a stuffed pink bear wearing a bib that said, I HEART HONEY.

"I think you could go to an orphanage that already exists and help them get new beds and clothes and toys for the kids that already live there," I said. "And maybe you could also bring in some new orphans through whatever network they already have in place?"

He was so excited by this idea that I thought he was going to propose. I worried about this for a few seconds because I wasn't sure I wanted to get married. Not yet, even if I did love him. My parents were divorced. They were the kind of couple that had gotten divorced, then decided they'd made the worst mistake of their lives and got married again a few years later, only to get a divorce eight months after they'd signed the second marriage license. In my head, I thought this was like taking your car to the junkyard, selling it to the scrap metal guy, and then going back a little while later to see if it was still there and buying it back for more than the guy had paid you for it in the first place.

"That's what I'm going to do," he said. "You're a genius."

I blushed. "No one's ever called me that before."

He looked at me, smiling. "Well, that's their problem, not yours."

I blushed harder. "Yeah, I guess it is."

I thought he looked especially handsome right then, and if I had been the type of girl who sometimes forgot to take her pill in the morning, later that day I would have gotten knocked up three times. But I never forgot to take my pill because I set an alarm in my phone, and I also didn't think I wanted kids so I always remembered the pill, alarm or not. There were enough kids on the planet already, and as I had been learning through being with Josh, more than enough orphans to go around too.

He found an orphanage in Rogers Park, a neighborhood on the north side of Chicago. It was more than an hour away from our community college, but they had kids living there who were refugees from the wars in Africa and they were so cute and made mistakes in English that I loved. Instead of *button*, one of them said *billion*—as in, "I lost my billion in the garden!" And another one said *cot* instead of *cat*. "That's just their accent," said the tough nun in charge.

"But if you have a cat and a cot in the same room, how can you tell the difference?" I asked her.

She just looked at me and blinked before saying, "That's a good question." She didn't go on to answer it, and later I complained about this to Josh, but he didn't care. He was worrying that the nuns would use the money he planned to give them the next day in the form of a big green cashier's check from his bank to buy themselves fancy salon haircuts and new Birkenstocks instead of bedsheets, yo-yos, gym shoes, Halloween costumes, and cases of coconut-and-chocolate protein bars (Josh's favorite), along with the occasional ice cream cone and movie ticket for the Congolese kids. The orphanage was close to a convenience store and a movie theater—ice creams and Disney movies wouldn't have been hard to get if the nuns were serious about giving their orphans these treats.

"Why don't you give them the money in the form of gift cards to GNC, Target, Jewel, and Sears maybe?" I suggested. "That way, they can't buy themselves haircuts at some chichi salon on Michigan Avenue, and they won't be able to buy fancy shoes for themselves either. But Josh, I really don't think the nuns would do that anyway."

"Why?" he said. "Because it's against their religion?"

I looked at him, not sure if he was joking. "That's one reason."

He thought over my gift card idea for what felt like a long time before shaking his head. "I can't see myself walking into GNC, buying three thousand dollars in gift cards and doing the same thing at those other stores. They might think I'm using drug money if I come in with cash, and the next thing I know, the manager puts the cops on my tail and my mom is coming downtown to bail me out."

"You don't have to use cash. Just use your debit card," I said. "Why wouldn't you call me to bail you out instead of your mom if you got arrested?"

He made a hiccuping sound, which was his way of showing how annoyed he was. "It's just an expression, Kim. God, chill out."

I ignored this. "The other thing you could do is buy all the stuff you want the kids to have and give it to them in a U-Haul truck."

"But then the nuns would know that I didn't trust them, don't you think?"

"Just give them the cashier's check and be done with it," I said, about to lose it. "You can't control what they do after you give them the money. You'd probably be happier if you kept the money for yourself. Or else just wrote out fifty-dollar checks every week for the charities you like and give all your money away that way."

"Jesus, this really sucks."

"What, winning the Little Lotto?"

He rolled his eyes. "Well, yeah, what else?"

That was the problem with being a generous type like Josh, I guess. If you won the lottery, then you wanted to share all your money with the people you knew and didn't know. I felt kind of bad for him, eating my rib-eye steak and baked potato with sour cream and chives later that night, which he was eating too but with a sad look on his face. We had gone to the bank before I made dinner and gotten the cashier's check cut. It was worth fourteen thousand dollars, and I'd never seen so much money before, but it looked so flat, as if it were kidding, as if it were play money, but it wasn't, and the teller kept staring at us and was probably wondering how a guy with bangs growing past his eyebrows and a girl with a palomino head tattooed on her forearm (I regretted it, which my mom said I would, but at the time, I hadn't believed her) could have so much money and why they were making it out to the Sisters of the Sacred Heart. The teller said as he handed the big green check to us, "Don't spend it all in one place. Ha!"

Josh just looked at him. I sort of laughed and said, "Oh, no, we won't. We're just giving them half the check."

The teller blinked and probably thought I was serious because he must have thought I looked dumb. "Just kidding," I said, and then we left, and Josh was quiet all through dinner and he kept glancing over his shoulder to where the check was now in an envelope on the kitchen counter. I had one of those black-and-white cat clocks from my grandmother, the kind with the big round eyes that roll back and forth, and it was there above the countertop, leering down at Josh and me and the nuns' and orphans' check.

"I just hope it helps make their lives better," said Josh in a small voice after he'd pushed away his plate, the steak mostly eaten, the potato barely touched, only the sour cream and chives raked off the top.

"It will, Josh," I said, feeling like I might cry. "You're such a good person."

"You don't have to say that," he said.

"I know I don't, but it's true."

* * *

What happened after that, I guess some people would say, was a comeuppance or a slap in the face or else just life, plain and kind of simple, maybe. Idealistic young kids being taught a lesson by some tough nuns.

Well, we don't know. We don't have proof, but what happened was, Josh and I drove down to Chicago again the morning after the rib eye and the bank and gave the flat money to the nun in charge, who invited us to stay for lunch. There were about eighteen kids at the orphanage and they were all jumping up and down in the back near the garden with the seedlings the nuns had planted a couple of weeks earlier, and they were told from time to time by a little nun who was sitting in a chair watching the kids not to go near the plants because they might fall on them and crush them and then there'd be no tomatoes and cucumbers in August.

A little boy kept wanting to hold my hand, which led to other little boys, and some little girls, wanting to hold my hand too. I had bought a bag of Tootsie Pops for them but had to ask the nun in charge first if it was okay to give them the suckers, and she said, "Yes, but only after lunch." So after lunch, which was grilled cheese, white milk, and carrot sticks, I gave the kids the suckers and it was as if I had suddenly turned into Santa Claus right before their eyes, they were so excited.

Or, wait, maybe they didn't know who Santa Claus was. Not yet anyway.

One of the boys from Africa kept running around in a circle after lunch, his arms flapping. He was yelling, "Whatshisname, whatshisname!" until one of the nuns grabbed him by the shoulder and made him sit in a chair.

"Cool down, Peter," she said. "Cool down."

"Calm down, Peter," said another nun. "Calm down."

It was all a little strange, but I got a kick out of it.

We left after that and Josh seemed okay for a while, but a week or so later he wanted to go back down to see the kids with their new yo-yos and gym shoes, and so we drove again into the snarl of city traffic, knocked on the orphanage door after we found parking four streets over, and the little nun who had been sitting on the chair near the garden the week before let us in. She smiled and said the head nun was out getting her nails done. Josh and I looked at her, Josh's face a crumpled-up mess all of a sudden. The little nun laughed and said the head nun was actually at the doctor getting her blood pressure checked. I wondered if this nun was off-kilter, because she probably wasn't supposed to tell us why the head nun was at the doctor, but what did I know. Maybe they were all very open about their health problems? Maybe it was one of the things they were taught in nun training.

We waited and when the head nun returned, she was in a new-looking blue Ford Focus; the last two times we'd been there, we'd only seen a dented old Camry with the orphanage name on the driver's door, its bumpers scratched and gouged. For a second she didn't seem happy to see us, but then she rearranged her expression and smiled. "Are you here for the letter for your taxes?" she asked. "I haven't yet had a chance to prepare it, but Sister Jean and I could type it up for you right now if you don't mind waiting a few minutes."

"No, no, we just thought we'd come by and say hi. We were in the neighborhood," said Josh.

I looked at him, worrying that if there was an actual hell, he'd be sent there for lying to a pair of nuns.

"Oh, how thoughtful of you," said the head nun. Then she and Sister Jean just peered at us, waiting for whatever one of us would say next. We could hear the kids screaming and laughing in some room out of sight and the voice of one of the other nuns scolding them but laughing too. Josh looked at me, and I worried he might cry or else say something strange like he had two days ago when we were leaving our college's parking lot—"The sow is blinding me." I knew he'd meant the sun, but the nuns would not have known this.

He said nothing though, and I said we should probably get going.

I glanced at the head nun's and Sister Jean's feet and saw that the head nun had pink-painted toenails. Her dress wasn't quite long enough to cover her sandaled feet. Sister Jean's feet I couldn't see. Her dress dragged on the ground just a little bit. Later, Josh told me it was called a habit, not a dress. I had forgotten this, I guess. "I'm not Catholic," I said.

"Even so, you'd think I'd know," said Josh.

"*I'd think you'd know*," I said, irritated.

"That's what I said," he said, angry too.

That night and the next day, Josh didn't say much else. I was at his house for dinner the next night and his mother gave me two placemats she'd sewn with crooked seams, something that happened once in a while. They had flags on them and were for the Fourth of July. "Thanks," I said. "You can't really tell there's any problem with them "

"Oh, you're so nice to say that," she said.

Josh was staring into space and then he left the table and went to his room. His mother and I looked at each other for a minute before she said, "I tried to tell him that if he's going to do nice things for people, he isn't going to be able to control how they respond. It's called growing up."

She was so right, but I wondered what he'd said when she'd told him this.

"Do you think he's going to be okay?" I asked.

She nodded. "Yes. That was only his first lottery payment. He has nine others coming to him. He'll learn not to be such a mope about his good fortune."

"Do you think those nuns took advantage of him?"

She was quiet for a few seconds. "Maybe, maybe not. But it's not like they're in New York on that Wall Street, stealing people's life savings and getting the government to pay them a billion dollars because they're such good, upstanding criminals. Those ladies take care of orphans, for Pete's sake."

She had a point, but when I said this later to Josh, he wasn't impressed. "I might go out West after the semester ends. I need to do some thinking. I'm not sure sometimes if I want to be with people. I'd rather live with coyotes and lizards. They don't have wallets or cars."

"You could come too," he said. I was glad to be invited but wasn't sure I wanted to go. How would I get my pills out in the desert, for one? I had to think about it.

"You could get a vasectomy, you guess," he said.

I didn't mean to laugh, but I did. "Yes, I suppose."

"I'm serious."

"I know. It's nice of you to offer."

He nodded but said nothing.

In my head, I saw the little kid in the garden again, yelling "Whatshisname, whatshisname!" He'd looked so happy, as if he liked everyone and everyone liked him. I didn't know if I'd ever felt that way in my life. I didn't know if I ever would either. I didn't say this to Josh, who was staring at his phone, his forehead crimped and serious, probably trying to decide if he should call the nuns.

THE COUPLEHOOD JUBILEE

THE FIGURE SHE CAME up with wasn't staggering, at least not in terms of the amount that some people might have spent, those with greater means or no fear of credit card debt. Nonetheless, it was much more than she felt comfortable with, and so much more than she had spent on travel and movies and dinners out for herself and Glen in any given year. She did her best to keep track of where her money went, hoping to discourage herself from spending three or four times more on temporary pleasures than she deposited into her retirement and rainy-day savings accounts. A dense bubble of resentment began to form beneath her breastbone as she stared at the sum: $24,900. This was the approximate amount that she had spent on friends' bridal showers, engagement and bachelorette parties, hotels, plane tickets, dresses, and other wedding-related expenses over the past eight and a half years.

During that entire time, she had been working as a high school French teacher and had earned an average annual salary of thirty-nine thousand dollars.

Twenty-five thousand dollars on weddings: well over half of what she earned in a year! The resentment bubble threatened to asphyxiate her. Why had she allowed this to happen? And about half of the people she had shelled out so much money for were already divorced!

Eventually the bubble migrated to her head, and for a few midday hours, it tried very hard to summon a migraine. At the all-day, end-of-year school meeting where she had surreptitiously added up these wedding-related expenses, she kept thinking, *I wouldn't even spend a third of that amount on my own wedding.* Despite their interest in monogamy, she and Glen, her boyfriend of six years, were not interested in marriage nor in what seemed to be the feverish American imperative to marry everyone off, tuck them into minivans and bring on infant-induced sleep deprivation as soon as biologically possible.

"Why don't you want to get married?" some of Karen's unhappily unmarried friends had asked. "Do you think that you or Glen can't be faithful?"

"It's not like we need to be married to cheat on each other," she had replied.

Her friends remained doubtful. "Then what is it? Are you both holding out for someone better?"

That wasn't it either. Their reasons were more complicated than their bemused friends and relatives suspected, but if Karen tried to explain her feelings and convictions, their eyes grew hazy with boredom and suspicion or else they argued that she was wrong, possibly egomaniacal, to resist this rite of passage that was good enough for millions of other couples.

Even so, she did not feel wrong or egomaniacal. She did not understand why she and Glen needed to buy a license and recite certain phrases in front of a judge in order to be declared a committed couple. As if, like someone who wanted a driver's license, a couple needed to be declared fit and legal to love each other.

Karen's parents, however, were worried about her unmarried status for other reasons. Didn't she know that if she or Glen ever became sick and choices had to be made about medical care and money, the existence of this license was the only way that they were guaranteed the right to make these critical decisions?

"Common law," Karen would usually reply to her parents and other critics, brandishing the phrase like garlic in front of a vampire.

"Sure," her father said, agreeably enough, "but common law marriages don't often hold up in court. You're young now so you don't care, but wait until the first time one of you has to go into the hospital for something unforeseen, and I guarantee you'll feel differently."

Despite his depressing predictions, she knew that her father meant well. Almost everyone meant well when they told her to march straight to the nearest courthouse or altar and marry herself off. She was thirty-five, for Christ's sake! What if Glen got tired of her when her breasts plunged to her navel and her knees started to look like a bloodhound's face?

"So what if he does?" she'd retort. "Good riddance to him if he's going to be that damn shallow. Why would I want to hold on to someone who doesn't want to hold on to me?"

Another open question that no one seemed willing to acknowledge: If you really were worried about being dumped by your boyfriend, couldn't you see that you were using marriage as a stand-in for a jail cell? Keep each other locked up in the invisible bonds of matrimony and all will be well . . .

Friends sometimes badgered her about her lack of a wedding ring, but the last Karen had heard (from Dr. Phil, from Oprah, from her dentist and hairstylist, and from, well, almost everyone), more than half of the marriages out there ended in divorce. These unfortunate facts were everywhere a person cared to look, glaring and as ghoulishly fascinating as a car crash, yet, so many otherwise-rational souls still continued to invoke the wedding march as if it were music flung down from heaven, meant to relieve them of all of their earthly sorrows.

Nonetheless, she did not feel smug about her decision to remain unmarried, despite what some people thought. She was happy when a friend or a colleague announced an engagement that he or she had been hoping for. A few of her friends and family members seemed to be happy enough as husbands and wives, and many weddings were joyful gatherings filled with laughter and good food and music and funny speeches, ones where, by the end, Karen's face hurt from smiling so much, and she couldn't help wondering if she too might want to get married.

But the feeling did not last for more than a few days, and eventually something would remind her that most everyone she knew believed they had a right to advise and judge her for how she had chosen to conduct her personal life, as if she would ever seriously consider telling them what to do with their own sex lives and finances.

Glen was more relaxed about this oppressive rigmarole, but as far as Karen could tell, men weren't prone to needling other men about their decision to stay unmarried. Men could shack up or sleep around and spend as much time as they wanted to making up their minds about who should be having their babies. Men could relax, because when it came to reproductive urges, they had no ovaries to worry about going out of business in middle age. Men could continue to make their offerings to the gene pool until, in many cases, they were coffin-ready.

Staring at the horrifying figure (almost twenty-five thousand bucks!) that had materialized before her during the meeting's midday lull, Karen decided that it was time to get her married (and, in a few cases, recently divorced) friends to return a few favors. She would ask Glen to help her throw a party, a "Couplehood Jubilee," where gifts were tacitly required, along with suits and ties, fancy dresses and elaborate hairstyles, and hotel rooms and rental cars and designated drivers. She would have to spend some money too, but she would do it. It was time for the married (and divorced) people of the world to understand that they weren't going to be able to keep skating by when it came to showing a little fiscal affection for their unhitched friends.

There could be no waffling either. Guests would have to fork over the cash and goodwill for her and Glen's non-wedding whether they liked it or not, because otherwise, like anyone whose friends and neighbors made up excuses not to attend their weddings, she would resent them. She would not issue any guilt-trips like the kind she had suffered as a bridesmaid, however: "If you can't afford them . . . um, I guess we could settle for the cheaper shoes even if they look like something my grandmother would wear." Or as a guest: "I know Hawaii is really, really far for everyone to travel, but it's just so beautiful and you can take a vacation there just before or after our wedding, right?" If people said no, she would tell them bluntly that she was disappointed, that they were, melodramatic as it sounded, breaking her heart. She would not smile and say, *No problem, I completely understand*, while giving the finger to their backs as they slunk away.

On a grander scale, with her Couplehood Jubilee, she hoped to inspire a social revolution: mass elopements. She single-handedly wanted to bring down the billion-dollar wedding-industrial complex, with its empty promises and guilt-inducing advertisements and wedding-planning mercenaries who seduced newlyweds and their parents into taking on years of high-interest debt.

But according to Glen, she would be massacring the starry-eyed dreams of little girls and grown women everywhere. And what about all of the jobs that would be lost if she brought down the wedding industry? Had she thought about the repercussions of such an outcome?

She laughed. "You're kidding, I hope." They were in the kitchen eating dinner, which was carryout pizza, because she had a coupon, one that would expire in two days. When she picked up their pepperoni-and-mushroom, the boy behind the register had thrown in a free bottle of Mountain Dew, which Karen loved but Glen thought disgusting.

Glen smiled, his brown hair flopping over his eyes, sheepdog-like. He needed a haircut, but the stylist he preferred charged sixty dollars a visit, and because he was even more frugal than Karen, he often waited three months between cuts. "Of course I am. Rock on with your assault on the wedding industry."

"I hope you mean that, because it's time to call our married friends' bluffs."

He pried up another slice from the pizza box and put it on his plate. "What are you proposing?" he asked and smiled. "No pun intended."

She described her idea for the non-wedding party. "I think it'll be a lot of fun if we can pull it off. We've been together longer than some of our friends have been married. Bill and Ella both, for one. And I wonder about Meg and Freddy now too." Bill had been married and divorced twice during the time that Karen had been with Glen, and Ella's marriage had lasted five weeks, but to her credit, it was the only marriage she'd had so far.

She showed Glen the rough draft of the invitation she'd written after returning home from the meeting:

THE COUPLEHOOD JUBILEE

PLEASE SAVE THE DATE!

In honor of our six years together,
Glen Calhoun and Karen Quinn
are pleased to host a Couplehood Jubilee!
We request the honor of your presence for our reception
on July 20 at our home, 2344 W. Pratt, Chicago
Wine and hors d'oeuvres: 5 p.m.
Dinner: 7 p.m.
Dancing: 8:30–11 p.m.
Black Tie Optional

We have registered at Macy's, Pottery Barn,
Tiffany & Co., and Neiman Marcus

Blocks of rooms have been reserved in our last names at
the Four Seasons, the Drake Hotel,
and the InterContinental

Please RSVP by July 5
kquinn22@hotmailspot.com or
MisterG@hotmailspot.com

Both Glen and I very much hope to see you at our celebration!

"When did you become such an advocate of the exclamation point?" he asked.

She smiled. *"J'adore le point d'exclamation."*

Usually he loved it when she spoke French, but his expression showed misgiving. "'Couplehood Jubilee,'" he said. "What exactly is that? And the Four Seasons and Neiman Marcus? Who are you planning to invite? George Soros?" He handed back the invitation. "Aren't you supposed to send out save-the-date cards before the actual invitations?"

"Yes, but we don't have a lot of time and I'm not going to send out both. Save-the-date cards are another way the wedding-industrial complex gets people to spend money they don't have. I'm going to do it all over email anyway."

"Karen," he said quietly. "This Couplehood Jubilee thing is, pardon my French, a fucking scam. If our friends figure out what we're up to, they might be amused at first, but then they'll probably feel like they're being conned."

"It is not a scam," she insisted. "It'd be a scam if we said it was a real wedding but when they got here, we said, 'Ha, fooled you!'"

"I still think some of our friends will feel like it's a scheme to get gifts out of them."

"I'm never getting back a penny of all the money I've spent on other people's weddings. It's an investment with no returns, especially because most of them will probably get divorced. I'd have been better off giving that money to charity and sending my friends cards saying that I made donations in their names instead of buying plane tickets and presents."

"You make donations when someone dies," said Glen. "Not when they get married."

"I know, but we should do it for weddings too."

He looked skeptical. "Okay, do whatever you want, Karen. Send out the invites and we'll see what happens. But if anyone asks whose idea this was, I'm going to tell them it was all you."

"That's fine," she said. "I'll be the trendsetter. I wouldn't be surprised if a lot of people start throwing couplehood jubilees. I should call the *Tribune* and get someone to write a story about us."

"Yes," he said. "And I'll stay home to clean up the broken glass when bricks start flying through our windows."

"Ha ha."

"You think I'm kidding, but people feel as strongly about their right to weddings as the right-to-lifers do about abortion."

"And I feel as strongly about my right to make my friends and relatives spend some of the money on me that I've spent on them."

"Do me one favor," he said. "At least change Tiffany's to Target."

She looked at him, knowing that he wouldn't insist if she refused. "All right," she finally said. "But that's it."

The first bemused inquiries about the jubilee arrived within an hour after she sent out the email invitation.

One of her college roommates asked, "Are you and Glen really getting married? I thought you were opposed to marriage!!"

The twice-divorced Bill wrote, "Is Couplehood Jubilee some new term for a wedding? I kind of like it, but it makes marriage sound like it's a nonstop party, which I can tell you it's not (not like I want to discourage you and Glen from getting hitched though. You guys are so great together. Heroic, even). This is embarrassing to admit, but I'm not sure I can afford any of those hotels. Would you see if you could get a block of discounted rooms at a Best Western or a Motel 6 too? I was also wondering if you invited either of my ex-wives. If you did, could you let me know if they're coming?"

Her friend Julia, another teacher at the high school, who taught biology, wrote, "Isn't a jubilee a religious celebration? I thought I remembered hearing it used in church when I was dragged there a few times a year by one of my aunts. Are you Catholic? I thought you were agnostic . . ."

Her mother called instead of emailing. "Sweetie," she said, her voice grave. "What on earth is a Couplehood Jubilee? It sounds like some sort of April Fool's prank."

Karen told her about the twenty-five thousand dollars, trying to keep her voice from taking on the whine of pouty affront.

Hearing this story, her mother sighed. "That's the price of having friends, honey. It's one we all pay willingly. Or should pay willingly. If we didn't have friends, I shudder to think what our lives would be like."

"I don't think friendship should have a price tag."

Her mother laughed. "I agree, but sometimes it does. You're old enough to know that. Are you really expecting your brother and Rae and the kids to fly in from Denver for this?"

"I thought it'd be nice. They can stay with you, can't they?"

"Of course, but the plane fare and your gift and dress clothes for Peter and Sam won't be a small expense for them."

"I spent a small fortune on his and Rae's wedding."

"He's your brother, Karen. Your only brother. Your father and I bought your plane ticket, didn't we?"

"Yes, you did. Thank you again," she said. She felt guilty now, but tried to shore up her weakening convictions. "I probably won't ever get married, so if Glen and I want to have this party, I don't think that's so bad."

"You can do whatever you want, but if people refuse to come, don't get too upset with them. Your idea is, well, I suppose it's very original. But I worry that your grandmother won't be very pleased when she gets her invitation."

"I'm not inviting her," said Karen. "I'm only inviting my friends, you, Dad, and Kevin." She had gone to three family weddings over the past eight and a half years, but the expenses had been modest compared with those for her friends' weddings. She had stayed with other family members and had only had to buy gifts and fill her car with gas. No plane tickets, no hotels, no bachelorette parties in Las Vegas, no gaudy bridesmaid dresses, jewelry, or shoes that she would never wear again. She had even managed to sidestep the bridal showers by sending a gift with her mother, who always liked to go to these kinds of family parties.

"If she finds out about it, she'll feel left out," her mother said.

"Who's going to tell her?"

"Kevin might let it slip. He talks to her from time to time."

"I'll tell him not to."

"All right," said her mother. "Go ahead and try."

"Are you and Dad coming?"

Her mother gave a small laugh. "We wouldn't miss it for anything." She paused. "Do you want your father and me to pay for any part of this? I suppose I should offer if it's the closest you'll get to having a real wedding."

"No, that's okay. But thanks for asking."

Later, Glen looked at her like she was a lunatic when she told him about her mother's offer. "She was willing to give you money for this thing and you turned her down?" he said. "How *are* you planning to pay for all of the food and the booze people are going to expect if they're crazy enough to come?"

"I'll take it out of my savings," she said. "You don't have to pay for any part of it." But even as she said this, she knew that she'd resent him if he did let her pay for everything.

"Call her back and ask her to pay for the food. Or at least buy a case of wine."

"I already told her no," said Karen, querulous.

"So? She knows you're fickle. Tell her you changed your mind."

"I am not fickle," she said, suddenly furious. No wonder marriages didn't last. The wedding planning was probably the beginning of the end! What an unfair grouch Glen was being. And why were so many of their friends acting so old-fashioned? More emails arrived that night and the next morning, many of them with negative replies. Poor Ella with her five-week marriage, whom Karen had always defended to all detractors, had written an odd, almost-hostile refusal: "I've never heard of a Couplehood Jubilee. Is it some sort of cult thing? I'm sorry, but I can't attend—already have plans that day. But you know, good luck to you guys. Except if you're not actually getting married, why are you bothering with this jubilee thing? Isn't it a lot of work?"

"Just hit delete, Karen," Glen advised. "Fogettaboutit. Adios. Sayonara. Did you call your mom back yet?"

"No."

He shook his head but said nothing.

"I will," she said. "Maybe. You need a haircut."

"I know." He was in his running clothes, on his way to the gym, and he left her sitting in her office, glowering at the computer screen. Glen had better things to do with his free time than try to collect imaginary dues from his friends or make an ethically questionable point. School was finally out for the year, and instead of relaxing in the backyard with a novel about perky shopaholics or exuberant divorcées in Paris, instead of bingeing on dopey movies for three days straight, she was making plans for a party that she now suspected might turn out to be a big mistake.

But the invitations had already been sent. It seemed, alarmingly, too late to change her mind. She had a feeling that this was how people felt when they went through with marriages that they absolutely knew were doomed. The irony was, she wanted to be with Glen—it was the party that brought on the jitters, not her choice of a partner. She must be going around the bend, as her friends' emails tactlessly implied. Nonetheless, several of them, a dozen or so over the first weekend after the invitations were emailed, had said Yes!! they would attend. How exciting! How intriguing! How unique! How very Karen and Glen it all was!

Why did the prospect of a wedding (or in this case, its substitute) bring out the same feverish enthusiasm that often accompanied the viewing of a very cute baby or a new puppy?

She knew, however, that people persisted in being optimists despite so much evidence of marital failure. Or else they just didn't have any critical thinking skills. Like many of her students, she thought, like the people who voted for politicians based on how handsome they were.

For the next four weeks, she kept track of RSVPs to her and Glen's email accounts; most came to hers, because Glen's guest list had been about a quarter the size of her own. "Guys don't keep in touch like girls do," he said, defending his humble offering of his mother's and twenty-seven friends' email addresses, most of which Karen already had on her own contact list. She also compared caterers' fees (Thirty-eight dollars a plate for a piece of salmon, a scoop of rice, and green beans almondine? Who were they kidding?) and decided to do most of the cooking herself, with her mother's help. She pored over grocery-store sale papers and started a hoard of paper cups, cans of mixed nuts, bags of pretzels, and bottles of inexpensive but drinkable red and white wine in their garage. She bought bags of M&Ms too, the peanut, crispy, and plain varieties, to go with the mixed nuts and pretzels, cramming the candy into her and Glen's freezer, not wanting it to melt or go stale in the weeks before the jubilee. Glen thought that she had become a little obsessive-compulsive and teased her regularly, but eventually ninety-two people committed to attending their wedding hoax, as he sometimes called it, and Karen could tell that he was more excited than he had expected to be. "I can't believe Frank is flying in from San Francisco and paying for a room at the Drake," he said. "When I knew him in college, he was so cheap that he'd ride his bike over to the power company to pay his bill because he didn't want to put a stamp on the envelope. Five miles each way. But I miss the guy. He's smarter and more honest than just about anyone I've ever known."

"Except for me," she said, mostly serious.

"Of course. That goes without saying." He winked. His winks reminded her of her grandfather, something she had told him once, and to her surprise, he had smiled.

"Do you think we should write vows?"

He hesitated. "Vows? Like as if we were actually getting married?"

She nodded. "Yes, but something more quirky. Something to make people laugh."

"I don't know if I'm that clever."

"We could do it like Mad Libs. I'll give you a template and you fill in the blanks. That'd be a lot of fun."

"It could be," he said, unconvinced. "But I don't know if either of us is that much of a comedian."

"I can be funny," she said. "I make you laugh."

"I'd scratch the vows. Don't you think your hands are full enough already?"

"When did that ever stop Bridezilla?"

In spite of himself, he laughed. "You might be having a little too much fun planning this. Don't get any ideas about having a real wedding if the jubilee's a success."

"I won't," she said. "You'd better not either, especially when you see me in my dress."

He blinked. "You're buying one?"

"Already did."

"Oh God. I hope you didn't dip into your retirement fund to buy it."

"I didn't. I got it for thirty bucks at Macy's. Marked down from ninety-five."

"Do I need to buy a new suit?"

"Only if you want to. But it might be best if we rented you a tux."

"No," he said. "Really?"

"You need to look like a groom. I put 'black tie optional' on the invitations too."

She hadn't told him how much she had already spent on the jubilee. The total was over five hundred dollars, and at least another eight or nine hundred would probably be necessary, especially if she bought flowers for the tables and for her and Glen to wear as a corsage and a boutonniere. Her parents were paying for a deejay and the tent rental, and her mother had also offered to buy the chicken breasts, pesto pasta, and four cases of inexpensive champagne. It was perhaps an unwise financial decision to try to recoup some portion of the original twenty-five thousand wedding dollars by spending another two thousand or so with no guarantee that she and Glen would receive something other than the inevitable decorative candles and picture frames, but the jubilee seemed to have developed an acquisitive force all its own—every time Karen paid for one thing, ten more rushed to mind, clamoring for her to buy them too.

Just what was the point of all of this? Glen asked after the RSVPs had crept past the seventy-five-guest mark. What exactly was she thinking?

In truth, she no longer knew. As she accumulated more party goods and crafted more plans, she acquired a vision of the perfect counterfeit wedding, a whole unruly pack of hopes.

To her surprise, she also began to understand the friends who had gone through a similar transformation—how much hope could be invested in the cake design, the seating arrangements, the playlist for the deejay! And how important location was: those exorbitant Hawaiian weddings were, Karen could see now, a means to what might actually turn out to be a remarkably beautiful end. The Hawaiian brides had doubtless hoped that their guests would remember their weddings as the pinnacle of their Chicken-Dancing, chicken-eating, champagne-toasting experiences. It was not exactly a modest hope, but how could they have resisted it? So much of the wedding propaganda they had ingested from childhood on exhorted them to make their weddings the most memorable day of their lives.

"I guess I just want us to have fun," she told Glen.

"That's a bit different from what you said when we first talked about having this party."

"If we get some nice gifts, that'd be good too. I haven't forgotten about the twenty-five grand."

He regarded her. "It might be best if you did."

She was with him in part because he said things like this, because he tried to help her overcome her jealousies, both the petty and more substantial ones, and her frequent anger over nothing that she could hope to change. He was the opposite of a hardened cynic: he tried to save whales and wolves and the starving elderly. He drove an electric car (one of the few things he had splurged on in the time they had been together) but also rode a bicycle when the weather allowed it, which, in Chicago, was about seven months out of the year, though he did ride in the snow and rain and sleet when he ignored her demands that he not. He was tolerant and kindhearted and loved her. He held her hand in public and did the dishes without complaint when it was his night off and she was too tired to do them herself. He told her often that she was pretty and let her listen to Madonna and the Smiths without complaint. She could not imagine meeting a better man. Except, maybe, for Robert Redford when he was thirty-five and perfect, but there was no chance of that.

The day of the jubilee arrived with rain clouds and tornado warnings in Chicago and three adjacent counties, but when Karen checked at nine A.M., flights were leaving and arriving at both O'Hare and Midway with few delays, and her brother and his family had flown in two days earlier and were staying at his and Karen's parents' house, all of the adults grumbling about the usual things after the first two hours together, Karen suspected, her mother confirming this when she arrived with four plastic coolers filled with the chicken breasts and pasta she had promised to buy. "Your brother and father shouldn't be allowed to talk about anything other than basketball and barbecuing techniques. They started yelling about some Tea Party character in Arizona this morning and upset Rosie so much that the poor dog threw up her food all over the kitchen floor."

"Does Kevin like the Tea Party?"

Her mother pursed her lips, trying not to smile. "Yes, I think he does."

"It's not funny, Mom. He's not supposed to be an idiot."

"I don't think you can call everyone who supports the Tea Party an idiot."

"No, I think you probably can."

"It's more complicated than that," her mother insisted.

Karen shook her head. "No, it's really not. You either care about other people's well-being or you don't."

"Let's not argue, sweetie. I want this to be a fun day."

"I do too, but we have so much work to do. I should have hired a caterer."

"We'll be fine," said her mother. "I already cooked the pasta and the chicken can be baked a dozen breasts per tray."

"I'm supposed to get my hair done at ten thirty. I can't believe I thought I'd have time for this."

"You should go. Don't worry. I'm sure you won't be too long. Would Glen be able to help me for a little while?"

"I'll go ask him."

He was outside in the wind, trying to string up tiny white lights around the perimeter of the giant tent that had been set up the previous afternoon by three college-age men, ones who'd expected a tip and were not happy with the five dollars Karen gave them. But it was all that she had in her wallet; she had not known that she would need to the tip them. "We take checks," one of the guys had said, not bothering to pretend he was kidding, but she awkwardly laughed off his comment. Glen assured her later that as far as he knew, you tipped movers, not tent rental people.

The tent was unearthly in its dirty-white vastness; it took up four fifths of the backyard, and the dance floor had to be squeezed into one corner, next to where her father would be pouring drinks as the volunteer bartender, because there was no room on the lawn for any dancing. When Glen saw her enter the tent, he shook his head, a string of lights tangled around his right hand. "Remind me again why we're doing this? The wind keeps blowing these goddamn things loose. Maybe we should just elope."

"My dad's supposed to be here soon. He'll help you. But right now, my mom asked if you'd give her a hand in the kitchen while I'm at the hair salon."

"You're leaving?" he asked. "There's no way we're going to have everything ready before the guests start arriving."

"I'll only be gone for an hour. The salon's six minutes away."

"It's too windy to get your hair done. Just put it up in a bun."

She shook her head. "No, I have to look good."

"Yes, I know, I know," he said wearily. "Because today's an important day."

They had spent most of the three previous days cleaning and decorating the house, making several trips to Home Depot and Target, and trying hard not to fight in a way that would damage them for good. He'd been right but she refused to admit it aloud: the jubilee was a crazy idea. She didn't know why she'd thought that after the planning was done, everything else would be easy. Because this was decidedly not the case.

While she was at the salon submitting to the expert hands of Miriam, her grandmotherly hairstylist of the past four years, the winds picked up even more and it started raining hard, everyone inching along four-lane Sheridan Road when usually they sped heedlessly through the daisy chain of stoplights. By the time Karen was home again, her French twist had wilted and the wisps that Miriam had curled on the sides of her face had gone limp. Glen was right—a wasted effort in every way. And things only grew more nerve-racking as the day progressed. Her father arrived in a foul mood, still angry, it appeared, over an argument with Kevin, barely managing to say hello to Karen and her mother before he stomped outside to the tent to help Glen with the lights. "This is the most fuss I've ever seen for someone who's not actually getting married," he grumbled as he left the kitchen.

Her mother gave her a sympathetic look. "He'll be fine once he eats lunch. His blood sugar is probably low."

"Why do people have parties?" asked Karen, peevish. "Everyone hates them."

"I don't hate them, but I do wish they were easier to prepare for."

By one o'clock, there had been two funnel-cloud sightings—the first near Geneva in Kane County, the second in

Lake County near McHenry. O'Hare had suspended takeoffs and landings, and although Midway hadn't, not yet, it would likely do so soon. Several of her and Glen's out-of-town guests called or sent texts to say that their flights were delayed or canceled, and they didn't know if they would make it at all now. Would Karen call the Drake and the Four Seasons to see if she could get full refunds on their rooms because the rate, even with the discount, was just a little too much for them to swallow whole?

Other disheartening questions followed: Would she think about postponing the couplehood jubilee until next weekend? Since it was at their home, not at a reception hall that had to be reserved months in advance . . . since the airlines would be willing to let them use the same plane tickets because of the bad weather . . . since they had been looking forward to seeing her and Glen so much and didn't want to miss their big day!

The messages and requests kept coming, her phone chiming and ringing and blinking like a frantic miniature robot. Glen's phone was doing the same frenetic dance, his friends also writing or calling to say they were delayed at the airport, or the highways weren't safe, and although some of them had always wanted a Dorothy-and-Toto moment, they doubted that they would have the same happy fate as the girl from Kansas if they were sucked into a tornado too.

By three o'clock, the sky had turned a soupy green, the maples in the front yard had lost dozens of leaves to marauding winds, and the red and violet-blue impatiens had been flattened by hard rain. Her father and Glen had managed to set up the tables and chairs in the tent and attach the lights to its interior perimeter by stapling them to the vinyl, which was probably not allowed, but in grim frustration, the two men had done it anyway. Karen didn't complain because they both looked exhausted and bedraggled, her father's wispy gray hair swirled high on his head like a meringue, Glen's closely resembling the wet pelt of the lake-loving collie she'd had as a girl.

"If anyone shows up for this thing," said Glen. "I'll be amazed. But Frank made it. He's camped out at the Drake already. I think he got in last night."

"Don't worry," said Karen's mother. "More food for us if only a few guests are able to make it."

"What are we going to do with a hundred and ten chicken breasts, Sue?" Mr. Quinn asked his wife. "And who's going to eat all of those goddamn cupcakes?"

Instead of a big layer cake, Karen had baked two hundred cupcakes—chocolate, strawberry, and vanilla—which she and her mother had just spent the last hour and a half frosting and adorning with black and white sprinkles.

Glen was eyeing the cupcakes. "You can have one," said Karen. "Two if you must."

He chose a chocolate one and ate it in three bites. "Let me make sure this one's all right too," he said, reaching for a strawberry.

At four thirty, Karen went into the bedroom and put on her dress. Glen had not yet changed into his rented tux, nor had her parents put on their party clothes, but when she went back to the kitchen in her new white dress with its small lavender flowers embroidered around the hem and bodice, her mother was dressed and combed, and her father, Mrs. Quinn informed her, was changing now. "Did Glen see you in your dress?" her mother asked. "He's not supposed to."

"He hasn't yet," said Karen. "I don't know where he is."

"He's outside talking to his friend Frank. He arrived a few minutes ago."

"I didn't hear the doorbell ring."

"I think it's broken," said her mother. "The storm must have done something to it."

"No," said Karen, tears surging hotly to her eyes. "It's been broken for a while. I completely forgot about it. Glen must have too. Or else he didn't feel like doing anything about it."

"Don't say that, honey. He's been working hard all week." Her mother hugged her, enveloping her in the scent of roses. "Everything'll be fine. It's time to have some fun now. I put a sign on the front door telling your guests to come around to the back. The grass is a little wet, but I'm sure they'll be fine."

"I bet only ten people will make it," Karen said moodily. "We had ninety-two yeses before the worst weather of the year picked today to show itself. This is such a disaster."

Her mother pulled back and looked at her, trying not to smile. "Spoken like a true bride. I said the same thing about a hundred times on the day your father and I were married."

"Glen and I aren't getting married."

"I know. Believe me, I know. Between you and your father, I haven't forgotten for one second."

Someone was knocking on the front door now, and Karen turned to run to the front of the house, but her mother held on to her arm. "I'll get it. You go outside and talk to Frank and Glen. Kevin and Rae and the boys just got here too. I think they'll all be glad to have you out there to mediate." She paused. "You look beautiful, honey. Try to enjoy yourself a little. Don't worry about who can and can't make it. Have some wine, eat some nuts, and relax."

"I can't," she said, her voice catching.

"Yes, you can. Go out there and have fun. Everyone here loves you."

Later, after thirty-seven intrepid guests had arrived and were eating chicken breasts and pesto-laced penne with what seemed to be great cheer, the storm having been outwitted, Karen looked up from the table where she and Glen sat with her two ebullient, sugar-addled nephews and Glen's friend Frank and knew that she needed to make a speech. Her eyes, in weak homage to the sky, had been leaking tears all evening, and seeing these heroic relatives and friends before her (including the twice-divorced Bill, who was relieved that neither of his ex-wives had made it), she started to cry in earnest. They had all risked their lives and nicest clothes and coiffed hair in order to deliver themselves and their be-ribboned boxes or sober white envelopes to the gift table with its vase of pink roses and crystal candy dishes with three different kinds of M&Ms. They had all willingly consented to offering her and Glen a whole day of their lives, a whole weekend, in some cases, and had brought them presents and agreed to observe the social contract that stated you should celebrate your friends' good fortune as if it were your own.

She'd drunk three and a half glasses of red wine and had not eaten a real meal since the previous night, other than a few bites of chicken and two cupcakes that had fallen on the floor and were not fit to serve to guests. She was tipsy and tearful and a little dizzy as she stood up from the table, Glen smiling at her uneasily. She tried to give him a reassuring look but her face felt rubbery, her lips huge and gummy when she smiled.

"I just want you all to know that I'm really grateful you're here," she said, her voice quavering. "I don't care that weddings are so expensive." She felt Glen put a cautioning hand on the small of her back but didn't look down at him. "I mean, I don't care that this wedding, even though it's not really a wedding, cost my parents and Glen and me so much because many of you have had real weddings and spent a lot more on them than we did on this party. I'm so happy you were able to come, and if you want to take your gifts back, you should. You being here is gift enough for us."

Glen had stood up and was trying to get her to sit down again. A number of the guests were chuckling, but others regarded Karen with a mixture of confusion and concern. At the next table, she noticed blearily that her father was staring at his plate and her mother's cheeks had turned very pink. Glen managed to get her back in her chair, and he laughed uncomfortably before saying, "I think the stress of planning this party has gotten to Karen a little. The weather certainly hasn't helped either." He laughed his pained laugh again. "Everyone, please have some more wine and thank you all for coming. It's almost time for cupcakes and then some dancing. Our deejay is stuck in St. Charles because the roads are flooded out by him, but my buddy Frank and I will spin some good tunes once we get the stereo set up."

Glen sat back down and took Karen's hand, squeezing it gently a few times. "Thank you," she whispered loudly. "You're so nice. I hope they believed me when I said that they could have their gifts back. I don't care about the money anymore. I'm just so happy we had this party."

"I am too," he said. "But maybe you should drink some water and leave the wine alone for a little while."

When she teetered inside a few minutes later to help her mother bring out the cupcakes, she felt lightheaded and asked if it would be all right if she sat down for a few minutes. Her mother nodded, and Karen walked very carefully into the next room, using the walls to keep herself upright as she moved toward the sofa. She took off her shoes and stretched out, and then suddenly it was very dark and she woke to find Glen and her mother standing over her, telling her that she should go upstairs to bed.

"Did I miss the dancing?" she asked, afraid to move because she knew that her head would protest. "Did everyone go home?" Her mouth was very dry and tasted strongly of peanuts.

"Yes, but don't worry," said Glen. "We'll have another party." He exchanged a smile with Karen's mother. "If your mother lets us."

"I'm sorry that I fell asleep and made you do all of the work," said Karen. "Why didn't you wake me?"

"We tried," her mother said, "but you told us to leave you alone. You don't remember?"

"I must have been talking in my sleep."

Glen smiled. "Likely story."

"I remember making a speech before I passed out. Or did I dream that?"

"Nope," he said. "That was real."

"Oh, shit."

"Don't worry, honey," her mother said, glancing at Glen. "You were very sweet."

"I was drunk," said Karen. "I hope everyone knew that."

"I don't think there was any doubt," said Glen.

It was after midnight by the time her parents and the last guest had driven off with extra cupcakes and chicken, Karen kissing them all good-bye, unsteady on her feet. The stormy conditions had departed too, the sky now punctuated with stars. As Glen helped Karen unzip her dress, his hands warm against her back, she wondered if any of their friends had reclaimed their gifts, but didn't ask.

"Do you think people had fun?" she asked instead, turning to look at Glen. He was already undressed, his tuxedo sheathed in plastic and hanging primly on his closet door.

"I'm sure they did," he said. "I did."

"I think I did too," she said. "But I worry that our friends hate me now because of my speech."

"No one hates you, Karen. They probably love you even more. It all went well, even with the tornados and the broken doorbell and your tipsy speech."

"I hope you're right," she said.

He yawned. "I'm exhausted. I'm glad we don't have to worry about the party anymore."

"God, it was a lot of work."

"Having fun often is," he murmured.

Within a few minutes, he was asleep, but after her three-hour nap, she lay awake for a while before getting up to drink a glass of water. In the bathroom, waiting for the water to run cold, she looked out the window and was startled to see the tent below her.

In the darkness, its peaked roof looked like a mirage, the work of fairies. If she closed her eyes and counted to five, she believed that it would be gone before she opened them again.

OLDER SISTER

BY THE BEGINNING OF her second year in college, Alex had learned that she did not like what happened when she drank, nor did she like to be around people who were drinking competitively. Something else she learned was that she had an older sister—technically, a half sister. It was her mother who told her that she and her younger brother, Chris, had a second sibling, even though Mrs. Fiore was not the woman who'd given birth to her. The girl's mother was an ex-girlfriend of Alex and Chris's father's, a woman named Michelle, who, twenty-one years earlier, had punished him for his decision to marry someone else a year and a half after their daughter, Penelope, was born by moving to France, where she'd found work as an English teacher at a boarding school a few miles outside of Paris.

When Mrs. Fiore told Alex that she had a sister, they were having lunch at a large and noisy deli on the southern fringe of the Washington, D.C., college where Alex was about to begin her sophomore year. It was the last day of move-in week, which had been very hot and humid, and now it was raining hard. People kept entering the deli with dramatic exclamations, stomping their feet on the waterlogged mats and shaking out their umbrellas, some of the drops landing on Alex's bare legs.

Alex stared at her mother after hearing her embarrassed revelation. Mrs. Fiore's arms were crossed, hands clenching her elbows as if she'd caught a chill. She was small and dark-haired, a high-strung, smiling woman whose laughter was timorous but frequent. Finally Alex asked, "Does Chris already know? Why are you the one telling me this? Why not Dad?"

Her mother wiped under her eyes with the napkin she'd been using while they ate turkey sandwiches and the sweet potato fries the deli was known for. She had trouble meeting Alex's gaze, something that made Alex feel both impatient and sorry.

"Your brother doesn't know yet," her mother said. "But Dad's supposed to talk to him this afternoon. I'm finally telling you because for years your father and I went back and forth over when and how to tell you, but he could never make up his mind, and now Penelope is insisting on meeting you, so there's no more stalling."

Alex blinked. "Why did they name her Penelope? Why does she want to meet me?" She could feel her heart racing and tried to take deep breaths. She would grow light-headed if she breathed too shallowly; she might even faint, something that had happened twice in the past year, both times at parties with classmates who had drained a keg before moving on to a cabinet filled with hard liquor.

"She wants to meet both you and Chris, but it doesn't have to be at the same time. I think she's coming to Washington next month, which is why I'm telling you now. You have a little time to prepare yourself before she arrives."

"What if I don't want to meet her?"

Her mother hesitated. "Well, think about it for a little while. But I do think you should see her. At least once."

"Has Dad seen her since she and her mom moved to France?"

"Yes."

"He has?" said Alex, taken aback. "When?" She had no idea when her father might have seen this other daughter, nor any memory of prolonged and contentious silences between her parents. Her father's mood was so steady that behind his back, she and Chris sometimes called him Mr. Sunshine.

"He saw her a few times when Michelle brought Penelope over from France to visit with her relatives in Madison. But he can talk to you about that. Penelope lives in New York now. She graduated from NYU last year."

"She's still there?" Alex paused. "What does she look like?"

"I think she's working at a law firm as a paralegal." Her mother smiled. "She's a cute girl. But so are you, honey. You're prettier than both she and her mother are."

"Don't say that," said Alex, embarrassed.

"It's true, honey. You're the prettiest girl I know."

"I'm your daughter. You have to say that."

Her mother regarded her, less sheepish now, the paper napkin back on her lap. "No. I don't."

Alex knew her mother was being sincere; she also knew that this prettiness was one of the reasons why she wasn't going to drink anymore, even if the boys who liked her pressured her to do it, even if her girlfriends jeered at her, mascara and thick eyeliner smeared garishly under their eyes, their euphoric, drunken faces laughing at her sudden, unaccountable prudishness, especially after such a spectacular first year of strip poker and quarters and beer bongs wet with the spit of other lonely students who would throw up all over the sidewalk on the way home or at the foot of their beds or in the dorm hallway, where the prim, Sunday-mass-attending RA would emerge at seven A.M. and step in it on her way to the shower, to the great hilarity of the few students who were awake to witness it.

"Why does Penelope want to meet Chris and me all of a sudden?" asked Alex.

"I think she has for a while. Your father was dragging his feet because he felt bad about not having told you about her sooner."

"That's why he didn't come out here with you to help me move in," Alex said flatly.

Her mother regarded her. "He did have to work, but you're right. He was being a coward."

"What's he expecting Chris and me to do?"

"I think he hopes you'll be willing to meet her. He said to tell you that he'll call you tonight to talk about everything."

"No, tell him not to. I don't want to talk about it. Not right now. I have to think about my classes."

"You're going to do better this year, sweetie. The first year is always hard."

Alex shook her head. "No, it's not. I was a fuckup. My classes weren't that hard at all. I just didn't do enough work."

"Don't swear, honey."

Alex laughed in a harsh burst. "Why not? You've heard it before."

"I know I have, but I don't need to hear it again. Not from you anyway."

A few weeks before the end of the spring term of her freshman year, Alex drank so much at a junior boy's twenty-first birthday party that she was sick for three days and probably should have gone to the hospital, but Cathy, her roommate, managed to get her to drink water and eat saltines and eventually she was able to keep down peanut butter on toast, then Cheerios with skim milk, and after that, she could take a shower without feeling dizzy and weak. It also helped that Jennifer, their RA, was out of town for the weekend; otherwise, Jennifer might have called for an ambulance, and Alex's parents would then have been notified and they might have forced her to go to a school much closer to home instead of allowing her to return to her expensive quasi–Ivy League college in Washington, D.C., where a year earlier, to her and her friends' surprise (and in some cases, envy), she'd managed to get in two weeks before classes started because by then her number was high enough on the waitlist, and her parents hadn't yet mailed in the tuition check to the University of Illinois.

Something else that happened while she was at the junior boy's birthday party, something she couldn't confirm, having only a dim memory of the later hours of that night, was that two, possibly three, boys had taken her into one of the bedrooms at the apartment where the party took place and had sex with her. She didn't think, however, that she could call it rape. Not exactly. She did not remember a struggle, nor did she have bruises anywhere on her body. She also wasn't sore between her legs the next day, but there was some stickiness, and she knew that something had happened, something she probably wouldn't have allowed if she were sober. Even in her reduced state the next morning, she remembered laughter and whiskers biting into her cheeks and chin and two or three boys whispering to each other and a door being shut and she herself giggling and later feeling sick and throwing up in the bathroom before she left the party. Her roommate, drunk too but less drunk than Alex, had half-carried her home with the help of another boy who lived in their dorm, one who had been out with friends who lived next door to the guys having the party.

After she recovered, Alex avoided the boy whose birthday they had celebrated, and he, it seemed, was also avoiding her, not meeting her eyes when they passed in the student union, only perfunctorily saying hello, and she could see that it took an effort for him even to do this, and Cathy had confirmed that at the party, Alex had gone off with him and another boy for a little while, but Cathy wasn't sure who the second boy was, except that he was cute, cuter even than the host, whose name was Carlyle, though everyone called him Carl. As far as Cathy knew, there was no third boy, unless he was already in the bedroom, waiting. What made matters more complicated was that Alex had slept with Carl once before, just after returning to school for the spring semester on a night when she was more sober than on his birthday. If she had done it once, it seemed likely that he might have reason to expect her to have sex with him again.

Cathy thought that Alex should go to the school clinic to get screened for STDs, but Alex did not go until she was home for the summer and could discreetly take herself to the county health clinic. The results of her tests had all been normal, which she discovered upon opening the clinic's envelope, one with no return address, her hands shaking as she worked at the flap. Cathy also thought that Alex should confront Carl and ask him what exactly had happened, but Alex didn't want to. It embarrassed her, and what if nothing *had* happened, or at least nothing too serious, and then what if Carl thought she was a lunatic for accusing him of raping her? She worried that he would talk about her with other people and they would all say what a freak she was, what a freshman whore, what an idiot lush too—couldn't she learn how to handle her liquor like most everyone else did? No one was forcing her to drink either. Why didn't she just stop drinking before she got drunk if she was so worried about guys raping her?

Other girls, spreading the rumor, would probably be even crueler to her than the boys. The ones who were jealous of her, the ones who said nice things to her face but behind her back made faces and said catty things about her hair (which was fine) or clothes (fine too) or the way she laughed (a little high-pitched but not terrible), things she tried to ignore, knowing that the place they came from was small and ugly. She had places like this in her too, but she tried to keep them closed off as much as possible.

And now, her mother was compounding her anxiety by telling her that she had a sister, one hidden from view for the entirety of Alex and her brother's lives. The start of the school year—so much stress already, especially because she was adamant about not falling into the same patterns that had ensnared her the previous year, and now she had to think about a girl named Penelope in New York who wanted to meet her, who thought that she had an unequivocal right to meet her.

But Alex supposed that it *was* her sister's right, and privately, she did feel a little flattered, despite her irritation over her father's cowardice and the fact that his long-held silence had been a kind of shortchange. Because if she were being honest, it might not have been too bad to have known all along that she had a half sister in France, one she might have been pen pals with, one she might have been allowed to visit. This older sister whom she could have talked to about boys, this sophisticated girl who would teach her how to tie a silk scarf and wear a beret, and maybe, Alex thought, though this was stretching it, maybe she would never have become a lush her first year in college and had sex with eleven guys, possibly twelve, during those nine months, in addition to the four she had slept with before college. She hoped it had only been Carlyle and one other guy in that darkened bedroom, that there hadn't been a third guy waiting for her too.

Her brother, Chris, who was starting his senior year of high school, did not want to meet their sister. When Alex talked to him on the phone the night after their mother told her about Penelope, he said, "If she were to come here, what would we do? Go out for pizza and talk about how great Dad is? I mean, what am I supposed to say to her?"

"You just have to be nice to her," said Alex. "That's all."

"So you're going to meet her?"

"I don't know. I guess I'll have to if she comes down to D.C. and knocks on my door."

"You live in a dorm. She won't be able to get into your building."

"You know what I mean," she said. "What did Dad say when he told you?"

"I think he was kind of drunk. He just said, 'This is a little tricky for me,' and he kept clearing his throat until finally I said, 'Are you dying or something? Is Mom dying?' He kind of laughed and then he told me about her. Why did they name her Penelope? It sounds . . . I don't know. It's such a dumb name."

"I don't think it's that bad. She probably goes by Penny."

"See? You like her already. I bet you guys will be friends."

"She wants to meet you too. Probably more than she wants to meet me."

He snorted. "I bet. Anyway, it doesn't matter. I don't want to meet her."

"You might change your mind."

"You sound like Mom and Dad."

"Well, they might be right."

"Whatever. I don't want her to come here. I'll leave if she does."

"I don't think they'll force you to meet her."

"We'll see if they try."

* * *

After her mother left campus, Alex tried not to be absorbed into the familiar, now-ominous scene: classes by day, ambitious drinking by night. Her friends would drink anything too: Boone's Farm, malt liquor, the cheapest vodkas and tequilas and beer—anything they could find someone to supply for them, usually an upperclassman but sometimes one of their own with a convincing fake ID. The point wasn't the flavor of the alcohol, only the blurry euphoria, the sloppy, ephemeral feeling of godliness before the puking set in. The point was the stories that could later be told about these hazy, hilarious scenes. She had trouble convincing her friends that she was, in fact, serious about her intention to avoid the series of bad decisions that might lead her to the dispiriting squalor of some boy's dorm room with its piles of dirty laundry and clattering empty beer bottles and its distinctive, cloying smell: half sweet, half repulsive, one that Alex had never encountered anywhere else. She wasn't sure what accounted for it—soiled T-shirts and socks? Leftover food moldering under a bed or in a closet? Whatever it was, it now made her want to run heedlessly in the other direction.

Cathy, Alex's roommate, seemed to understand her sudden and startling abstinence, because she was one of the few people who knew about what had probably happened to Alex at Carlyle's party, but her other friends' responses ranged from bemused skepticism to outright hostility. What, did she think she was better than they were? Had she turned Mormon or become a Jehovah's Witness or something over the summer? Just what was so wrong with wanting to go out and get shit-faced once or twice a week when college would be such a drag otherwise? Did she really think that she would be able to stand around and drink Diet Coke while everyone else was having a great time playing quarters?

Cathy was also smart enough to recognize that the boozy parties weren't the best way to spend her time, but she was not as popular as Alex and not very confident intellectually either, despite her good grades in high school and the obvious fact that she was there, enrolled at their elite university, one that received many thousands of annual applications, not even a quarter of these applicant-supplicants accepted. Cathy told Alex to ignore the kids who gave her a hard time, and also said that she would show her support by going to fewer parties herself. "I could stop going altogether if you wanted me to," Cathy said.

"I don't want you to have to do that for me," said Alex, though she did. "You should go out whenever you want to. I'll still go to some things."

"You should," said Cathy hopefully. "I'll make sure you don't get too crazy whenever you do go out."

Alex knew that she probably wouldn't but said nothing. Cathy was a well-meaning, nervous girl with a soft heart and wealthy parents who seemed mostly to want her out of their hair and firmly established in her own independent adult life. But Cathy did not want to be an adult, not yet. She still slept with a blond-furred teddy bear and ate animal crackers with the peanut butter and jelly sandwiches she made for herself in their room when she stayed up late studying. She collected heart stickers and flowery stationery and used a pen with purple ink when she sent birthday cards to her friends, most of whom had stayed in Tallahassee and enrolled at Florida State. Alex felt a sometimes-painful affection for her, along with a desire to protect her, but she was also occasionally irritated by her roommate's artless enthusiasms and unforced wholesomeness. Cathy seemed to like everyone and did not understand why some of their classmates were not particularly nice to her. And about Alex's abrupt acquisition of a sister, Cathy was predictably enthusiastic. "Could I meet her too?" she asked. "I think she sounds so cool. Growing up in France, how awesome is that?"

"I guess you could meet her," said Alex. "But maybe I should meet her by myself first."

"Oh, sure," said Cathy, blushing. "I'm sorry. I didn't mean to seem pushy."

"You're not," said Alex. "You're so sweet sometimes it kills me."

Her roommate looked at her uncertainly. "I guess you mean that as a compliment?"

It was a Friday afternoon, the end of the second week of classes, when Penelope called from New York, no trace of a French accent in her voice, which sounded more girlish than Alex had expected from someone who was raised in France and had attended college at chic NYU. The warmth of her message also surprised Alex: "I'm just so glad that you know about me now, Alexandra. I've known about you and Chris most of my life and it was so strange to have you guys out there, completely unaware of my existence. I hope we can meet soon. I'm going to be in D.C. next Thursday through Sunday and I'd love to take you out for dinner and whatever else you think might be fun, if you have time. Please call me back as soon as you have a chance. I can't wait to talk to you."

Alex listened to her sister's message five times, her stomach leaping each time she hit repeat. She'd had one stilted conversation with her father (*their* father, Alex realized with a start) since the lunch when her mother had told her about Penelope. On the phone, Mr. Fiore had sounded almost defiant, as if he had had nothing but good intentions in keeping the news of Penelope's existence to himself until now. As if Alex and Chris would have been grievously scarred by the knowledge that they had a sister, that their father had had sex with another woman before their mother's advent. It wasn't until the end of their conversation that he had said something self-effacing and sincere. "I didn't want you and Chris to think badly of me," he said quietly. "I know it was cowardly to wait so long to tell you."

For several seconds, Alex said nothing. Her father eventually cleared his throat, about to speak again, but Alex interrupted him. "You didn't tell me," she said. "Mom did. But I guess I understand why you wanted her to do it."

He sighed heavily. ". . . if you knew how much anxiety all of this has caused me. I almost started seeing a therapist."

"Maybe you should have."

"Yes, maybe so."

"You still could."

"I know," he said patiently, as if he and Alex's mother had argued many times over his reluctance to make an appointment. "Do you want to see one? Your mother and I will pay for it if you do."

"I don't know. Probably not."

"If you change your mind, the offer won't expire."

"Thanks, Dad. I'll see."

She hadn't told him or her mother or brother, only Cathy, that she did plan to see a therapist, that on the first day of classes, she'd called the counseling service on campus and made an appointment, but none of the therapists, most of whom were Ph.D. candidates in psychology, could see her right away. She had to wait until the following Friday, which, as it turned out, was the same day that Penelope called for the first time. It was upon her return from her first meeting with Dr. Abbott that she was greeted by her sister's warm, almost giddy, message.

Alex's intention had been to talk with Dr. Abbott (who looked only five or six years older than Alex, wore her hair in a long, dark braid, and, startlingly, had clear braces fastened to her teeth) about her decision not to drink at parties anymore and that she still thought about Carlyle's party and the hazy events of that night more than she wanted to. But when she had taken her seat across from Dr. Abbott—Sylvia, she had told Alex to call her if she wanted to—she hadn't wanted to talk about the party. It was too embarrassing, and Dr. Abbott would probably dismiss her as a nitwit drunk, as Alex knew others would, the date-rapists in particular. She was thinking of them in these terms now, more and more. But she wanted to make a good impression on Dr. Abbott, make this solemn young woman like her. Alex wanted to seem smart and sophisticated, as if she were courting her—something that she could also imagine herself doing with Penelope. It was she whom Alex talked about instead, this unexpected half sister, and her father's cowardice, her mother's collusion, her brother's disaffection.

Dr. Abbott nodded sympathetically as Alex spoke, saying that she understood, of course it was hard, of course Alex was surprised and disoriented and a little angry at her parents. Dr. Abbott would not tell her what to do though; she would only ask questions or nod encouragingly as Alex spoke. "Do you think I should be happy that she exists?" Alex asked.

But Dr. Abbott would not say. Instead she said, "I want to know how you feel. That's all that matters. My opinion isn't important."

"I think I'm glad," Alex said after a disappointed pause. "I think I probably am."

Dr. Abbott nodded, crossing her legs, which were covered by a navy blue skirt, and looked expectantly at Alex.

"Why do you think she wants to meet my brother and me?" Alex asked.

Dr. Abbott hesitated. "I suppose she likes the idea of having siblings. A lot of people do. But I shouldn't be speaking for her. You can ask her if you meet her. Do you plan to?"

Alex nodded.

"Do you think you can forgive your father for waiting so long to tell you and your brother?"

"Yes, I already have, I suppose."

It wasn't until the last five minutes of the appointment that Alex found the courage to mention the party and the two boys, possibly three. "I really don't remember that much, but I know something probably happened. I don't want to go to parties anymore, unless I know they're not going to be about getting wasted. I'm not going to drink much anymore either. My friends are giving me a hard time about this. Except for my roommate because I'm her only friend. At least, the only female friend she can count on here. Most of the other girls are pretty fake with her. They think she's a dork."

Dr. Abbott was looking at her with a mixture of suppressed alarm and concern. "Have you talked to anyone else here about what happened at that party? Your RA? She's trained to handle situations like the one you just described."

Alex shook her head. "I didn't want to. I didn't really like my RA last year. The one I have this year is better but it's too late now."

"It's not too late," Dr. Abbott said quietly. "It's really not. You should talk to her. Those boys should be called before an adjudication board if you know for sure who they are."

"Carlyle's the only one I'm sure about." She paused. "But I think it was his friend Jack too."

"Alexandra," Dr. Abbott said, her tone more forceful. "You really should talk to your RA. Women keep quiet about these sorts of crimes all of the time and it does no one any good."

At last, an unequivocal directive. But it was not one that Alex felt comfortable acting on. She had not used the word "crime" in her thoughts, even if she had begun to think of what the boys had done to her as rape.

As Alex was picking up her bag and stuffing a wadded tissue inside, Dr. Abbott said, "I want you to come again. Let's talk next week. I'm sure I can find a slot for you."

"Okay," said Alex, feeling chastened. It was obvious that Dr. Abbott would not let her off easy. But Alex did not think that she was ready to act. It was too overwhelming to contemplate—the accusations put down on the university's official record, the names spoken in an office somewhere to some school official's stony or possibly admonishing face, the circumstances of that now-distant night described over and over, the rumors that would leak out like poison contaminating groundwater, the shame and embarrassment of her transgressions of the past year being discussed in detail, her reputation henceforth defined by her freshman-year excesses, predictable and average as they were. There were other girls who drank more, and more often, than she had, other girls who had had sex with more boys, but as far as she knew, they had not been taken very drunk into a room by two or three classmates who, aside from their hoarse breathing, had made no other sounds as they fucked her. And if these girls had had the same experience, many of them had probably remained silent about it too.

Alex made the appointment with Dr. Abbott for the next week but later canceled it. She called Penelope the morning after receiving her message but was routed directly to voicemail. Her sister called back that night, a Saturday, when Alex was sitting in her room, contemplating Monday's homework and wishing that Cathy would return very soon from the party that she had gone to with three other girls who lived on their floor, or else she might have to go out and find her, which she knew would be a bad idea.

Penelope's voice, hearing it live for the first time, made Alex's eyes well up. She sounded so warm and kind, so genuinely pleased to hear Alex's own voice on the other end of the line that for several seconds it was hard for Alex to speak. Until that moment, she had not understood how deeply entrenched her misery was, how confused and forsaken she felt at this university, which, she'd believed, would be the setting for her greatest feminine and scholarly triumphs, at least up to this point in her life.

"Alex? Are you still there?" asked Penelope, tentative.

"Yes," she said, her voice breaking.

"Hey, are you all right?"

Alex found that she could only breathe in small gasps. "Yes," she whispered.

"You don't sound like it. Have I upset you? I'm so sorry if I have."

"No, it's not you," said Alex, clearing her throat. "I'm happy that you called." She tried to laugh but it came out sounding as if she were choking.

Penelope wavered. "Do you want to tell me what's wrong?"

". . . I don't know."

"You don't have to, but if you want to, I hope you will."

"We hardly know each other," Alex croaked. "I can't unload all of my problems on you."

"You can, Alex. I want us to be sisters, for real, and whatever we talk about, tonight or on any other night, I'll keep to myself."

"It just feels a little strange to be talking about it over the phone. I can wait until you're here next week."

"Do you want me to come down sooner?"

Alex did want her to, but she couldn't bring herself say it. "It's okay, I can wait."

"No, no, it doesn't sound to me like you can or should. I could come down tonight," said Penelope. "I think there's an Amtrak that leaves for D.C. at ten. I'd get there around one thirty if it isn't delayed."

"No, no, I can't ask you to do that."

"You're not asking. I'm offering. I could ask my boyfriend to lend me his car too."

"You have a boyfriend with a car? In New York?"

"Yes." Penelope laughed self-consciously. "He's a little older than I am. He's got a much better job than I do." She paused. "I could come down, Alexandra. Really, if you need me to, I will."

It was absurd, Alex knew, but she did want her to come down. She wanted very badly for Penelope to appear before her and tell her what to do. Go to the R.A. or not? Risk ruining her chances for lasting friendships and good boyfriends and witty stories she might one day publish in the college alumni magazine or try to forget the events of that night?

"If you don't say anything in the next few seconds," Penelope murmured, "I'm going to assume that you want me to come down there."

"You're coming next weekend."

"Yes, but I can see you both this weekend and the next."

Alex took a long, shaky breath. "I do want you to come but it's such a long—"

"Good. I'm glad you can say it. This is about a boy, I'm assuming."

"Yes," said Alex weakly. "Well, more than one."

"Wow," Penelope breathed, laughing a little. "A woman after my own heart."

"No, it's not like that. It's actually pretty bad."

"It is? Oh no. Well, we'll straighten it out." She said this with such confidence that Alex could almost believe her.

* * *

It was a little after two A.M. when Penelope called Alex's cell phone to announce that she was downstairs and needed to be signed in at the dormitory's security desk. Cathy had returned from the party only a half an hour earlier and was now passed out on her bed, alcohol fumes rolling off of her in fetid waves. Alex had tried to tell her that she was expecting her sister to arrive soon, but Cathy hadn't seemed capable of processing this news and Alex had given up and let her fall asleep, Cathy's eyelids drooping even as she struggled out of her suede boots and corduroy miniskirt. She fell asleep on top of the covers, her gauzy peasant blouse still on, her skirt in a tangle on the floor, her bikini underwear white with big pink polka dots. Alex had to struggle to get her under the covers, not wanting her sister's first impression of her roommate to be such an undignified one.

Her palms and underarms were damp when she walked the two flights down to the security desk to sign Penelope in. She felt fully awake; also, guilty. She worried that it was very selfish of her to have allowed her sister to take the train down from New York in the middle of the night so that she could tell her a humiliating story, one that Penelope might even insist she tell their father. She hadn't thought of this possibility until Penelope was already en route, long past the point where she might have said, "No, never mind. Let's just wait until next weekend."

But then, seeing her sister standing in front of the security desk with an oversize black handbag slung over her shoulder, her small body belted into a tailored red raincoat, a delighted smile on her pretty, flushed face, Alex knew that Penelope wouldn't force her to reveal any of her secrets to their father. Alex liked the look of her instantly. She was already a little infatuated with her anyway (her brother's suspicion that she might eventually favor Penelope over him not necessarily unfounded)—her Parisian pedigree, her NYU diploma and big-city lifestyle, whatever this lifestyle actually was.

"Thank you so much for coming," said Alex, abashed, walking into Penelope's open arms, surprised by how firmly her sister hugged her.

"It wasn't a problem," said Penelope, brushing a few strands of dark hair out of her eyes. She wore it shoulder-length, with a slight wave to it. Alex had the same hair, from their father, unless Penelope's mother had it too. "I slept the whole way. It's a good thing that I couldn't get Tex on the phone. Driving would have been harder."

"Tex? Is that your boyfriend?"

Penelope nodded, laughing a little. "His real name is Frederick, but he's gone by Tex since he was twenty. It's a little silly because he's from New Jersey, but he went to college in Austin." She paused. "It's so good to finally meet you, Alexandra. You're so pretty! But I knew that you would be. Dad showed me pictures of you and Chris the last time I saw him."

It was disorienting to hear Penelope call their father Dad, though of course she would, Alex realized. Unless she addressed him by Mark, but it didn't seem like she did.

"Dad still hasn't shown me any pictures of you, even though I asked him to send me some," said Alex, promptly regretting it, not sure if Penelope would be hurt.

"He's so weird about all of this. You probably know that I finally had to force his hand. There were so many times when I thought about calling you guys in Chicago and telling you who I was, but I didn't want to seem like a crazy person."

"Let me take your bag," said Alex, leading her into the stairwell. "I wouldn't have thought you were crazy."

"Chris probably would have. And your mother too."

Alex paused. "Chris might have. He tries to be so macho all of the time but he really isn't. He cried when he read *Night* for his history class, but he wouldn't admit it, even though I know he did."

"I cried when I read it too."

"I'm sorry Dad didn't tell us about you until now. I feel bad that you had to wait so long."

"My mother didn't really encourage it either though. I think she was pretty jealous."

"She didn't marry someone in France?"

Penelope shook her head. "She dated some guys but she didn't end up marrying any of them. I think she thought Dad was her soul mate." She laughed a little, seeing Alex's disconcerted expression. "No need to worry. He was smart to get away from her. She's kind of nuts. I love her and every-thing, but there's a reason I'm here in the States and not back in France with her."

At the door to her room, Alex gave Penelope a look of apology. "My roommate went out earlier and she's passed out on her bed now. The room sort of smells like alcohol too. I really hoped she wouldn't get wasted tonight."

Penelope smiled. "Don't worry about it. I'm sure I've seen worse. I've probably done worse too."

"It's hard not to. Who's going to tell you to stop?"

Her sister nodded. "I know. Thank God college is only four years. Otherwise half of us probably wouldn't make it. Why weren't you out tonight too?"

"I guess I was just tired," said Alex.

Penelope looked at her gravely. "What is it you wanted to tell me?"

"It's—" said Alex exhaled shakily.

"We should go somewhere and talk. Is there a diner or something near here that's open all night?"

"There's a café on M Street, but we should put your bag in my room first. Are you sure you have the energy?"

"I do if you do. We can sleep in tomorrow. Unless you go to church?"

"No. Do you?"

Penelope laughed. "Not if I can help it. My mother goes three times a week. She became very Catholic a few years before I left for NYU. I'm not really sure why, especially because she was raised Lutheran. France isn't even that Catholic anymore. It used to be, but I think less than half the population goes to church now."

"I think it's the same here." Alex put her key in the lock and tried to open the door quietly but the hinges creaked and she could see Cathy stirring on her bed, but she didn't sit up or say anything when Alex put Penelope's bag, heavier than she expected, at the foot of her own bed. She would have to sleep on the floor and let her sister have the bed. She couldn't imagine the two of them sharing it, not so soon.

At the college's front gates, Alex looked uncertainly at the deserted streets. M Street was about a ten-minute walk away and at two thirty in the morning, Georgetown was not the safest place for two women to be walking by themselves. But when she said as much to Penelope, the older girl waved a hand dismissively. "I have pepper spray," she said. "I'll use it too."

"Isn't pepper spray illegal?" Alex asked. "I think it is in Chicago."

Penelope laughed. "I don't know, but I'd rather risk a cop arresting me than some drug addict mugging me."

Alex could feel her face burning; Penelope probably thought that she was an enormous loser. Yet, her sister, two inches shorter and ten pounds lighter than Alex, said nothing more and took her arm, holding it just above the elbow, and didn't let go until they reached M Street, where a few people were still loitering in front of the bars, music crashing out of their open doorways. Alex could feel some of the bouncers' eyes following them as they passed and shook their heads at these burly men's exhortations to come inside. It was a chilly night but the bouncers were in T-shirts, apparently impervious to the brisk air.

Only five other people were inside the all-night café when they arrived: two young couples at a small round table, along with a boy with a blond mustache who stood behind the register, waiting without interest for their order. Alex ordered hot chocolate, Penelope a hummus plate and sparkling water. While the boy made Alex's drink and went into the kitchen in search of Penelope's hummus, the faint strains of an old Van Halen song emerging from behind the kitchen door when the boy opened it, Penelope told her about Tex, who was tall (six foot four! she exclaimed), and thirty-five, and a designer of video games.

"He's a vegan too," she added after the boy had returned with her food, a generous serving of garlicky hummus and raw vegetables. "I could never even be a vegetarian. For one, it's pretty hard not to eat meat in France. It's such a huge part of the diet there, but we do treat our animals a lot better. No factory farms. Or at least not very many."

"I've never been to France," said Alex.

Penelope looked up from her plate, her gray eyes bright with surprise. "Oh, you have to go. You'd love Paris. Maybe we could go together sometime."

"You know all of the best places to shop, I bet."

"Some of them, yes," said Penelope. "There's no shortage. Okay, no more stalling. Tell me about your man troubles."

Alex had to look away from Penelope's curious gaze. It was all so unsettling: the middle of the night and here she was several blocks from campus with her sister, this previously unknown woman who now sat less than two feet away, waiting for her to reveal the most shameful secret of her life.

And, Alex realized, she was going to do it.

As she told Penelope about the birthday party, her sister tried to maintain a look of kind encouragement, but there were moments when anger, even outrage, pulsed across her eyes and mouth, something that made Alex apprehensive because she understood then that, like Dr. Abbott, her sister was very likely to insist that she talk to her RA or the dean of students, someone who would start an inquiry and change her life. This upheaval was what she feared most, but she also realized that she had been courting it ever since her return for sophomore year. Otherwise, why would she have gone to talk to Dr. Abbott or asked her sister to come down from New York, spur of the moment, to immerse herself in what had become, Alex also realized, her life of controlled hysteria? Well, not hysteria exactly, but watchful anxiety, permanent unease. Even when she slept through the night, she woke up feeling tired, and sometimes her dreams were violent, waking her before dawn, her heart beating wildly, her empty stomach leaping sickeningly.

"Something like that happened to one of my friends at NYU," Penelope said quietly when Alex finished her story. She reached across the table and took Alex's hand. "I'm so sorry."

Alex shook her head, her eyes tearing up. "I feel like such an idiot. I don't know why I had to drink so much every time I went out. It was so stupid."

"Don't blame yourself, Alexandra. It's what kids do in college. No parents, no rules. At least not the kind that are easy to enforce. I drank a lot too sometimes. But you're tired of that now, it sounds like. That's something positive."

"But I don't know what to do. I saw a therapist and she told me that I had to talk to my RA, but I don't want to."

"You don't? Are you too embarrassed?"

"Yes."

Penelope sighed. "Of course you are. Have you told your boyfriend? What did he say?"

"I don't have one right now."

"No? I thought you would for sure. Did you have one when it happened?"

"No. I went out with a few guys last year but no one long enough to call a boyfriend. I partied too much."

"You're not pregnant, are you?"

Alex shook her head.

"Did you get screened for STDs?"

"Yes, I was fine."

"Thank God." Penelope looked at her steadily, her expression unreadable. "You could talk to your RA like your therapist said. Or not. It's up to you, obviously. It depends on how much muck you're prepared to get yourself into. Especially if you had sex with one of the guys earlier in the semester."

"What would you do?"

Penelope touched the edge of her plate, avoiding Alex's eyes. "I would probably go talk to the guys who did it to me. I would tell them that they're assholes and that I've told my friends to stay away from them. I don't know if I'd tell my RA or the dean though. I'm not very brave. But that's just me."

Her words summoned something complicated that it took Alex several seconds to sort out. But then there it was, as uncompromising as a brick wall: disappointment. She wanted Penelope to command her to go to the dean and set things in motion against Carlyle and his friend, but her new sister, older and more worldly, had not said this. As Alex sat looking down at her empty mug, chocolate syrup drying at the bottom, she felt a powerful wave of exhaustion. She needed to get back to campus and go to sleep, even if it would have to be on the floor. It had been stupid to insist that Penelope come down from New York a week early, to expect her to have all the right answers, to fold her into a sisterly embrace and march her off to the dean's office, where Alex would tell the whole embarrassing story of that hazy night when something bad had happened, but well, maybe it hadn't? Though she knew it had.

How stupid, for the thousandth time in her life, she had been. Was being.

"Alex," said Penelope, her voice gentle. "If you think you should go to your RA, I'll go with you. We can do it first thing in the morning."

"I don't know what I think," said Alex. "I feel like such an idiot."

"What happened isn't your fault."

"It is my fault. I shouldn't have drunk so much." She could feel tears pricking her eyes hotly and looked down at her lap. Her hands were clenched, her knuckles and nails glowing whitely. She worried that she might throw up.

"Not every girl who drinks too much ends up in a room with three rapists. You should be able to go to as many parties as you want and not worry that you'll be taken advantage of."

"That's not—" She hesitated. "I don't know if that's realistic."

Her sister looked at her, fatigue showing in her kind, pretty eyes. "Let's go back to campus. We can talk more in the morning, okay?"

As Alex pushed back her chair, the tears she'd been holding in for the last hour began flooding down her face, an enormous lump rising in her throat. Penelope put an arm around her and steered her toward the door, out into the street, where they stood in the cold night air as Alex sobbed and Penelope hugged and murmured to her, the voices of the bouncers down the block reaching them in short gruff bursts, cigarette smoke hanging in wisps before their hawkish faces. Alex felt emptied out, on the brink of something terrible and necessary. Her sister's neck smelled like rose soap and cloves.

It was almost four in the morning and there were no taxis. They turned and started back to campus, to Alex's room, where her drunken roommate snored softly in the tensile dark. Penelope held her hand as they moved north toward the university's front gates, neither of them speaking. There was no one else on the street, and they walked fast, eyes on the block ahead of them. Alex wished they were already inside her dorm, the door closed and locked behind them.

CLEAR CONSCIENCE

Wᴴᴱɴ Sᴀsʜᴀ, Mɪᴄʜᴀᴇʟ's sister-in-law, was offered a consulting job at a big teaching hospital that needed help setting up its new outpatient facility, she had to commit to spending half the week in Chicago. Her home was in Madison with Jim, Michael's brother, and their twelve-year-old daughter, Quinn, who loved horses and shopping and had plans to become a hostage negotiator after college, if not before, something Michael and Jim found amusing, Sasha preposterous. After she accepted the job at the hospital, there had briefly been talk of her staying at Michael's place three nights a week during the six months she would need to commute to and from Chicago. Ultimately, his offer was rebuffed: she rented her own apartment, one closer to the hospital than was his place, which was in a neighborhood several miles north of the medical campus.

Whether Sasha or her employer was paying the rent on her small, opulent one-bedroom in a high-rise that overlooked Lake Michigan, Michael didn't know, but he suspected that regardless of who paid the bills, it was his brother who had insisted that Sasha find her own lodgings. It was also possible that she wanted her own place, an eventuality that bothered Michael slightly more than his brother opposing their occasional cohabitation.

A year and a few months before Sasha was hired for the Chicago job, Michael went through an unpleasant divorce, his ex-wife, Tess, adding extra enmity to the proceedings by writing, under a pen name, acerbic blog posts about her view of the divorce and its causes. The pen name was a mockery of anonymity—all of their friends and family knew of the blog, which made scathing fun of Michael's perceived shortcomings and infuriating habits. The one scrap of good fortune in his marriage's demise was that there had been no children to argue over along with everything else.

After Sasha settled into the routine of her three nights and twenty-seven weekly hours of work for the hospital, Michael met her for dinner on Wednesday evenings. This was usually the third night of the three she spent in his city, and often an air of subdued festivity permeated their meetings. Sasha claimed not to read Michael's ex-wife's blog, where he was referred to alternately as the Tightwad and the Crocodile, and sometimes, more inexplicably, the Mole. In addition to serving as the focus of his ex-wife's virulent frustration over the scale of her accomplishments so far, he was the supposedly spoiled younger brother to Jim, who was five years his senior. Jim was also four years older than Sasha, and Michael liked that he and Sasha had grown up listening to the same music and seeing the same movie matinees, whereas his brother, with his half-decade handicap, was sometimes teased for being an old man when they were all together—how could he not remember who Pauly Shore was? Or Blind Melon and Mazzy Star? That Jim could recall dialogue verbatim from *Casablanca* and *Apocalypse Now* and all three of *The Godfather* movies, that he favored the classics over the junkily ephemeral, that he was wittier and more cultured than Michael and his entire graduating high school class combined (as Jim, slightly drunk on strong eggnog, had once claimed during a fractious family Christmas party)—these qualities were thrilling to Sasha when she met Jim, but now not so much.

"I shouldn't talk about him when he's not here to defend himself," she said, looking down at the second fish taco on her plate, deciding, Michael assumed, if she should eat it. If she didn't, he would ask her for it. Jim would have started eating it without permission, but he was her husband, and also always ravenous, in part because he claimed to be too busy to eat lunch, or else decided to make do with an apple and handfuls of raw, unsalted almonds at his desk while the other attorneys in his office went down the street for sandwiches and fattening, over-dressed salads: full of sodium and bad calories, he said, with a disapproving shake of his head. ("Nutrition density is hardly given the time of day in this country," he also said. "Lentils! We should all eat lentils at least every other day.") He ran forty miles a week, more when he was training for a marathon. Michael was fit too, though not as disciplined or, as he had said to some of his friends, as obsessive; he exercised only a couple of days each week, with weights at the gym and halfhearted five-mile bouts on the treadmill. "The dread-mill," his brother liked to say with a frown. Jim ran outside, rain or snow or sweltering sun.

"You know I won't tell him," said Michael, feeling a little uneasy despite his desire to hear Sasha say critical things about his older brother, disclosures that always interested him.

She met his gaze, her dark eyes clear and unblinking. "I know. But I don't want you to feel like you have to put up with me. I can go to a shrink." She laughed softly. "I do go to a shrink."

This was new, somewhat startling information. Michael glanced again at her leftover taco, unable to look at her for a few seconds.

"That's a good idea," he said.

She laughed again. "I suppose so, yes."

"Does Jim see one too?"

She shook her head. "No. You can just guess what he says. Running is his therapy."

"I went with Tess to a marriage counselor for a few months. It was like getting kicked in the ass for an hour straight."

Sasha made a face. "That doesn't surprise me."

"On the way home, Tess kept the kicks coming." He paused. "Sorry. I'm the one who shouldn't be bothering you with this stuff."

She smiled. "Not at all, Mike. Don't worry."

"If you've looked at her blog, you already know that we saw a therapist." He hadn't visited her blog in a couple of weeks. He knew that he should never, under any circumstances, read it, but some nights, angry or embittered by the memory of an old argument or petty humiliation, he did look, and then he lay awake for hours feeling furious and half awed by his ex-wife's vindictiveness. "Doesn't she have other people to hate?" his friend Jon, who had been his best man, once asked. "Like Donald Trump? What about Pol Pot?"

"I haven't looked at her blog," said Sasha.

"Thank you."

She regarded him steadily. "I didn't like her. You know that."

"I was glad that you still managed to be nice to her though."

"I guess I was? But I didn't have to see her as often as you did."

Michael laughed. "That's true."

The bartender had turned up the restaurant's stereo system, loud enough that everyone had to raise their voices to be heard across the narrow tables with their faltering tea lights. It was a few days before Halloween, and the song playing was

"Thriller," which Michael still remembered the words to; as a boy, he thought it was a mark of distinction that he shared a first name with the song's flamboyant performer. "Quinn just saw this video for the first time," said Sasha. "She loved it. She's going to be a zombie this year."

"I keep seeing previews for zombie movies. I'm not really a fan but they seem to be everywhere now."

"I'm not a fan either," said Sasha. "Jim told her that she'd make a very convincing zombie. He thought he was being funny. Quinn was offended, but she's twelve and everything her father and I say now offends her."

"At least she didn't want to be a stripper or a sexy witch."

"She has a friend who's allegedly going as a porn star."

"I bet her parents are proud," he said dryly.

"His parents." She smiled again, seeing Michael's surprise deepen. "Yes, I know. He's using fur from an old teddy bear for chest hair and a potato for—" She pursed her lips. "To quote Quinn, 'for his thing.' Do you think she knows the word 'dildo' yet?"

"She talks to you about this stuff?"

Sasha shook her head. "She talks to her friends about it. I eavesdrop when she's in the living room and I'm in the kitchen. She doesn't realize how loud she's talking most of the time." She pointed at her taco. "Want it?"

"Thank you," he said, lifting it off her plate with his fork. As he cut into it, her phone rang and she pulled it out of her handbag and sighed.

"Jim," she mouthed.

He looked down at the taco, the strings of lettuce and sour cream oozing from its corners as he cut another piece. The speakers howled and a woman at a nearby table released a loud, answering cackle. Her friends guffawed. The woman cackled again, louder. Sasha stuffed a finger in her ear, a useless attempt, Michael was sure, to mute the drunken uproar. "I'm at dinner," she yelled into the phone. "I can't hear you very well, Jim. Can I call you back in a little while?"

Then, "I'm with your brother." After this, she said good-bye and gave Michael a sheepish look. "He said that I forgot to pay the water bill. He was annoyed, as you can imagine."

"Did the city shut it off?"

"No, no, of course not. You get at least two warnings. That was only the first. He was just mad that I'd forgotten."

"I'm surprised he hasn't had you set it up for auto-pay."

She laughed. "He doesn't want our banking information in their system. He's a little paranoid sometimes."

"Tess was like that too."

"I think I'd like one more margarita. It's been a hard week."

She ordered a large lemon-lime with salt, larger than the other two she'd already had. Thirty minutes later, she was drunk, her eyes pink and heavy-lidded, her movements abrupt and unmeasured. Michael looked at her anxiously from across the table. He would have to drive her back to her lakeside high-rise and see her upstairs, where he would also have to make sure that she locked the door behind him after, as he imagined it, he left her sprawled across the couch or clinging to the granite countertop in the kitchen. He could remember seeing Sasha this drunk only once before—at his and Tess's wedding, where Jim stayed sober and gave him unnerving, sardonic looks much of the evening, as if he could foresee the results of Michael's marital gamble. Quinn was there too, six years old and sugar-stoked from several kiddie cocktails, her pink headband askew, her cheeks also glowing pink.

Tess and he had started dating in college during the last several weeks before graduation and dated on and off for five years before marrying—the marriage happening only because Tess had pushed for it. When Michael proposed, he had silently reasoned that if it didn't work out, they could get a divorce. After all, what would be the big deal? Millions of people had married and divorced and more or less survived both ordeals. Since his own divorce, however, he'd grown cynical: about his naive and carefree former self, about the changeability of other people, about long-term commitment in general, sexual or otherwise—several of his old friends also having grown inattentive to their friendship, rarely bothering to return his occasional emails or phone calls. They had disappeared into parenthood, into exhausting jobs that required frequent air travel and overtime and onerous social commitments of their own, but one or two did apologize (often in an aggrieved tone that made him feel worse) when he did catch them on the phone.

Since the July night when Tess had demanded that he get out out out! and had thrown his keys from their second-story bedroom window into the dense rosebushes on the west side of the money-pit colonial they'd bought four years earlier, he had gone on dates with two women. One he'd met online, and when they went on their first and only date, she'd brought along a friend. She informed him in a voice devoid of irony that the friend was there as a safeguard against boredom. The other woman he went out with was the cousin of a co-worker; she was cute and fit and had a good sense of humor, but after they had sex on the second date, she confessed that she was probably going back to her ex-boyfriend. As she smoothed her black pantyhose over her calves and pointed her toes coquettishly into the carpet, she gave him an appraising look and said, "But that was really fun. I don't think you'll have any trouble finding someone to take my place." He felt disoriented and bereft, watching mutely from the door of his new apartment building as she drove her little blue VW down the street and away from his rumpled bed for good. He retreated inside and made himself feel worse by eating an entire bar of dark chocolate with bacon and calling Tess to demand that she return his deluxe-edition Monopoly and Trivial Pursuit games immediately or she would soon be hearing from his lawyer.

A week later, her blog went live, and he became infamous among their small galaxy of friends and family members as the contemptible ex who snored and growled in his sleep and "snapped his jaws like a crocodile," which she thought especially disgusting because he had bad breath. He often left the door open when he used the bathroom (a lie) and had insisted during their courtship, always, even on her birthday! that they go dutch (another lie).

That Sasha claimed never to have read the blog was generous of her, but Michael didn't believe it. She had once suggested that he counter with his own blog about Tess's failings, something he considered but then dismissed because it would seem a feeble rejoinder, as if he were yelling at a schoolyard bully, "I know you are, but what am I?"

With his arm around her shoulders, Sasha sagged against him while they waited outside the restaurant for the valet to reappear with Michael's car. He wondered for a second if she would get sick before he got her home, and if she did, whether she would remember it later and feel embarrassed and not want to see him when she was in Chicago the following week. He had looked forward to their weekly dinners in the same way he used to anticipate a snow day or a Christmas package, one sent by his grandparents from Tucson in a brown-paper-wrapped box, and he knew this Sasha-related suspense to be a problem, or a soon-to-be-serious problem. It wasn't so much that he wanted to have sex with his brother's wife, though he did. Yet, this was hardly an original impulse, he felt sure. Sasha was attractive and smart, and among other things he liked about her, she often spoke with thrilling and knowledgeable fury about people, dead or alive, who she detested. She also loved Peter Gabriel's *Us* more than *So*, which was true of no one he knew other than himself. What probably endeared her to him the most, however, was that she asked him questions no one else asked: If suddenly you could buy anything you wanted, anything at all, what would it be? If you were the last man on earth, whom would you want to be the last woman?

On the drive back to her apartment, he glanced over at her twice and both times she was staring at him, a half-smile on her lips. The third time he looked in her direction, her face had collapsed into a suppressed sob.

"What's wrong?" he asked worriedly. "Should I pull over?" They were on Lake Shore Drive, hemmed inside a herd of speeding cars, and he could see that it would be difficult to safely pull over. It was drizzling too, the blades scraping the glass with a plaintive moan.

"I'm so tired," she said, her voice cracking.

"I'll have you home in a few minutes, Sasha. Can you hang on?" he asked, reaching over to pat her shoulder, but she shifted in her seat, and instead his hand came down on her left breast.

She let out a hiccup of laughter.

His face burned. "I'm sorry. I didn't mean—"

She laughed and waved a hand in front of her face. "Are you sure that was an accident?"

"Yes, I'm so sorry," he croaked.

"I'm not tired tired," she said after a moment.

He glanced over but she had turned toward the window. "You're not?"

"I'm just tired of being a wife and a mother. I make more money than Jim does. Did you know that?"

"No, I didn't, but there's nothing wrong with that."

"I know, but he won't let me take a year off. He actually makes enough to support us but he says, 'What if I lose my job?' He never will, but he still won't let me take any time off. So I work. In the one-in-a-billion chance that he gets laid off and we end up in the gutter." She laughed angrily.

"There's really no danger of that?"

She snorted. "No. He's ridiculous. I deserve a fucking year off if I want one. I only took off two and a half months when Quinn was born."

"I think you deserve a year off too."

"If I were married to you, you'd let me have one, wouldn't you?"

He wondered if before tonight she had ever thought about what it would be like to be his wife. "Of course I would," he said, pulling off Lake Shore and turning onto Monroe Street before turning again onto her street. He hoped that her doorman would let him park his car in the circular drive for a few minutes while he helped her upstairs. She did not seem very drunk anymore, but he knew from the thickness of her voice that she wasn't yet sober.

"You wouldn't bitch at me for forgetting to pay the water bill, I bet."

"No, probably not," he said.

"I think I might have kissed the father of Quinn's porn star friend," she said.

Michael turned into her building's driveway, his eyes on the front entrance, on its windows with their wafers of inviting yellow light. "You think you kissed him?" he said, keeping his voice level. "Or you know you kissed him?"

"I know," she said and laughed. "I suppose."

He said nothing.

"But for Quinn's sake, I'm not going anywhere, other than to Chicago every week for the next four and a half months."

"Do you have feelings for the guy you kissed?" he asked, not sure if he felt more jealous than upset—for his brother and for himself. If Sasha divorced Jim, she wouldn't want to bother with him, the younger brother who had also married a woman who divorced him.

"Forget I said anything," she said quietly. Her hand raised, then dropped to her lap. "I shouldn't talk about it."

"But you must want to. I would, probably."

She fixed him with a bleary stare. "Nothing ever happens anymore. That's what you and Tess missed by not staying together: nothing."

"I don't know," he said slowly. "You could say that in our case, too, much happened. Her bipolar diagnosis, the cats she kept adopting without asking me first. Then I caught her trying to sell our cars for two hundred dollars each to the con man down the street before she tossed my keys out the window and kicked me out. It was time for me to leave anyway, but I would have preferred not to have to paw through a rosebush for my keychain in the middle of a thunderstorm." He put on the hazards and opened his door. "I'll help you upstairs. I think I can park here for a couple of minutes."

"You're such a gentleman, Michael," she murmured. "Really, you're so nice to me. If I'd met you before—" Her voice trailed off.

"Don't say that," he said.

"I can say whatever I want," she said flatly. They were out of the car and she was leaning against him more heavily than she had on their way out of the restaurant.

In the elevator lights, trying not to look at her, he realized that he was angry with her.

As if reading his thoughts, she mumbled, "I can kiss whoever I want to too."

"You can," he said, "but I don't think it's a good idea if you want to stay married to my brother."

She had turned her whole body toward him; her breasts pressed against his arm now, and she was talking into his shoulder. "I don't want to," she said. "But I will. At least until Quinn goes off to college. God, I hope she does."

"She will," he said.

Sasha sneezed. "She could become a drug addict, for all I know. She could get knocked up and drop out of high school."

"She's not going to do that."

"She could, especially if I can't wait six years to tell her father I want a divorce."

"It sounds like you've already made up your mind."

She nodded, her head bobbing next to his chin. Lavender and the street scents of wind and dust rose from her hair.

"You've maybe had a little too much to drink," he said. "I think you'll feel differently about everything tomorrow."

"Tess was crazy to kick you out." She smiled crookedly. "No pun intended."

He tried to return her smile. "In fairness to her, a lot of people are bipolar. Our problems stemmed from other things too."

"See how nice you are?" she said. "Your ex-wife was such a bitch to you, even when she was on meds, and you can still see her point of view."

He said nothing. The elevator stopped and disgorged them onto the sixteenth floor, with its taupe carpet and eggshell-colored walls. Her apartment was at the end of the hallway, away from the noise of the elevator shafts. She dug into her purse, and after some struggling that included a fumbled wallet and two lipsticks dropping to the carpet, she unearthed her keys. Michael took the keys and opened her door. The apartment smelled of something recently burned and was messier than he expected. Two blouses, one white, one pink, along with a pair of gray dress pants, were strewn across her sofa. A half-dozen empty Diet Pepsi cans and an open box of Cheerios, with a dirty bowl and spoon next to it, sat on the island in her kitchen.

"It's a pit," she said. "Sorry. I never spend any time here. I'm always at work or on the way to work."

He looked around, spotting two pairs of high heels, one pair beige, the other navy, in a small heap next to the kitchen island, gray nylon stockings snaking out from the mouth of one of the navy pumps. "Maybe you should have a cleaning service come in once a week," he suggested.

"I thought of that," she said.

"I'd better get going," he said. "I've got a meeting at seven tomorrow and still have an hour or so of prep to do for it."

She yawned, her jaw popping. "The young executive."

"No, not really," he said, embarrassed. He was one of the two main people who managed his university employer's financial software and he was good at it, but he didn't plan to do it forever. He was thinking of going to culinary school but had told no one. It seemed a shameful secret, like binge drinking or bulimia. He could already hear Jim's droll comments about how you couldn't trust a skinny chef, so, did Michael plan to get fat?

At the door, Sasha kissed him good-bye, her lips pressed wetly against his cheek for several seconds. "I want you to meet someone nice," she said, pulling back to peer up at him. "I can't have you, but you should have someone better than me anyway."

He looked at her, taken aback. "How long have you wanted a divorce? I should have said earlier that I'm very sorry to hear this."

"Oh, I don't know. A while," she said.

"I'm not going to say anything to Jim. This is between you and him, obviously."

She blinked. Her face sagged with fatigue, as if in that moment she could scarcely hold her head and body upright. "I didn't think you would."

"I won't," he said quietly.

The following Wednesday they did not meet for dinner. Sasha sent him an email on Monday afternoon saying she had a meeting that would include dinner on Wednesday evening, but next week she'd be free again, if he would be in town and wanted to go out for steak at Ruth's Chris? Or did he like Morton's better?

Yes, he would be in town, he replied. He asked how Halloween had gone, if Quinn had in fact dressed up as a zombie. Had her friend gone as a porn star? Had Sasha kissed the kid's father again? This last question he typed but then deleted before sending the email.

Halloween was rainy, Sasha replied the next morning, and Quinn and she had gotten into a bad argument that resulted in Sasha grounding her for a week. Quinn had ignored her curfew of ten thirty on Friday, the night of the party to which she had worn the infamous zombie costume. And she hadn't answered her phone when Sasha called at ten forty-five to ask where she was, and therefore, Sasha had gone seething to the house of the porn star boy and hunted down her twelve-year-old daughter, who was in the backyard eating candy corn held before her by the front teeth of the porn star, potato still obscenely visible in his tight jeans.

There was no mention of the father Sasha had once kissed, nor what he thought about his son pretending in a semi-public place to advertise a large, tumescent penis. Michael guessed that there would never again be a mention of this man, unless Sasha left Jim for him. He and his brother had had no contact since before the night Sasha had too much to drink and mentioned wanting a divorce, but Michael didn't usually talk to or email Jim more than once or twice a month, unless it was to discuss something related to their parents, who were retired and often preoccupied with golfing in Florida and photographing birds and trees in Canada, where they took frequent road trips in their Airstream RV.

When they met at Morton's for dinner, Sasha ordered an iced tea. "No margaritas for me this time," she said with a sheepish smile. "I had an awful hangover after our last dinner." She had on a tight black V-neck blouse, a strand of gray pearls, blue jeans, and her hair was pinned up into a makeshift bun. Michael found himself consciously averting his eyes from her breasts and sometimes also from her direct, assessing gaze. He had gone out with a new woman over the weekend, a friend of the co-worker's sexy cousin's, who had gotten in touch with him based on the cousin's recommendation. Her name was Sparrow, which he wasn't sure he believed, but she was attractive and articulate and liked to laugh, and several times he had noticed his heart beating hard during the meal. She had long dark hair and slipped in and out of rooms with feline grace; she'd studied acting in college and in the past year had been cast in supporting roles in two of the bigger productions at the Chicago Shakespeare Theater. He liked her upon sight but did not invite her to his place or accept her offer to go back to hers. When he kissed her good-bye by the gate outside her redbrick Wrigleyville apartment, she smiled up at him and said that next time he would have to come in or she would be forced to slip him a roofie at dinner.

Michael told Sasha about Sparrow's forthrightness, and Sasha rolled her eyes. "Well, so much for playing hard to get," she said dryly.

He glanced at his water glass, a lemon wedge still impaled on its rim. "I guess so."

"You don't think it's a good idea to exercise a little restraint?"

He looked at her, wondering if she was being ironic. "I do, but you could say that's not always necessary."

"Well, I suppose you're not getting much sex right now."

They had never talked frankly about his sex life or hers, and he did not want to start. He regretted mentioning Sparrow. By making Sasha jealous, he was exposing them both in a shabby, underhanded way.

"I know it's none of my business," said Sasha, looking down at the Caesar salad she'd been picking over for several minutes. "Sorry to sound like such a shrew. But at least your conscience is clear."

"She invited me over," he said, not sure what she meant. "Not the other way around."

"You could easily have gone home with her," she said. "But you decided not to take advantage of what I'm sure she was offering you."

He had trouble reading her expression: was it distaste or impatience? Possibly both.

"Maybe, but if she offers again, I probably won't turn her down."

"No, I didn't think you would."

They ate in strained silence after this. He tried to tell her about his boss's son's elaborate bar mitzvah preparations—a trapeze artist, fiery hoop-jumping poodles—hoping to make her laugh, but she hardly smiled, and after another few minutes she asked their waiter for the check, which she insisted on paying. They parted ways outside the restaurant, she refusing a ride back to her building. "I'll take a cab," she said. "I have to call Jim and Quinn. If I do it in the cab, it won't take as long as if I wait until I get home." She paused. "I'm a bad mother."

"No, you're not," he said. "You're just tired."

"That's true," she said, nodding. "But I'm also a bad mother."

The next afternoon she sent Michael an email while he and Sparrow were exchanging flirtatious instant messages. He had plans to see Sparrow that night, and at lunchtime he had gone out to buy an expensive fine-spun cotton shirt he'd been eyeing for a few weeks at Macy's, along with several pairs of boxer shorts, the kind he remembered from high school, the brand's ad campaign with a rapper-turned-actor and his gym-built abdominals nearly ubiquitous.

Sasha wrote in the email that she thought they should stop meeting for dinner, at least for a few weeks. It was a strange time for her and she felt embarrassed by her disclosures of two weeks ago. She was afraid of becoming emotionally dependent on him and couldn't trust herself. Did he understand? She was sorry, and maybe he shouldn't come up for Thanksgiving either—could he think of some excuse?

An hour later, before he replied, she wrote again. *You should come for Thanksgiving. I don't mean to be so selfish and cold-hearted. I've just been having a hard time lately. Please ignore/forgive me. Love you, S*

She had never before signed off with those two words. He was thirty-six and at loose ends romantically and trying not to do something stupid. It seemed to him then that this was how his life, any life, should be measured. His obituarist might write: *It went all right, overall, because he didn't do anything too stupid.* Or else: *He tried, but was, unfortunately, often very stupid.*

Sparrow's message window popped up again: *Want to see you in those CKs. Then in short order see them on my bedroom floor. : P*

His cell phone began to ring, Sasha's name and number appearing on the screen. His stomach leapt; he didn't pick up.

Me too, he replied to Sparrow's message. *See you soon.* After he hit return, he signed out of his messaging account.

Sasha's voicemail was brief: *Call me when you have a chance? Bye, sweetie.*

Instead of calling her back, an hour later he called Jim and confessed to his brother's voicemail that he was thinking of going to culinary school. Jim didn't return his call, but before long sent a text, one that hinted at nothing: *Busy today. Talk soon.*

He went out that night with Sparrow without calling Sasha back. They had dinner at a Japanese restaurant near her apartment, where she doused their shared rice in soy sauce, but then asked him, her brow furrowing, "Do you have a problem with sodium?"

"No, but after I eat some of that, I might," he said wryly.

"Oh shit. Should we ask the waiter for another bowl?"

"No, it's okay," he said. "I'm teasing you." The flirtatious woman of their first date was nowhere in evidence. Sparrow also kept glancing at her phone as they ate. "I know it's a terrible habit," she said with a nervous laugh. "But it's like I'm on drugs or something."

He realized within thirty minutes that he wanted to be at home, alone with the Bulls game and a lightly salted dinner, one made in his own kitchen. The new shirt, the new underwear, the afternoon's sexual suspense—none of it mattered. He was tired and he understood now exactly what Sasha had meant when she'd claimed to feel the same debilitating fatigue. Aside from his bad marriage, most of his life had been a committed exercise in the avoidance of suffering. He had no children, no dependents, no responsibilities other than to himself, and marginally, to his parents. Despite what the attractive woman sitting across the table from him seemed to be offering, he wanted to be alone and unbothered by anyone, pretty or no. *Okay, so he wasn't stupid, but he was a little . . . strange.*

When the check came, he had already pulled out his credit card and handed it to the server without looking at the total.

"Would you still like to see my place?" Sparrow asked as she watched him sign the receipt a few minutes later.

He lifted his eyes to meet her hopeful gaze, but before he'd spoken a word, she shook her head and glanced away. "If it takes you that long to decide," she said quietly, "I can tell that the answer is no."

"That's not what I was going to say," he said, his face reddening. But he was lying and she knew it.

"Don't bother. It's okay." She laughed sadly.

"It's not you," he said. "I swear, it's not."

She gave him a weary look, her dark eyes glistening. "It isn't? Then who else is it?"

In the cab on the way home, he stared down at his knees unseeingly, wondering if he should stop at Binny's for a bottle of vodka and some orange juice and get drunk in front of the TV. He hadn't done that in a while, and the last time had not been on purpose. He and Tess were still together and she was in the next room, playing online backgammon. He decided not to ask the cabbie to stop and sent a text to Sasha saying he was sorry that he hadn't yet called her back. She replied within a minute to say that he shouldn't worry.

A few seconds later, his phone rang. "Come over," she said, matter-of-fact. "Or I'll come up to you. I didn't go back to Madison today. I had to put in some extra hours this week."

He closed his eyes; he could feel his heart beating harder. The cabbie hit the horn, cursing at a man crossing against the traffic light. "I don't know if that's a good idea," said Michael, trying not to shout into the phone over the cabbie's own shouting.

"You were with that girl, weren't you. The one with the stupid name."

"We went out for dinner, but I'm not with her now."

She exhaled. "I'm not saying we'll have sex if you come down here."

"I didn't think that."

"But we could," she said.

He was so startled by this that he blurted out a question that under other circumstances he would never have been bold enough to ask. "Have you read Tess's blog? Please tell me the truth."

"Not for a while." She paused. "Why are you asking me that?"

"So you have read it?"

"I've glanced at it once or twice, but I didn't read any of her posts the whole way through. She's not a very good writer. Quinn could do better."

"Yes, she probably could."

"I really doubt she'll keep writing it for much longer," said Sasha. "I bet she's already getting tired of it."

The cabbie had pulled up to his building and was waiting for the fare. Michael gave him a ten and a five and motioned for him to keep the change. The streetlight directly in front of his building flickered dispiritedly; it had been doing that for two weeks, the bulb somehow holding on.

"I have to get to bed," he said, walking up to his building. "I have to be at work again at seven tomorrow."

"You're not coming down here?" she asked.

"Sasha, you know I can't."

"Jim won't know. I'd never tell him."

"Did you have sex with that guy you kissed? The one with the son who used the potato?"

She exhaled. "I don't want to talk about him."

"Did you?"

"Michael, come on."

After a moment, he said, "I really should let you go."

"Okay," she said and hung up.

He felt drained and depressed but could not relax enough to fall asleep after he got into bed. After the narrow, ghostly clock hands moved past two, he got up again and tried to turn on his laptop, but the battery was dead and he realized that in his haste to get home to shower before meeting Sparrow, he'd forgotten the power cord at the office.

I'm sorry, he texted to Sasha, not sure what he meant.

She didn't reply, but he could sense that she was awake five miles south, that his message had been seen and ignored.

Did you pay the water bill? ;) he asked in a second message. She ignored this one too.

If you're awake, you could come over. He hit send before he could change his mind.

Again, no reply. Maybe she was asleep after all. Maybe at Thanksgiving she would kiss him in the kitchen when everyone else was in the dining room waiting on the pies. Or maybe he would have Sparrow with him because she'd decided to give him another chance, and when his brother tried to flirt with her, she would not respond, at least not in the way that Tess had, smiling and blushing, every single time. She would not tell him in front of everyone that he needed to use dandruff shampoo because who did he think he was kidding? the others at the table trying not to stare at them as they argued, everyone thinking, he was certain, how they would never let themselves be this petty, this unhappy.

He remembered a question that Sasha had asked him not long before she began working in Chicago. If he had a choice between losing one glove or two, which would he choose? Because it seemed to her that if you had to lose a glove, you might as well lose both—this way, whoever found them could keep wearing them, whereas one glove was useless for both the loser and the finder. What did he think?

Well, sure, it did seem like it'd be best to lose both. That was fine with him. What would she do?

She pursed her lips, trying to hide a smile, and said that because she was a mother, she bought two sets of everything. She'd rather just lose one glove and keep the remaining one in reserve.

That's hardly fair, he said, laughing a little.

I know, she agreed. But it's practical. I'm allowed to be practical. So are you, for that matter.

At five A.M. she sent a text: *Jim said you want to be a chef. Why didn't you tell me?*

I guess I forgot to, he typed but didn't hit send. Instead, he used his phone to check Tess's blog. Aside from the older humiliating posts about the divorce, there was only a review of a rock concert she'd gone to with an undisclosed male companion two nights earlier:

> *The lead singer (Wilder Peeples, in case you weren't sure) forgot some of the words to the best songs ("Pink Plastic Poodle" & "Please Me") and told us at the end of the show (instead of doing an encore, which was pretty lame of him to skip) that he had some advice for us: "Don't lie. Buy local. Drink more water." Later, on the way to the car, R. said, "He forgot to remind us to*

*change our underwear too." I burst out laughing. But then I
thought it was okay, that Wilder only meant to be nice even if
he was completely wasted?*

Michael posted a comment: "You're both idiots." Afterward,
he went back to bed but still could not fall asleep.

THE NEW, ALL-TRUE CV

24 April 2010

Dr. Sandra Matheson, Ph.D.
Executive Vice President of Human Resources
Elite Industries
4200 N. Prairie Blvd.
Omaha, NE 68182

Dear Dr. Matheson:

I am writing today to apply for the position of Chief Recruiter, Manufacturing Division, at Elite Industries, which I know from my research is the number one luxury T-shirt manufacturer in the Midwest, possibly in the United States, if not in all of North America. Your T-shirts are the most stylish articles of clothing in my closet, and I have been wearing your products for many years. My first Elite shirt was long-sleeved and purple, and I purchased it at a Prince concert with a month's worth of babysitting money when I was thirteen. I attended this concert with my friend Elizabeth Pelsen, who no longer speaks to me, but I'll save that story for later on in my application. The Prince T-shirt, which is more than twenty-five years old now, is still in excellent condition. On the front is a picture of the diminutive rock star sitting on a motorcycle (the same image is on his *Purple Rain* album cover, one you might also be familiar with), and the dates and cities of his tour are printed on the back. The fabric and stitching have held up very well through countless washings, even if the silk screening hasn't fared as well. If you'd like, I can bring this shirt with me if you call me in for an interview (which of course I hope you will).

After thinking for a long time about the stressful process of applying and interviewing for jobs, and all that these tasks entail, I have come to some conclusions about the methods employed by many HR departments in their day-to-day business of finding the best possible candidates for their companies' available positions. As the attached curriculum vitae details, I have a degree in both finance and management organizational behavior from The Ohio State University (the "the" with its capital "T," for some reason, is very important to OSU functionaries, though I'm still not sure that I understand why), and I have some unorthodox (but potentially revolutionary) ideas about how to make more lasting hires for every position in any company. Like you, however, I am most interested in helping to ensure the ongoing success of the hiring process at Elite Industries. Vetting potential employees is a fraught undertaking, of course, and during the interview period, a recruiter can never be sure if a candidate is what he or she appears to be, either on paper or in person.

Although I realize that my CV should stress only the positive, my scholastic and professional accomplishments in particular, this document's efficacy is doomed from the outset because it omits some of the most remarkable formative events of my life, whether they are personal successes or humiliating but character-building failures. With this in mind, the attached document is my attempt to offer you a more detailed and genuine picture of who I am. Most of the following information would ordinarily never be a feature of any job application, but because I had a near-death experience not long ago (which is detailed on the attached, ref. Disasters Averted or Otherwise), the same experience that eventually led me to come up with my innovative recruiting strategies, I have decided to dispense with the usual self-promoting subterfuge. As long as this impulse endures, I intend to embrace it, and I hope that you will be impressed and engaged by what you learn from my CV. (It should be noted that, on the whole, co-workers learn what a new hire's shortcomings are only *after* he or she begins working alongside them. If I am offered the position I'm applying for today, I will do my best to help ensure that future Elite Industries job candidates will also be properly vetted.)

Please feel free to contact me at your earliest convenience at either 464-0021 or FanofElite@goodjob.com. I do hope to hear from you soon.

Sincerely yours,
Camille Roberts

ENCL: experimental CV
      sample interview questions

(PROTOTYPE: THE NEW, ALL-TRUE CV)

Camille Roberts
1624 N. Madison Dr.
Winfield, NE 68140
FanofElite@goodjob.com
464-0021

OBJECTIVE: To acquire a prestigious and lucrative position in Elite's Human Resources department that will allow me to revolutionize hiring practices for current and future generations of workers. Also, to find love and marry above my current economic and social class. Husband-to-be will ideally have good teeth, a taut and well-muscled midsection, no kids from previous wives or girlfriends, no credit card or gambling debts or outstanding student loans, no history of consorting with prostitutes, no substance-abuse problems, including but not limited to cigarettes, alcohol, fatty foods, intravenous drugs, and prescription pills; he will not have any visible disabilities such as a limp, an overbite, or psoriasis, will own his own home, and will not spend whole weekends staring at the TV, cursing and cajoling various millionaire athletes as if he were their bipolar father. He will rarely, if ever, snore.

FORMATIVE YEARS/EDUCATION

Elementary & Junior High School
Northborough Elementary and Junior High Schools, Northborough, MA

– *1978–79*—I don't think I was any more of a misfit than most, but I did have an unfortunate tendency of breaking out in facial hives whenever a teacher asked me a question, and although I usually knew the answer, I hated to have everyone's demonic eyes staring at me, and soon they started to expect me to get hives and I always did, on some level not wanting to disappoint them, I guess, and also, I was so young and nervous by temperament, and had to eat ham-salad sandwiches for lunch more often than not, their smell aggressively permeating the orange-walled room where we all kept our sack lunches and coats and hats. On top of this, I had a well-meaning, sartorially conservative mother who dressed me in plaid skirts and buckle shoes and pigtails with ribbons. What young girl isn't painfully anxious about everything having to do with school and with boys who stepped on shy girl-classmates' toes to get their attention and called them Pimplehead and Piss-Pants for reasons that will not be explained here?

– *1979–80*—All families have similarities and differences, the voice on the filmstrip said, just as all girls and boys have similarities and differences. Something else I learned that year: it is never a good idea to walk into your parents' bedroom without knocking first, especially if you've had to skip your after-school Young Bible Scholars class because of an upset stomach, and therefore you arrive home early to discover what some of the main differences between boys and girls are. It is even more alarming if you walk in on your parents and one of them isn't actually your parent but the parent of a classmate who is known for stealing small, valuable objects from neighbors' houses, which, as an adult, you will later understand to be an act meant to punish his own parents rather than the people he stole from.

– *1982–83*—If you were female and grew to be five feet seven inches tall by sixth grade and had largish front teeth that made you look, in some people's opinion, like a fur-bearing, rapidly reproducing creature, and you needed a bra as big as a few of your classmates' mothers' bras, bigger in a few cases, you learned early on that life isn't fair, that life is actually a cosmic joke played out over and over on the young, who are sometimes desperate enough to consider suicide by mixing bleach and chocolate milk but (luckily) never find the guts to drink this lethal, disgusting beverage.

High School
Somerville High School, Somerville, MA

- *August 1986*—Shelley Zenk's party between freshman and sophomore year is a classic example of an event that is supposed to be lost in the sands of time but fiercely refuses to be buried for any extended period. At Shelley's house, I suffered the indignity of getting my monthly visitor while wearing a white skirt and having to call my parents to pick me up early, along with a second, worse indignity of first having allowed myself to be felt up by a buffoon named Steve Lish, who was known for eating oranges with the peels still on them, often forgot to wear deodorant, and at a talent show in the eighth grade burped the chorus of "Jessie's Girl" to great acclaim and eventual detention.
- *April 1987*—While babysitting for the Monroes, who lived on Paradise Lane in a split-level with a stained-glass window embedded in their front door that looked as if it had been stolen from a church, I went for a walk with the boy and girl I was in charge of for the night while the Monroes ate dinner at a fancy Indian restaurant near Harvard Square to celebrate their twelfth wedding anniversary. The boy and girl, Kyle and Alyssa, were riding in a wagon that I was pulling behind me, and they soon began giggling like asylum inmates. When I looked back to see why they were laughing, Kyle made an obscene hand gesture. In my embarrassed

surprise, I accidentally overturned the wagon, both kids falling out, Kyle smacking his head on the sidewalk and unfortunately never being quite the same again. His parents didn't sue my parents because we weren't yet as litigious a society as we are today and Kyle's grades didn't get any worse; somehow they actually got better, but he acquired the habit of shouting at inappropriate times, often racial epithets or curse words that caused his parents to turn red and rush him out of movie theaters or away from the Fourth of July parade, and apparently caused his sister to avoid him more and more as they grew older.

- *October 1988*—There was morning-after remorse but no unplanned pregnancy. There was a minor flare-up of something that required antibiotics and a seriously awkward conversation, conducted over the phone, with the boy in question, who, to my amazement, did not go out and tell forty of his closest friends, but this might have been due in part to the motorcycle accident he had later that day, one where he broke his collarbone and the femur of his left leg. While he was in the hospital being plastered over, his parents found out what else was wrong with him, and too cowardly to admit to his own faults, he blamed the bacteria and burning sensation on me. His stepmother soon called my parents and demanded that they stop letting their whorish daughter out of the house. Shelley Zenk was once again implicated: it was through her that I'd met this diseased coward who had, along with a motorcycle, three pairs of football cleats, two pairs of soccer shoes, a father with three DUIs, and a mother with a second husband and another two sons all living in a different state in a far coastal city.
- *March 1989*—I let a boy in the afternoon senior English class plagiarize my *Hamlet* paper, which turned out to be a

very bad idea because Mr. Weir and Mrs. Pottsfield didn't believe that either of us had written it. Mr. Weir thought that Alex Crouse and I had gone in together and paid a smart kid from a nearby university to write it for us, because even though I earned good grades every quarter, I wasn't supposed to know who Laurence Olivier was, let alone enough about theater performance to comment on his interpretation of Hamlet, because what high school kid knew anything about the English stage, let alone Sir Laurence Olivier? What Mr. Weir and Mrs. Pottsfield didn't believe was that my parents had made me watch Olivier's *Hamlet* on PBS, and I had taken notes on the way he portrayed Hamlet's mental state. Was the Danish prince as crazy and hysterical as Ophelia? I thought he was, but to make such an argument at age seventeen is to risk teacherly censure, especially when just a year earlier Mr. Weir had caught me taking a roll of toilet paper out of the girls' bathroom because I had a bad cold. But he thought that I planned to t.p. the trees outside the school, which had been happening a lot that fall term.

College

The Ohio State University, Columbus, OH, Bachelor of Science Degree, May 1993

Major—Business: Concentrations in Finance and Management Organizational Behavior (I have no clear idea why I ended up majoring in these two disciplines. My temperament was probably better suited to a foreign language or an English literature degree, but from eighteen to twenty-one, it is very hard to know what you're truly interested in, aside from looking pretty, avoiding public disgrace, having sexual relations with people who might or might not hurt you [badly], and making friends with people who might or might not hurt you [badly] either.)

- *Fall and spring semesters, Freshman year, 1989–90*—Freud, Jung, and Poe: The id, the ego, the superego, the anima, the doppelgänger, the telltale heart. These were costumes some of us learned to dress up in at will. In tandem, we were trying on promiscuity, duplicity, scorn, madness (real or imagined), genius (real or imagined), self-destruction, alcoholism, Catholicism, individuality, Judaism, classism, racism. In many cases, during high school, we had already developed an early mastery of these disciplines, but if not, back then college allowed us the ideal breeding grounds for our lifelong obsessions and foibles. I also realized once and for all that I loathed my stepbrother (who is also the former classmate who stole small, valuable objects from neighbors), in part because when he came to visit me at The Ohio State University during his spring break from the tonier Colgate, he flashed my roommate and me, and when we both screamed, told us with a smirk to stop being such f**king prudes because it was just a joke and didn't we know that college was supposed to be about letting it all hang out, despite the fact we had chosen lifeless and backward Columbus, on the lame eastern fringes of the boring Middle West, as the location of our coming-of-age experiences? (The previous sentence is a paraphrase, but the general tenor and meaning of his tirade have been preserved.)
- *Spring semester, Sophomore year, 1990–91*—Even under penalty of tears and tantrums, do not agree to go if your roommate pleads with you to take part in a ghost-hunting expedition in downtown Columbus, not only because it is overpriced and a criminal waste of time, but also because you might, to your still-great disbelief, bring an actual ghost home with you. How this happened, we weren't sure, but in fact, it did happen. For the remaining seven weeks of the semester, the mirror over the sink in the corner of our

dorm room took on a cracked aspect after the hour of eleven P.M., and each morning when we awoke, we'd find our underwear had been herded into the back of my room-mate's closet, some of it disturbingly damp, as if worn by a profusely sweating girl-ghost. Were we being taught a lesson in the vanity of our ways? Some of the underwear was made from lace and worn solely with the intent of being flaunted before dumb boys who would not have cared if we were wearing underwear stitched from a potato sack, as long as it came off as easily as any other fabric did.

– *Fall semester, Senior year, 1992–93*—"The main reason why you should get a college education," Professor Randall Dixon said near the end of the semester in European History from 1900 to WWII, "which is the same reason why you should study history, is to learn humility."

A student with a Southern accent who had lived in my dorm freshman year raised her hand and said, "Isn't that also the main purpose of life? Aren't we supposed to learn to bow down to the government, to our bosses and husbands and police officers and politicians, from here on out?"

Professor Dixon blinked for several long seconds before answering. He smiled and shook his head. "Submission, humility, self-abnegation, self-immolation, suicide." He paused. "Not that I'm advocating anything but humility. Still, people have killed themselves for far less than bad govern-ment and a surfeit of murderous stupidity."

A few days later, Professor Dixon was reprimanded by his department chair for this minor blip of a political protest speech, after an aggrieved student filed a complaint. It had seemed to him that his professor was advocating suicide and was probably a nihilist or maybe even a Satanist. At the time, I was dating the self-righteous idiot who filed this complaint. His name was Mike Post and he ate chicken Kiev every

Thursday and fish sticks with mashed potatoes every Friday. He had a big p*n*s and, needless to say, a small brain and heart.

- *Spring semester, Senior year, 1992–93*—When my closest friend from home, Elizabeth Pelsen, came to visit over her spring break, which was one week before my spring break (half of which I had planned to spend at her college), I made the mistake of having relations with my boyfriend in the same room where Elizabeth was asleep, or had been asleep until our indelicate noises awoke her. I didn't know that she was in the room because I had been drinking my classmate Yasmina Pujoles's "Toxic Waste Dump Punch" and stayed later at Yasmina's birthday party than Elizabeth wanted us to, which meant that E. walked home alone, deciding as she walked the several blocks between the party and my apartment that she no longer wanted to have anything to do with me. I was a shallow, sometimes-bulimic, weekend lush who had developed an annoying laugh and a falsely breathless way of talking that she thought made me sound like a parodic Marilyn Monroe impersonator. At the time, I thought she was being prudish and mean, but after several years of calling her uncharitable names to a diminishing number of mutual friends, I finally realized that I had behaved like a self-absorbed idiot who was more interested in trying to please boys who would never really love me than maintaining the most meaningful friendship (so far) of my life.

CULTS

- *May 1995–July 1998*—Member, G. Don Dinkman's Church of the Divine Truth. Personal schism with church occurred when the suggested tithe went up by 18 percent overnight because of a roof problem that was the dipsh*t minister's own fault. He tried to create a refuge for bald eagles on top of the church by attempting to grow scrub and pine trees and installing a miniature lake and a 1/10,000-scale model of a mountain range meant to duplicate the Canadian Rockies, which cost more than a hundred thousand dollars and caused the aging roof to collapse just after a birthday party for Mr. Dinkman (who has been dead for a long time, but a party is still held in his honor by many ministers each year because Mr. Dinkman is the Divine Truth robots' own personal Jesus figure, but without the crucifixion and loaves-and-fishes stories—just the alien ancestors and millionaire adherents who are so easy to brainwash it might be hilarious if it weren't also so sad).

– *February 1996–present*—Member, Nicolas Cage Fan Club.* Despite a hairstyle that fluctuates between silly, seriously balding, and chic-retro-minimalist, Mr. Cage is a supreme thespian who is known for taking risks with the roles he has chosen to promulgate his genius in the world, *National Treasure* and *The Rock* notwithstanding. His early triumphs in *Valley Girl* and the tonally opposite but equally seductive *Wild at Heart* remain signal achievements in the Hollywood pantheon. The one time I was in the same place at the same time as Mr. Cage, he was chatting up an underage waitress and also seemed to be drinking a lot of sake, but he was kind enough to kiss my hand and then autograph my forearm when I introduced myself; he also winked at me with his swoon-inducing blue-green eyes.

---

*The Nic Cage Fan Club isn't, technically, a cult, but I recognize that devotion to a celebrity, especially one who isn't likely ever to befriend you, more or less does put you in the same realm as cult membership.

WORK EXPERIENCE

- *September 1991–May 1993*—**The Ohio State University Bookstore**, Columbus, OH
  * **Cashier.** Duties included ringing up purchases; making change; keeping the checkout area free of trash and general debris, along with loiterers, drunks, dogs of the non-seeing-eye variety, smokers, loudly laughing people, Christmas carolers, panhandlers, and trick-or-treaters.
  * Awarded Employee of the Month in April 1992, despite unfortunate clash with energetically sweating Hallmark vendor over stale chocolates the Kansas City–based company (which has since successfully diversified itself as a viable multimedia entity, though what it mainly sells is feel-good or tearjerker-type movie flotsam) had believed it could sell along with its puppy and kitten stickers and birthday and Boss's Day cards.
  * Won holiday brownie bake-off for all bookstore employees, December 1991. Never admitted that half of the brownie mix was taken from a Betty Crocker box. Other key ingredients included peanut butter, mini-marshmallows, walnuts, and Baileys Irish Cream. (Alcohol wasn't supposed to be used either.)
- *August 1993–November 1997*—**Dublin Animal Hospital**, Dublin, OH
  * **Receptionist/Bookkeeper.** Not really a job related to my college degree, but I did work with money and wrote out receipts for those who paid in full after their once-carefree animals had been worked into a terrified frenzy by the two veterinarians, a husband-and-wife team who often bickered in the back rooms (a place where they thought no one in the reception area would be able to hear them), usually about who had spent how much on what useless

object or who had been rude to or leered at the other's best friend, or, would Dr. Calvin ever stop stuffing his face at one in the morning and watching garbage TV until four A.M.? He was disgusting, just disgusting, nothing like the man Dr. Kimberly had met in vet school and fallen in love with and didn't he know it was such a sad joke that he thought their neighbor's teenage daughter looked at him with anything but revulsion?

— *November 1997–July 1998*—Dublin, OH

   * **Unemployed.** Minor nervous breakdown three months into unemployment stint, precipitated by two back-to-back incidents. The first: a hotel-room burglary that occurred during a weekend trip to New York City, where my plan was to see as many museums and off-Broadway plays as could be squeezed into two and a half days. Was very disappointed that I could not get tickets to see *Hamlet* with Ralph Fiennes, the British actor who, for years, along with Nicolas Cage, I had the strong sense I was destined to marry. Items lost included passport, grandmother's filigreed silver locket with picture of grandfather from boyhood, laptop with compromising photos on it taken by ex-boyfriend, six pairs of underwear (three of them unwashed—the thief must have been a pervert), one small jar of peanut butter, four sheets of flower stickers and pink writing paper, one green-marble calligraphy pen, one box of Ritz crackers, assorted toiletries including a big bottle of Anaïs Anaïs perfume, several tampons, one tube of Crest toothpaste (travel size), one contact case, one bottle of contact solution, one pair of toenail clippers, tweezers. The worst was that they also stole $142, money that I had borrowed from the ex-boyfriend, a guy who insisted that every cent be paid back whenever he lent me money, which he continued to do even after we broke up because he dumped me for someone else and his guilty conscience made it difficult for him to say no when I asked for a loan, but not so difficult to demand repayment. It took me three months to pay him back because of my unemployed status. I earned a small amount of money during that time by selling my CDs and my favorite clothes (**except** for the **Elite Prince T-shirt**) on consignment at Out of the Closet.

The second: A drugged-out nutcase accosted me at a U2 concert. It's painful for me to recount the circumstances in full, but here is a short summary: I had on a new dress, one that I bought on sale. It was Laundry and beautiful, the kind of dress you're sure will change your life. I realize that a U2 concert is not the ideal place to wear a marvelous new dress, but I couldn't wait. The druggie/nutcase grabbed me from behind, unzipped the dress all the way down, and tore it from my body in one violent motion, like someone pulling a curtain from a rod. I had on a bra and a pair of underwear that didn't match and there were holes in the underwear. I don't know why I didn't bother wearing a nicer pair, considering how spectacular the dress was. People all around me started shrieking and staring when they saw me standing there in my disgraceful bikini briefs. The nutcase took off through the crowd with the dress while I cried and tried to cover my appalling near-nakedness. My assailant was a woman, a large, sweaty one with pink and blue hair. I think we might have gone to high school together, but that seems improbable now, considering the concert was in Ohio and I went to high school in Massachusetts. A well-meaning insurance salesman eventually gave me his Cincinnati Reds sweatshirt, which I tearfully pulled on. He also gave me his address so that I could return the sweatshirt, which he said was his favorite. The one good thing about it was that it almost matched the red high heels I was wearing.

– *July 1998–February 2007*—**Best Buy**, Lincoln, NE

* **Cashier** (7/98–4/00), **Assistant Manager** (4/00–3/03), **Manager** (3/03–2/07). (How on earth did I end up in Lincoln, Nebraska? Please refer to <u>Disasters Averted or Otherwise</u>.) I think you could say, in view of my nine years' experience at this large chain-store hellhole, that I have paid my cosmic dues, whatever they might be. First, for twenty-one long months, I rang up Britney Spears and Garth Brooks and remaindered Yanni CDs, Doom video games, big-screen television sets, exorbitantly priced printer-ink cartridges (what an effing con those things are!), cell phones, car stereos, Pilates DVDs, and impulse-buy king-size Snickers bars. I called for price checks and for managers to deal with the irate, emotionally fragile customers who were almost apoplectic when the advertised sale price did not ring up for their CD Walkmen and jump drives and *Seinfeld*, season 1 DVDs. I learned so much about human nature that I am now as qualified as your favorite therapist to counsel the disenchanted, the lonely and distraught, the beaten-down, the oblivious, the bankrupt/shopping-addicted, the selfish, the foolish, and the otherwise scarred-by-life.

I was looking for a different job, one in consulting, human resources, accounting, hospitality industry, etc., while cashiering, but no one was hiring. At least not me.

Wearing the **Assistant Manager** crown was slightly better. I got a few days of paid vacation every year, marginal health insurance, slight respect from the nicer customers, and the scornful envy of my former peers (those cashiers who were deemed unpromotable).

Lessons learned or re-learned included, but were not limited to:

a) Elderly churchgoers are as likely to shoplift as meth-addicted teenagers.

b) No one has any respect for the break room's cleanliness, no matter their rank and salary; the same for the restrooms'.

c) A pregnant woman might actually be a creative thief with a picnic basket concealed beneath her blouse instead of a growing fetus, one she has filled to the brim with CDs and DVDs.

d) Supervisor's children are, as a rule, spawn of Satan (which I guess makes the supervisor Satan).

I was promoted to Manager of Entertainment Media (a pretentious name for music and movies) because of the kindness of the supervisor who had two young children who were known for torturing household pets and pilfering coins and small bills from their parents' and their aunts' and uncles' wallets. I fell hard for this supervisor, despite his tendency to do bad Adam Sandler impressions and compulsively eat powdered donuts that left a fine sugar dust on his goatee. Needless to say, this seminal love affair did not end the way I hoped it would, and I soon left Best Buy for my next employer (details immediately below). I couldn't bear to look at the supervisor any longer because I kept imagining him in the throes of orgasm, which made me feel maudlin on some days, horny on others. This faithless, donut-addicted man is, as far as I know, still married to his chronically unpleasant wife, and likely will spend the rest of his life bailing his ingrate children out of one scrape after another, some of these scrapes financial, some of them personal and sordid, a few of them, most likely, also criminal.

- *March 2007–December 2009*—**Dogs in Suds**, Winfield, NE
* **Manager/Dog Groomer.** It is an open secret that once a dog falls for you, she will love you unconditionally until her death (provided you don't mistreat her—a crime that would earn you a place in hell with the rapists and serial killers, I'm absolutely certain). I loved this job and the only reason it ended in December of 2009 was because we went out of business. We had a problem with a combative German shepherd–spitz mix attacking an aging, asthmatic poodle that died the next day—whether from its wounds or an asthma attack, I've never been certain. Word of this catastrophe, in any case, traveled in a predictable trajectory: bad news flies/ricochets/exists in an eternal vacuum, ready to resurface at any time, whereas this dog beauty parlor of the first order had previously enjoyed a flawless reputation—ten years of solid business practices and solvency with devoted clients, its owner (Millicent Hart) the founder and annual sponsor of the Doggy Day Parade down Cherry Street and a generous donor to local animal shelters, where we went twice a year to give bubble and flea baths to the canine inmates, providing each grateful dog with his/her very own flea collar.

One of the few things I didn't like about this job was some of the dog owners: wealthy sourpusses who voted for the wrong candidates in every election and proudly affixed these gasbag candidates' bumper stickers to their SUVs' rear ends. And, not like there's anything wrong with plastic surgery (if you can afford it), but just because you have a snub nose and huge tits doesn't make you God's Gift to the Universe, Elisha H.!

Since Dogs in Suds went out of business, I have been temping for **Crème of the Crop**, doing secretarial work for ConAgra, mostly. I've found that after nearly two years of grooming and bathing dogs, cute as they are, it's nice to see men in pressed shirts again. Some of these professional guys smell of onions, others of talcum powder; some compulsively check their cell phones for texts (from mistresses?); one or two unaccountably have tears in their eyes when they think no one is looking. I want to take these sad, well-groomed men into my arms and offer them solace but am not sure how such a gesture would be interpreted.

IRRATIONAL FEARS

* Cobras (with hoods unfurled to their full glory even typing this makes me feel sweaty and light-headed)
* Seagull attacks
* Being killed with piano wire (a type of grisly choking death often used in violent movies, especially those of the '80s and '90s)
* Decapitation by a helicopter blade that flies off of a traffic helicopter and goes scissoring through the air to find me as I walk to the library or to the convenience store for chocolate
* The one week I don't play Mega Millions, my numbers are chosen (therefore, I always play)

SEMI-RATIONAL FEARS

* Rape
* Poverty
* Car crashes
* Food poisoning (especially in burrito huts, McDonald's, and roadside bratwurst stands in small Wisconsin

towns, including the one where my maternal grand-
mother lives)
* Identity theft
* Rabid squirrels, skunks, opossums, dogs, porcupines,
  armadillos, bats, cats, raccoons, mice, rats, shrews,
  chipmunks, ferrets, cows, sheep, bulls, llamas
* My parents' deaths
* My friends' deaths
* Dying alone and childless, incontinent, senile, and
  unloved
* Decapitation by the eighteenth-century guillotine on
  display in the Weapons of War and Instruments of
  Torture Museum in the Wisconsin town where my
  maternal grandmother lives (near the questionable
  bratwurst stands). The guillotine blade has, on two
  separate occasions, fallen down with a terrifying,
  vengeful *whhaapp!* while alarmed visitors looked on.
  The docent pleaded innocent to this mischief but could
  not stop laughing at the looks on her tour group's faces.

DISASTERS AVERTED OR OTHERWISE

– *Early August 1991*—**Motorcycle ride** with P.J. Wilczek,
  sophomore-year college crush. P.J. hit a dead opossum in the
  road, slammed on the brakes, and sent us both flying into
  a drainage ditch. I was wearing jeans, a leather jacket, and a
  helmet, and was all right, aside from about five hundred
  bruises and a chipped tooth; P.J. was wearing a helmet too
  but had on shorts and a T-shirt. Needless to say, his arms and
  legs and back looked like someone had gone after him with a
  cheese grater, but his brains were still intact. So to speak.
– *May 1993*—**Move to Los Angeles** to try to break into the
  movie business contemplated then decided against.

- *May 1993*—**Move to New York City** to try to break into Broadway musicals contemplated then decided against.
- *May 1993–April 1998*—**Minor disasters:**
  a) an adoption of a feral (?) cat (the shelter worker didn't mention how numerous and scary this cat's problems were; the cat was returned and probably, sad to say, sent into the next life in short order)
  b) feather instead of foam pillows at a B&B in Wheeling, West Virginia
  c) a collision with a deer while riding in Rich Dolzer's Ford Fiesta after a pool party while visiting college friends in Indianapolis
  d) the theft of my purse at a Dublin, OH, strip mall (but **overall**, these five years were fairly tranquil)

  April 1998—**Engagement** to Jesse Cates called off in favor of a relationship with Mitchell Cates (Jesse's cousin), which resulted in Mitch's and my abrupt departure for Lincoln, Nebraska, where Mitch had lined up a job at the University of Nebraska's Bursar's Office.
- *December 1998*—**Mitch dumps me for idiot** named Courtney Foster, who has big boobs, a fat ass, and a snorting laugh that for several years appeared in my nightmares. Her dad is loaded and she doesn't have to work, so she doesn't. When I knew her, she used to go around saying, "The world isn't as bad a place as some people who write for big-time newspapers would like us to think." Also, "New York City is the root of all evil." But instead of saying "root," she said it "rout," as in, "That army routed its enemies."

* Fast-forward to near-death experience:
- *March 2010*—**A road trip** to Arches National Park and the Grand Canyon with my friend Jane Garcia, who worked

with me at Dogs in Suds. We were parked at an overlook at Arches when a carload of teenagers wearing T-shirts with the names of pro-football teams on them showed up and dumped an ashtray of butts out the window next to our car. I was in a **rotten mood** because my stepbrother had just texted me to say that he needed to borrow three hundred dollars again (for some reeking dive's video poker machines, probably, or else to give to his **lame-ass girlfriend** who has cheated on him with at least two different guys). I picked up a handful of the discarded butts, some of them soggy, and threw them at the windshield of the teenagers' car, yelling, more or less, "Go eff yourselves. This is a national park. Can't you show some effing decency for once in your worthless lives?"

This did not go over well. Jane was still in the car, and she rolled up the windows and locked the doors, not realizing, I don't think, that I couldn't get back in now. Two of the teenagers, **miscreants** who looked like they each weighed twice as much as I did, picked me up like a suitcase (their friends drunk and laughing and shouting behind us) and carried me to the edge of the overlook, threatening to pitch me down the billion-year-old rock bed to my **probable death**. I looked down toward my last moments and said, I'm not sure why, "If you let me live, I promise never to tell another lie." They laughed like I was insane but stepped back from the ledge. They took me back to my car, dropped me on my knees hard, and said, "Get the f**k out of our faces, you crazy-a** b*tch!"

Needless to say, my vow not to tell any more lies led me to my idea that a cover letter and résumé shouldn't contain any lies either. Hence this **revolutionary** (?) job application that you hold in your hands (or else are reading on your computer screen).

HOBBIES

Books—I am not a devoted fan of any books about vampires, wizards, baseball, zombies, or ones that involve people transformed into insects, giant bananas, or VW Beetles upon waking.

- I greatly admire *Lolita* because I think V. Nabokov was a genius, if not also a bit of a pervert, but I think we all have a pervert strain in us, whether we like it or not.

Movies—*Leaving Las Vegas* (for which Mr. Cage won the Best Actor Oscar!), *Wild at Heart, Valley Girl, Bad Lieutenant: Port of Call New Orleans*

- *The English Patient* (for which Mr. Fiennes should have won the Best Actor Oscar!)
- *Monsters, Inc.* (This remains the best kids' movie around, even better than *Old Yeller*, and of course much different.)
- *Butch Cassidy and the Sundance Kid* (Paul Newman was originally considered for the role of Sundance. How our history would have been different if he had been cast as the sidekick instead of the man with all the [sometimes wrong] answers!)
- *The Graduate* (Every woman, after a certain age, has a bit of Mrs. Robinson in her.)

Music—Nothing country, please. Instead:

- Anything by Prince, pre-1993: e.g., *Purple Rain, Parade, Around the World in a Day, 1999, Controversy, Dirty Mind, For You, Prince*

- David Bowie (pronounced *Bo-ee*, not *Bow-ee*, as in bowwow)—*Let's Dance, Tonight*
- Duran Duran's *Greatest Hits*
- Peter Gabriel's perfect *So*
- Rick Springfield's *Success Hasn't Spoiled Me Yet* ("Jessie's Girl" is just fine, but who could forget the barely contained jealousy of "Don't Talk to Strangers"?)

You probably have noticed a pattern here. The '80s were a musically rich and diverse period, if not the most morally exemplary time in our country's history.

References Generally Available Upon Request

ADDENDUM

If offered the opportunity and the great privilege of working for Elite Industries, I would humbly request permission to redraft some of the more humdrum interview questions so many employers rely on—e.g., "Where do you see yourself in five years?" "What would you say your greatest weakness is?" "How well do you work without supervision?"—and instead ask future job applicants some or all of the following questions:

1. If you found a wallet that contained a few hundred dollars in cash and the driver's license inside revealed that the wallet belonged to a former mean-spirited neighbor who had ruthlessly clashed with you and/ or your family for years, would you return the wallet? Yes or no, please explain your rationale.
2. If you witnessed a co-worker you like and respect doing something illegal outside of the workplace,

such as shoplifting candy bars, or mistreating a small, defenseless animal (e.g., a declawed cat or a hamster), what would you do?

3. The same scenario as above but the co-worker is one you do not like and respect.

4. Do you listen to country music? Yes or no, please explain.

5. If reincarnation were real and you had to choose to return in your next life as one of the following, which would it be and why?

a) a lion   d) a flying squirrel
b) a Ferrari   e) Tennessee Williams
c) a glacier   f) a cockroach

6. Free-Association Exercise
What thought first comes to mind after you hear each of the following words?

a) construction zone   c) spendthrift
b) wig   d) prostate

7. Have you ever wanted to marry one of our presidents, congresspeople, or senators? Yes or no, please explain.

8. Have you ever wanted to assassinate one of our presidents, congresspeople, or senators? Yes or no, again, please explain.

9. If you had to watch one of the following movies every Sunday, which would you choose?

a) *Wayne's World*   d) *A Clockwork Orange*
b) *Smokey and the Bandit*   e) *Dirty Dancing*
c) *My Dinner with André*   f) *Weekend at Bernie's*

10. Which life do you believe has more value: a wolf's or a mosquito's? Please explain your rationale.

THE VIRGINITY OF
FAMOUS MEN

RAIN WAS FALLING FOR the fifth day in a row, the city layered with baggy, newsprint-gray clouds, the birds silent and chastened in their nests. Water poured or dripped from every awning and overhang onto the heads of sullen passersby.

The eighth-arrondissement apartment Will and his girl-friend Jorie had moved into the previous month, a three-bedroom on the fourth floor of a Haussmann-era building, overlooked the rose-filled Square Marcel Pagnol. Their place was advertised as a luxury property and the owner charged an exorbitant rent; Will paid for three months up front in order to beat out two other applicants for the same apartment. Jorie had assumed from the beginning that this prepayment was a greedy landlord's ruse, and Will did now too: as often as not, the elevator was out of order, and their unit had leaky windows, a flaw they discovered two and a half weeks after moving in. When it rained heavily, rivulets streamed down the interior panes and pooled on the ledges. Jorie had called the concierge, Madame Reiss, twice to complain, but a handyman had yet to appear.

She wondered if Madame Reiss was punishing her because of her dog, a Chihuahua named Coquelicot. No pets except for fish and small caged birds were permitted in the building, but the concierge had made a grudging exception for her and Will. If there were complaints from other tenants about barking, Coquelicot would have to go *tout de suite!* Madame Reiss sternly informed them, her dark eyebrows arching theatrically. They'd also paid an extra thousand-euro deposit for damages the dog might inflict on the baseboards and varnished hardwood floors.

Coquelicot had so far been a blameless tenant. She was eleven, with an arthritic hip, and when she wasn't being fed or walked or ferried about the city in a scuffed brown-leather shoulder bag by her mistress, she spent much of her time sleeping on a plush vermilion bed that in the winter months Jorie kept by the iron feet of a hissing radiator.

On the fifth and ultimately final day of rain, Will's father flew in for a long weekend from Toronto during a break in the shooting of *Occam's Razor*, a film he was directing and starring in ("If Clint can do it, I don't see why I can't too," said Renn). When he met Jorie and her dog for the first time, he joked that the Chihuahua might be Gloria Swanson reincarnated. "Those eerie eyes," he said. "I'm ready for my close-up, Mr. DeMille."

"Dad," said Will. "That's—" He wasn't sure what he was going to say. Cruel? He bit back the word.

"What?" His father laughed and glanced from Will to his girlfriend. "Don't you think the dog looks a little like Gloria Swanson?"

Jorie smiled fondly, her gaze on Coquelicot's tiny head and voluminous ears. The dog was pretending to doze on her mistress's lap, her protuberant eyes opening a fraction before drifting closed again. "What do you think about that, Poppy?" Jorie asked.

"Poppy?" asked Renn.

"*Coquelicot* is the French word for 'poppy,'" said Will.

"The dog answers to both?"

"She does," said Jorie. "She's very smart, Mr. Ivins."

"A bilingual dog," he said, amused. "Of course. Please call me Renn, Jorie. Only the police call me Mr. Ivins." He laughed again.

The dog opened her eyes all the way and peered up at him worriedly, her ears fully alert.

"I'll try," said Jorie. With one hand, she lightly stroked the smooth fur of Coquelicot's back. They were in the brightest room in the apartment, a salon with south-facing windows, sheer curtains tied back. On the coffee table next to the leather sofa where Will sat with Jorie, Renn in an adjacent armchair, their breakfast dishes were scattered with crumbs from the pastries they'd eaten with orange juice and cups of coffee.

Will watched his father hold Jorie's gaze until she looked away. Ordinarily, his girlfriend wasn't shy with strangers, and she already had some familiarity with celebrity. An aunt on her mother's side was the first-chair violin for the New York Philharmonic, and she had a cousin who acted in a popular police procedural on one of the networks, but Will's father was many times more well known than the aunt and the cousin put together.

Will had met Jorie in a French class for foreigners that he'd enrolled in not long after moving from L.A. to Paris, desperate to flee the long shadow his father cast over his and his younger sister Anna's lives. Jorie had remained amiable but aloof for a while, not pursuing his friendship the way the other students in the class did. She sometimes joined the group of four or five who invited Will to have drinks or dinner with them after class meetings, but he had to ask her out four times before she consented to having dinner with him alone.

He hadn't seen his father in more than a year and a half, and it was only in the last month that he'd started returning Renn's phone calls. Will's mother had played the peacemaker on her ex-husband's behalf, even though Lucy had also been offended by Renn's relationship with Danielle, a woman Will dated before moving to Paris. Danielle was no longer living with Renn, though it wasn't clear whether they were still seeing each other. Will hadn't spoken to Danielle in nearly two years, and he hadn't asked his father if they'd broken up for good.

When they finally did talk, Renn apologized about Danielle, but he didn't mention a second woman, Elise Connor, whom both he and Will were in love with when Will moved to France. It was Danielle who broke up with Will when his crush on Elise came to light the previous autumn. Despite their acrimonious breakup, Will didn't think it absolved Danielle and his father of their own eventual pairing-off.

In the end, Elise hadn't chosen Renn or Will. When she broke off her engagement with Renn, Will was hopeful that she would come to Paris to see him, but she didn't, and soon after, his father took up with Danielle and asked her to move in with him. If this was meant to be his punishment for competing for Elise, Will supposed that on some level he deserved it, but he hadn't admitted this to his father or anyone else. Instead, he'd quietly passed the time in Paris, fallen in love with Jorie, and occupied himself with screenwriting and seeing films he'd never seen at home in L.A.—*Taxi Driver, The Deer Hunter, Kramer vs. Kramer, Apocalypse Now, Two-Lane Blacktop, Five Easy Pieces*—despite having met some of their stars through his father.

By leaving L.A., he soon realized that he had stepped into a beautiful dream. Something that he knew some people assumed he'd always been living, but it was only now in Paris that this became true.

"Where do you two want to go to dinner?" asked Renn. "Do you have a favorite place? Or should I call a friend who I think could get us a table at Taillevent?"

Jorie stared at him. "Your friend could get us a table there on such short notice? I know you're a—" She stopped herself and looked helplessly at Will.

Renn nodded. "Yes, I think she could. Is that where you'd like to go?"

"Not tonight, Dad," said Will. "I'm sure you're tired from the flight anyway."

"Not at all," said Renn. "I slept the whole way here."

"You can do that?" asked Jorie. "That's amazing." She laughed.

"I'll call my friend at Taillevent then."

"Yes, please, that'd be great," she said.

"Dad, no. Not tonight," said Will, not looking at Jorie. "Let's do something a little more low-key, okay?" He hadn't known that Jorie wanted to go to Taillevent, France's most celebrated restaurant. If he had, he would have already taken her there himself. He was supposed to think of this sort of extravagant gesture on his own, he realized, embarrassed. To his father, of course, this kind of thing was second nature.

"What if instead I flew us all down to Aix-en-Provence?" asked Renn. "I have another friend who keeps inviting me to his cottage." He gave Will a wry look. "That's what Bob calls it, but I'm sure it's more like a château. We could stay down there tonight and fly back tomorrow, or else on Monday morning if we decide we'd like to stay an extra day."

Jorie again looked at Will, her expression at once bemused and avid. Of course she wanted to do whatever his father wanted to. Will could feel his head starting to throb. Every woman he'd ever met had always abruptly fallen for his father's charm and enthusiasm for the present moment, for his insistence on wooing every pretty girl he met with his bullying, jaw-dropping generosity.

"Dad," said Will, keeping his voice level. "Can we just stay in Paris? You're here for what, two, three nights? We can go to Septime for dinner and to Le Siffleur de Ballons for a drink afterward. They're both over by the Bastille, so we'll need to cab it, but I'm sure you'll like them."

"They're both very good," said Jorie. Will thought he heard a note of disappointment in her tone, but he ignored it. His father was supposed to be their guest. It was he who had flown in to see them. Almost a whole year and a half without speaking to each other and Renn was acting as if nothing was awry, as if Elise and Danielle did not lie between them like a dangerous chasm.

"I'll have my car service take us to the restaurant. Seven thirty, eight o'clock? No need to mess with cabs."

"Eight sounds fine," said Will, glancing at Jorie. She nodded.

"But if you change your mind about Aix or Taillevent, we could go for it," said Renn.

Will shook his head. "Let's just go to Septime and Siffleur. You'll like them."

"What are you doing this afternoon, Renn?" asked Jorie. It was almost noon, Renn having arrived at their door at ten thirty, straight from the airport, bearing gifts: a bag of fragrant croissants, two plain, two with marzipan filling, and two dozen yellow and pink roses, which he presented to Jorie, who was both flustered and dazzled, clutching the flowers to her chest, exclaiming, *Oh, my, this is—my goodness—*. The croissants he'd handed to Will, who had so far eaten only a banana, even though he'd gotten out of bed at six thirty to run seven miles in the rainy gloom. The run had helped to relax him before the storm of his father's arrival. He hadn't felt ready to see Renn, but he knew that he couldn't keep saying no. His father would probably have appeared eventually, invited or not. Will preferred a scheduled visit to an ambush.

"I thought I'd take you both shopping," said Renn. "Unless there's something else you'd like to do."

"Shopping?" asked Will, wary. "We don't need anything, Dad."

"How about a new sofa? Or some new dishes? Maybe you need a new bed—whatever you guys think."

"The sofa's only a year old," said Will. "It's fine. Our bed's fine too. We really don't need anything." He could feel his mouth going dry. He had plenty of money, but it came from the trust fund his father had set up for him when he was still a child. Neither he nor Anna ever needed to work, but Anna had been working without interruption since high school; she was now in her first year as a resident in internal medicine at Cedars-Sinai. Will, at present, was relying on his father's money, but he hoped to start filming one of his screenplays in the next year or two, after he found investors to help finance its production. He wanted to shoot his film in Paris, where most of it was set. It was autobiographical, and his father, Will suspected, would not like how he was portrayed. Everyone's names, ages, and professions had been changed, but Will was sure that his parents and sister would recognize themselves.

Jorie did not think that he was unkind to any of them though, only honest. The story made her sad, she said. His father's absences and egotism, his mother's anger and disappointment over her marriage's dissolution, his sister's half-blind love for Renn. Will thought that Anna had almost always been too easy on their father while they were growing up, either excusing or pretending not to notice his self-absorption.

What was his father's agenda, Will wondered, making this too-intimate offer to buy him and Jorie a new bed? Before he lost his nerve, Will asked him.

A tremor of unease passed over Renn's face when he heard the question, but his reply was casual. "The beds I remember sleeping in during my first couple of trips to Europe were sometimes very lumpy. And the pillows—Jesus, the log-like ones probably would have damaged my neck and spine forever if I hadn't slept on a balled-up sweatshirt instead." He paused, glancing at his watch, the platinum Cartier Lucy had given him after his first Oscar nomination. The time-check was a habit he'd had for as long as Will could remember. "I just thought you might need a new bed. Aren't a lot of Parisian apartments furnished when you rent them?"

"This one wasn't," said Will. "I brought the bed with me from our last place. I bought it new. It's a good one."

"It is," Jorie agreed. She reddened and looked down again at her dog. Coquelicot's ears were upright and alert but her Gloria Swanson eyes were closed.

"Let's go to the Musée d'Orsay or the Musée Rodin," said Will. "It's clearing up, and it'd be good to be outside with all the other tourists." He forced a laugh, which Jorie and his father ignored.

"All right, art it is," said Renn. "I'll go over to the Georges V and check in. Should I meet you at the Musée Rodin around one? If we feel like it, we could make our way to the Musée d'Orsay afterward and stop in some of the antique shops over that way."

"You really aren't jet-lagged?" asked Jorie, still shy. Her hand fluttered to her thick dark hair, freshly washed. She had grown it out in the last year, Will having told her once, early on, that he loved long hair, predictable as it was for a man to prefer it to boyish short hair. It fell past her shoulders now; he was touched when she'd started to let it grow. And for her, he had begun wearing brighter colors more often—greens, violets, and reds, rather than his habitual glum browns, blues, and grays.

Will could see something shift in his father's face, some decision being made about Jorie, that she was as susceptible as anybody to his charm.

"I feel great," said Renn, grinning. His whitened teeth glowed, a coded message from the alien land he belonged to.

"You're tough," said Jorie. "Every time I've flown here from the States, I've been ready to drop as soon as I get through customs."

"Dad, why don't you get going so that we can meet at the museum at once?" said Will. "I have a few things to do before we go too."

"Kicking me out already?" asked Renn. He smiled at Jorie and shook his head.

"Yes, but you'll live," said Will. "We'll see you at one at the Musée Rodin."

"Do you let him treat you like this too?" Renn asked, still looking at Jorie.

"Oh no, I'm the one who treats him like that," she said, laughing and turning to Will with a droll smile.

Renn hugged Will on his way out, his cologne the same one he'd been wearing for years—a scent blended for him specially by a parfumerie in Provence, its top notes sandalwood and cinnamon. The perfume was his father, in the same way that during Renn's long, oppressive absences in Will's childhood, a pair of his left-behind shoes or a scrap of paper with a note he'd scrawled that contained some request or directive was. The scent brought momentary tears to Will's eyes.

When Renn turned to Jorie and took her into his arms, a delighted titter escaped her as he pulled away, his day-old beard catching on a few strands of her licorice-black hair. He said good-bye and disappeared down the hall, in the direction of the faulty elevator.

For a few moments after Will closed the door behind his father, the apartment felt bereft. The shafts of sunlight knifing through the southern windows, the first glimpse of the sun they'd had in nearly a week, seemed to fall on nothing. Previously, each room had seemed happily, even blissfully, inhabited. Over the many months he'd lived in Paris, Will had collected a few pieces of furniture he expected to keep forever: a handmade cherry dining room table—an acquisition that his father had complimented him on, his large hand caressing its smooth surface; there was also a Danish chestnut-brown leather sofa and matching armchairs in the salon where they'd eaten their croissants. Thick, dyed wool throw rugs adorned the floors in the hallway and salon, and in the bedrooms were rugs that Jorie had chosen the previous August from the furniture department at Galeries Lafayette for the elegant but cramped one-bedroom they first lived in together across the Seine in the seventh arrondissement, their street cobblestoned, a bakery on one side of their four-story building, and a stationer specializing in the implements of Japanese calligraphy on the other.

She turned to Will with a guarded look. "He's nice," she said. "Nicer than I expected."

"He is nice," Will agreed. He would not let himself turn jealous and dour. He had her and he had his screenplays—his work, the whole point of his life, he believed, at last revealing itself to him after he'd moved to Paris.

And one thing, barring tragedy, that he had more of than his father did was time. Renn was in his mid-fifties, Will only in his late twenties. He could imagine, even feel, what was ahead—he would catch up to his father. It wasn't so much that he intended to replace him, but his own name would begin to matter at some point in the approaching future; people would know that he was someone other than a famous man's son. Hadn't this happened, in any case, for men like Michael Douglas and Jean Renoir?

Anna thought it was all so Oedipal and depressing—why did Will persist in comparing himself with their father? Why did he continue to see himself as a victim of Renn's successes? But Anna, in Will's opinion, was more driven and focused than he was—like their mother, she had been interested in medicine from an early age, and directly after college had enrolled in UCLA's medical school and graduated with honors.

"I can see what you mean, though," said Jorie. "He sucks up a lot of the oxygen in the room, doesn't he."

Will nodded. "Yes. He needs a lot to keep the party going."

"I don't think I'd want to be him."

"No, but he'd certainly rather be who he is than someone else."

"Don't you feel the same way about yourself?" she asked.

"Yes, I do, I guess." He picked up Coquelicot from where she was loitering near Jorie's feet. The dog stared at him, glassy eyed, before turning her head to look imploringly at her mistress. Jorie stood before the open refrigerator, the light making her fair skin glow. She wore a short khaki skirt and a flattering black V-neck blouse, and she'd been careful with her makeup that morning too. When he'd complimented her before Renn's arrival, Jorie demurred and said that she'd done the same things she did every morning.

"You and your father look a lot alike," she said now, taking out the water pitcher and closing the refrigerator door with enough force to startle Coquelicot. The dog squirmed in Will's arms.

"I didn't realize how much until I saw you side by side," she added.

"I thought you've always thought we looked alike."

She shook her head. "What I said was that I could see a resemblance, but today was the first time I could see it so clearly."

"Oh," he said.

"Don't sound so disappointed," she teased. "I thought you wanted to be your own man."

"I am," he said. "But my dad's a good-looking guy. I don't mind if we look alike."

Jorie laughed. "You're both beautiful."

"Oh, come on. Don't say that."

She was pouring out two glasses of water; she frequently berated him for not drinking enough of it. She set the pitcher down and looked at him. "You don't need to be coy. You know you're very handsome."

That wasn't what he meant, but he said nothing. He petted Coquelicot's soft head for another second before setting her back on the floor, her twiggy legs briefly shaking before she found her footing. He took the glass of water Jorie had poured for him, thinking that he should kiss her, but he didn't.

"I'm going to work at my desk for a little while," he said.

"All right," she said, turning back to the sink. "I've got some work to do too."

He went down the hall to the room with his writing desk and for several minutes stood before the window that overlooked the courtyard. Madame Reiss was down there, arms akimbo, dressed in a knee-length mouse-gray skirt and light-blue blouse, monitoring the portly, redheaded gardener, Serge, who had what looked like an unlit cigar clamped between his teeth. With a small watering can, he was giving what Will assumed was fertilizer to the potted fruit trees and geraniums lined up along the passageway that led to the street. They had likely received more than enough rainwater in the last five days.

The clouds had almost entirely dispersed, the sky now an arresting blue. In the streets that bordered their building, Will could hear the growl of motorcycles and the car horns of harried drivers. About a mile away was the Champs-Élysées and the weathered monuments built to commemorate the country's imperial forays, its wars and colonizing incursions. Or, as Jorie had once said, its burning and pillaging of faraway places and people.

He sat down to check his email, tuning his radio to a rock station that played more American music than French. Jorie passed by in the hall, speaking softly to Coquelicot.

Dad's here now. Everything's fine, he wrote in reply to an email his mother had sent in the night while he was sleeping fitfully, assailed by doubts about his father's visit. Jorie, however, had been completely submerged, as usual. He envied her seemingly effortless ability to fall quickly and deeply asleep. She was the cherished youngest child of a close-knit family of five; she rarely ever complained about her parents or older siblings. She loved her work too, freelance graphic design, which she did from the apartment in her own study. Her three steady clients were a Canadian medical supply company, an American fitness chain, and a coffee-roasting business based in Berkeley; they paid her well, and she had time to do whatever she and Will felt like doing in the evenings; many of her afternoons were free too. She was a year younger than he and, as often as not, in a lighthearted, teasing mood. He was still in awe of her.

Lucy had visited them a few months earlier with Michael, her new husband. He was a friend from college Lucy hadn't seen in close to thirty years when their paths crossed at a breakfast place on Colorado Boulevard in Pasadena one morning before she was due at the clinic where she practiced pediatric medicine four days a week. Will and Anna both liked Michael, who was funny and kind, this kindness deployed equally in his treatment of the people he loved and with strangers—poorly skilled waiters, people who accidentally stepped on his heels, store clerks who scowled at his awful French. He'd known Renn in college too, and like Lucy, he wasn't cowed by or overly envious of Renn's fame.

Dad's staying until Monday, then straight back to Toronto, I think. It's good that Jorie's here. She likes to talk. So does he, needless to say. You know that I'm not always so good at it.

I'll keep you posted. Hope you and Michael are doing well. Anna told me that she saw you two for dinner a couple of nights ago. I'm glad she's not seeing that Glass guy anymore. He was such a jerk to her. I know she's still pretty cut up about him though.

Let's hope she's on to someone better very soon.

Love, Will

When he and Jorie met Renn at the Musée Rodin, *The Thinker* glamorous and striking in its muscular familiarity as they rounded the garden path near the entrance, Jorie's compliment from earlier was still on Will's mind. He knew that it shouldn't matter if his girlfriend thought his father was a beautiful man, but her words bothered him, and he almost let out a harsh bark of laughter when the woman selling tickets at the museum's interior entrance recognized Renn and waved the three of them through, hardly glancing at Will and Jorie. "*Monsieur Ivins, bienvenue.* How nice of you to come to see Monsieur Rodin's art. Please let us know if there is anything you will need during your visit."

"Thank you. That's very nice of you," said Renn, smiling at the woman; her long brown hair, penciled eyebrows, and red lips were dramatic, but she wasn't pretty. He was always gracious, despite how often he'd experienced the same scenario. Will knew that this graciousness was one reason for his father's success—fans did not race to their blogs to publish acidic gripes about his father's refusal to sign an autograph for their paraplegic daughter or cancer-ridden brother because he was late for an appointment with his psychic or personal trainer.

"Let's go out to the gardens," said Jorie. "It's turned into such a gorgeous day." She looked at up Renn, smiling. "You must have brought the good weather with you."

Will could feel people looking sidelong at his father as they walked the path bordering the sprawling back gardens where sculptures stood on pedestals situated among the trees, but no one approached them, and Renn pretended not to notice that he was being noticed. Since moving to Paris, Will had observed that Europeans were generally more polite than Americans, but he knew it was inevitable that someone would eventually approach them, asking to shake his father's hand, asking for a photo and an autograph.

It wasn't until they were inside the museum again, in the room with the famous kissing couple, that someone did. Jorie looked on, amused, as a middle-aged Australian couple, the woman taller than her bearded companion, both dressed in shorts and T-shirts, his T-shirt a plain blue, hers black with the Eiffel Tower in silver sequins on the front. "Is this your favorite Rodin sculpture?" she asked Renn, her words emerging in a nervous rush, her face and neck turning pink as she spoke.

Will turned and fled the room. He heard his father pause and stare after him, his reply to the Australian woman spoken to Will's retreating back. "That's my son," he heard Renn say. "He's very serious about art."

He and the woman laughed. Will could feel his own face burning now.

The woman's reply was inaudible but her tone conciliatory. He was embarrassed to have descended so quickly into a fit of pique, and after a minute or two passed, he went back to join them, but Jorie and Renn were no longer in the gallery. Only the Australian couple remained, pretending to inspect *The Kiss*.

This time it was the man who spoke as Will passed them. "We're sorry that we interrupted you and your father," he said, contrite. His friendly face was more lined and sun-chapped than Will had previously noticed. Was he the tall woman's father rather than her husband?

"No, no, you didn't," said Will. "I just wanted to see what was in the next room."

The man apologized again, unconvinced. "Your father and his girlfriend went that way," he added. He pointed with a blunt, freckled finger toward the south gardens.

Will nodded, suppressing a sudden flare of confused panic.

The Australian opened his mouth, but then thought better of it. The woman hovered behind him, contrition also on her face. Will could easily picture them returning to the unimaginable town where they lived, telling their friends about how unpretentious, how charming, Renn Ivins was, but his son? What a surly git.

Outside a flock of starlings circled the garden before heading west. The air was more humid and warm than when they'd arrived; it felt to Will as if it were withholding damaging secrets. He spotted Jorie and his father immediately. They stood right in front of him, at the base of the steps leading down to the garden, laughing with three new strangers. Renn's hand was on Jorie's shoulder, her animated face filled with the pleasure of his attention—this man whose films, she'd sworn to Will, had never unduly impressed her, except for *The Zookeeper*, the first film Renn had directed. The one that had won him all the Oscars, *Bourbon at Dusk*, she'd found too manipulative. "Pure melodrama," she'd told Will, and until now he'd believed that she meant it.

He didn't know why he needed her bad opinion of his father. He had many other things to think about; his screenplay about his family was good, possibly very good. Jorie had read it and loved it, and so had Luca, Will's most trusted friend. Luca was lazy but also smart; he'd studied film in college and did not hand out undeserving praise.

And Renn, it seemed, was trying to be magnanimous. He had so far decided not to open the still-healing wound of his and Will's rivalry over Elise Connor. According to Lucy, his father was sincere about making amends with him. Their relationship would not recover, his mother worried, and apparently Renn worried too, if he and Will didn't try now, with real purpose, to reconcile their differences. A year and a half of not talking to each other—that was much too long. It could turn into another year and a half, and another after that. She knew how these things went.

Will walked down the steps to join Jorie and his father and the three strangers, two teenage boys with an athletic blonde woman who looked too young to be their mother. They all turned to watch him approach, five pairs of curious eyes. He had to look away.

With an accent Will didn't recognize, the woman exclaimed, "You are his son, yes? This is a most wonderful moment in our lives to meet you and your brilliant father." She thrust a hand with three ornate silver rings at him, and when he took it, she stood staring at him with adoration. "How wonderful you both are," she murmured.

He glanced at Jorie and found her smiling back at him, irony insinuating itself into her expression.

"Thank you," said Will, bowing his head to the blonde woman.

After a long second, she released his hand and turned back to Renn. "Will you sign my notebook for me?" she asked, unzipping a black messenger bag looped crosswise over her chest. A silver chain with a dolphin pendant glittered at the base of her throat.

"Yes, with pleasure, Mimi," he said. He glanced at the boys, red Dr. Dre headphones cuffed around the neck of the taller boy, his brown hair gathered into a stubby ponytail. The other boy pretended to be uninterested, but he kept stealing looks at Renn; Will guessed that the boy had seen most of his father's movies—the one he'd starred in instead of directed—and some more than once.

Will met Jorie's eyes again. *Mimi*, she mouthed, winking at him.

When they were back on the garden's perimeter path, Mimi and the two boys having disappeared into the house, Jorie grabbed Will's hand and pulled him closer. Renn was a step ahead, drifting toward the sculpture of Balzac a few yards away.

She stood on her toes and kissed Will. "Your dad's a hoot," she said softly. "But, wow. He really isn't ever off work."

"You looked like you were having fun," he said.

"Oh, I am, but—" She laughed. "You know what I mean."

He'd been with her for longer than he'd dated any other woman, but he still wasn't sure if all of her compliments were sincere. Twenty-eight years as a famous man's biographical footnote made it difficult for him to believe that anyone other than his mother and sister truly appreciated him.

"I can't believe he offered to buy us a bed," he said, glancing at Renn, who was now looking up into Balzac's affable face.

Jorie laughed. "I know. I was a little surprised too."

"I thought it was kind of creepy."

"No comment." She chuckled again.

"What are you two whispering about?" called Renn. "Are you ready to go?"

"Whenever you are," said Will.

"Should we head to the Musée d'Orsay, or do you want to do a little shopping?"

"Maybe you two should go ahead without me," said Jorie. "I need to get home and take Poppy out for a walk. With all the rain we had this week, she got shortchanged."

"Oh, come on," said Will. "She'll be fine for another couple of hours."

His father was watching them closely. "Let her go," he said. "Her dog needs her, Will."

"Yes, listen to your father," said Jorie, grinning, her dimples popping. She laughed, a fluting, rising octave of bright notes.

"Don't gang up on me, you guys," said Will.

"Don't get mad," said Jorie.

"I'm not," he said. "I'm just a little tired. I slept like shit last night."

"You can sleep in tomorrow," she said. "No early-morning run, okay?"

They put her in a cab, a black Mercedes, its driver appearing not to recognize Renn. Jorie's lips touched Will's firmly as they said good-bye, and he and his father took a second cab toward the Quai d'Orsay. When they were almost there, Renn said he'd changed his mind and wanted instead to go to Café de Flore.

"Let's have a beer together," said Renn. "We never do that."

"No, I guess we don't," he said. "That sounds good."

They were climbing out of the taxi, a siren droning in a nearby street, when Renn finally said her name. "Elise is still with Marek Gilson, in case you're curious." He looked at Will calmly, his lips parted slightly.

Will couldn't think of anything to say that wouldn't start a quarrel. He stared at his father, unable to reply. All around them the traffic surged, the lights changing from red to green, people moving about with blank faces, avoiding each other's eyes. He wasn't sure what he felt, if it was relief or resignation or sorrow.

"I understand that she was irresistible," said Renn. "I think I can forgive you for trying to take her away from me. I hope you can forgive me for what I've done too."

"Yes," he said quietly. There was an ashy taste in his mouth; if he said more, he was sure that his voice would break. He sensed strangers' eyes on them, his father's presence releasing its jittery electricity into the atmosphere. People were stirring at the sidewalk tables, faces turned toward them, expectant. A woman spoke his name loudly to her companions; they laughed and tried abruptly to hush each other but couldn't stop their elated laughter.

It was at this café, with its overpriced menu and restive tourists who hoped to spot someone famous, or the ghosts of the famous, that Renn's fans intruded in a large, insistent group. Since childhood Will had found this variety of public worship of his handsome, flawed father deeply enervating. A tour group of a few dozen Germans from Bavaria lined up for his autograph and a photo. His father also permitted the more daring of the giddy, swooning women to kiss his cheek while Will sat a few yards away with their untouched beers. It would probably be another fifteen or twenty years before his father's fame was likely to fade enough to keep these strangers from flocking to him, hoping that a few minutes with him would change their lives.

After an hour, Will paid the bill and got up from the table, waving to his father; four Germans, three women, one man, still clustered around Renn.

"See you tonight," he called. "Sorry, Will. We'll catch up at dinner."

Will nodded and left the café, turning north toward the river. A few miles away, Jorie was waiting for him, watering their plants or eating an apple while she looked down into the courtyard and wondered again if she should get a bicycle. He was sure that despite her sympathy for him, her steadfast willingness to love him too, she would want to hear every detail of the futile trip to Café de Flore. But she never asked him the kinds of questions a couple of his past girlfriends had, one in particular he hadn't yet managed to forget. That girlfriend, a sweet but witless acting major who would end up becoming no one but the mistress of a film studio executive, asked who the lucky girl was that his father had lost his virginity to. Will stared at her for a few seconds, wondering why she thought he would have any idea. He opened his mouth to ask her this, but instead found himself making up a lie. "Some girl who lived down the block from him in high school, I think," he said.

His girlfriend had believed him, and Will still didn't know why her gullibility had so infuriated him.

ACKNOWLEDGMENTS

Thank you to my generous and inordinately hardworking editor, Nancy Miller, and to everyone at Bloomsbury; and thank you to Lisa Bankoff, Berni Barta, and Daniel Kirschen at ICM Partners.

Likewise, my deep gratitude to the editors who first saw merit in these short stories and published them in their literary magazines; especial gratitude goes to Carolyn Kuebler at *New England Review*, who published four of these stories. It is always a privilege to appear in their pages. A heartfelt thank-you also goes to Laura Furman and Heidi Pitlor for their recognition of my work.

Thank you to my patient and supportive friends and family, particularly to my parents, Susan Sneed and Terry Webb, and to Boppy-dot. Much gratitude to Sheryl Johnston, Randy Albers, Eleanor Jackson, Sara Mercurio, and my colleagues at Northwestern University, DePaul University, Regis University, and the University of Illinois at Urbana-Champaign, who have offered me teaching jobs and kept me solvent during the past several years.

PUBLICATION INFORMATION

"Beach Vacation" appeared in the *Southern Review* and received a special mention in *Pushcart Prize XXXVII*.

"The First Wife," "Clear Conscience," "Older Sister," and "The Couplehood Jubilee" all appeared in *New England Review*. "The First Wife" was reprinted in *The PEN/O. Henry Prize Stories 2012*, and "Clear Conscience" was named one of the year's distinguished stories in *The Best American Short Stories 2015*.

"The Prettiest Girls" appeared in *Ploughshares*.

"The Functionary" appeared in *Great Lakes Review*.

"Words That Once Shocked Us" appeared in *Fifth Wednesday Journal* and won the 2012 *Fifth Wednesday* Editor's Prize in Fiction.

"Five Rooms" appeared in *New Ohio Review*.

"Roger Weber Would Like to Stay" and "The New, All-True CV" both appeared in the *Literary Review*.

"Whatshisname" appeared in *LUMINA*.

"The Virginity of Famous Men" appeared in the *Southern Review* as "Café de Flore." An earlier story titled "The Virginity of Famous Men" was published in *Cream City Review*.

A NOTE ON THE AUTHOR

Christine Sneed has published the novels *Paris, He Said* and *Little Known Facts*, and the story collection *Portraits of a Few of the People I've Made Cry*. She has received the Grace Paley Prize for Short Fiction, *Ploughshares'* John C. Zacharis First Book Award, the Chicago Writers Association's Book of the Year Award, and the Society of Midland Authors Award for Best Adult Fiction in 2013. Her stories have appeared in *The Best American Short Stories, The O. Henry Prize Stories, New England Review, Glimmer Train,* and elsewhere. She lives in Evanston, Illinois.